THE BEST OF
RHYS DAVIES

Rhys Davies

DAVID & CHARLES
Newton Abbot   London   North Pomfret (Vt)

British Library Cataloguing in Publication Data

Davies, Rhys
 The best of Rhys Davies.
 823'.9'1FS   PR6007.A78A15

 ISBN 0–7153–7756–6

Printed in Great Britain
by Redwood Burn Limited, Trowbridge & Esher
for David & Charles (Publishers) Limited
Brunel House Newton Abbot Devon

Published in the United States of America
by David & Charles Inc
North Pomfret Vermont 05053 USA

CONTENTS

THE CHOSEN ONE

A letter, inscribed 'By Hand', lay inside the door when he arrived home just before seven o'clock. The thick, expensive-looking envelope was black-edged and smelled of stale face powder. Hoarding old-fashioned mourning envelopes would be typical of Mrs Vines, and the premonition of disaster Rufus felt now had nothing to do with death. But he stared for some moments at the penny-sized blob of purple wax sealing the flap. Other communications he had received from Mrs Vines over the last two years had not been sent in such a ceremonious envelope. The sheet of ruled paper inside, torn from a pad of the cheapest kind, was more familiar. He read it with strained concentration, his brows drawn into a pucker. The finely traced handwriting, in green ink, gave him no special difficulty, and his pausings over words such as 'oral', 'category' and 'sentimental', while his full-fleshed lips shaped the syllables, came from uncertainty of their meaning.

Sir

In reply to your oral request to me yesterday, concerning the property, Brychan Cottage, I have decided not to grant you a renewal of the lease, due to expire on June 30th next. This is final.

The cottage is unfit for human habitation, whether you consider yourself as coming under that category or not. It is an eyesore to me, and I intend razing it to the ground later this year. That you wish to get married and continue to live in the cottage with some factory hussy from the town is no affair of mine, and that my father, for sentimental reasons, granted your grandfather a seventy-five-year lease for the paltry sum of a hundred pounds is no affair of mine either. Your wretched family has always been a nuisance to me on my estate and I will not tolerate one of them to infest it any longer than is legal, or any screeching, jazz-dancing slut in trousers and bare feet to trespass and contaminate my land. Although you got rid of the pestiferous poultry after your mother died, the noise of the motor cycle you then bought has annoyed me even more than the cockerel crowing. Get out.

Yours truly,
Audrey P Vines

He saw her brown-speckled, jewel-ringed hand moving from word to word with a certainty of expression beyond any means of retaliation from him. The abuse in the letter did not enrage him immediately; it belonged too familiarly to Mrs Vines' character and reputation, though when he was a boy he had known different behaviour from her. But awareness that she had this devilish right to throw him, neck and crop, from the home he had inherited began to register somewhere in his mind at last. He had never believed she would do it.

Shock temporarily suspended full realization of the catastrophe. He went into the kitchen to brew the tea he always made as soon as he arrived home on his motor bike from his factory job in the county town. While he waited for the kettle to boil on the oil stove, his eye kept straying warily to the table. That a black-edged envelope lay on it was like something in a warning dream. He stared vaguely at the familiar objects around him. A peculiar silence seemed to have come to this kitchen that he had known all his life. There was a feeling of withdrawal from him in the room, as though already he were an intruder in it.

He winced when he picked up the letter and put it in a pocket of his leather jacket. Then, as was his habit on fine evenings, he took a mug of tea out to a seat under a pear tree shading the ill-fitting front door of the cottage, a sixteenth-century building in which he had been born. Golden light of May flooded the well-stocked garden. He began to re-read the letter, stopped to fetch a tattered little dictionary from the living room, and sat consulting one or two words which still perplexed him. Then, his thick jaw thrust out in his effort at sustained concentration, he read the letter through again.

The sentence 'This is final' pounded in his head. Three words had smashed his plans for the future. In his bewilderment, it did not occur to him that his inbred procrastination was of importance. Until the day before, he had kept post-poning going to see the evil-tempered mistress of Plas Idwal about the lease business, though his mother, who couldn't bear the sight of her, had reminded him of it several times in her last illness. He had just refused to believe that Mrs Vines would turn him out when a date in a yellowed old document came round. His mother's forebears had occupied Brychan Cottage for hundreds of years, long before Mrs Vines' family bought Plas Idwal.

Slowly turning his head, as though in compulsion, he gazed to the left of where he sat. He could see, beyond the garden and the alders fringing a ditch, an extensive slope of rough turf on which, centrally in his vision, a great cypress spread branches to the ground. Higher, crowning the slope, a rectangular mansion of russet stone caught the full light of the sunset. At this hour, he had sometimes seen Mrs Vines walking down the slope with her bulldog. She always carried a bag, throwing bread from it to birds and to wild duck on the river below. The tapestry bag had been familiar to him since he was a boy, but it was not until last Sunday that he learned she kept binoculars in it.

She could not be seen anywhere this evening. He sat thinking of last Sunday's events, unable to understand that such a small mistake as his girl had made could have caused the nastiness in the letter. Gloria had only trespassed a few yards on Plas Idwal land. And what was wrong with a girl wearing trousers or walking bare-foot on clean grass? What harm was there if a girl he was courting screeched when he chased her on to the river bank and if they tumbled to the ground? Nobody's clothes had come off.

He had thought Sunday was the champion day of his life. He had fetched Gloria from the town on his motor bike in the afternoon. It was her first visit to the cottage that he had boasted about so often in the factory, especially to her. Brought up in a poky terrace house without a garden, she had been pleased and excited with his pretty home on the Plas Idwal estate, and in half an hour, while they sat under this pear tree, he had asked her to marry him, and she said she would. She had laughed and squealed a lot in the garden and by the river, kicking her shoes off, dancing on the grassy river bank; she was only eighteen. Then, when he went indoors to put the kettle on for tea, she had jumped the narrow dividing ditch on to Mrs Vines' land—and soon after came dashing into the cottage. Shaking with fright, she said that a terrible woman in a torn fur coat had come shouting from under a big tree on the slope, binoculars in her hand and threatening her with a bulldog. It took quite a while to calm Gloria down. He told her of Mrs Vines' funny ways and the tales he had heard from his mother. But neither on Sunday nor since did he mention anything about the lease of Brychan Cottage, though remembrance of it had crossed his mind when Gloria said she'd marry him.

On Sunday, too, he had kept telling himself that he ought to ride up to the mansion to explain about the stranger who ignorantly crossed the ditch. But three days went by before he made the visit. He had bought a high-priced suède windcheater in the town, and got his hair trimmed during his dinner hour. He had even picked a bunch of polyanthus for Mrs Vines when he arrived home from the factory—and then, bothered by wanting to postpone the visit still longer, forgot them when he forced himself at last to jump on the bike. It was her tongue he was frightened of, he had told himself. He could never cope with women's tantrums.

But she had not seemed to be in one of her famous tempers when he appeared at the kitchen door of Plas Idwal, just after seven. 'Well, young man, what do you require?' she asked, pointing to a carpenter's bench alongside the dresser, on which he had often sat as a boy. First, he had tried to tell her that the girl who strayed on her land was going to marry him. But Mrs Vines talked to the five cats that, one after the other, bounded into the kitchen from upstairs a minute after he arrived. She said to them, 'We won't have these loud-voiced factory girls trespassing on any part of my property, will we, my darlings?' Taking her time, she fed the cats with liver she lifted with her fingers from a pan on one of her three small oil stoves. Presently he forced himself to say, 'I've come about the lease of Brychan Cottage. My mother told me about it. I've got a paper with a date on it.' But Mrs Vines said to one of the cats, 'Queenie, you'll have to swallow a pill tomorrow!' After another wait, he tried again, saying, 'My young lady is liking Brychan Cottage very much.' Mrs Vines had stared at him, not saying a word for about a minute, then said, 'You can go now. I will write you tomorrow about the lease.'

He had left the kitchen feeling a tightness beginning to throttle him, and he knew then that it had never been fear he felt towards her. But, as he tore at full speed down the drive, the thought came that it might have been a bad mistake to have stopped going to Plas Idwal to ask if he could collect whinberries for her up on the slopes of Mynydd Baer, or find mushrooms in the Caer Tégid fields, as he used to do before he took a job in a factory in the town. Was that why, soon after his mother died, she had sent him a rude letter about the smell of poultry and the rooster crowing? He had found that letter comic and shown it to chaps in the factory. But something had told him to get rid of the poultry.

He got up from the seat under the pear tree. The strange quiet he had noticed in the kitchen was in the garden too. Not a leaf or bird stirred. He could hear his heart thumping. He began to walk up and down the paths. He knew now the full meaning of her remark to those cats that no trespassers would be allowed on 'my property'. In about six weeks he himself would be a trespasser. He stopped to tear a branch of pear blossom from the tree and looked at it abstractedly. The pear tree was *his!* His mother had told him it was planted on the day he was born. Some summers it used to fruit so well that they had sold the whole load to Harries in the town, and the money was always for him.

Pacing, he slapped the branch against his leg, scattering the blossom. The tumult in his heart did not diminish. Like the kitchen, the garden seemed already to be withdrawn from his keeping. *She* had walked there that day, tainting it. He hurled the branch in the direction of the Plas Idwal slope. He did not want to go indoors. He went through a thicket of willows and lay on the river bank, staring into the clear, placidly flowing water. Her face flickered in the greenish depths. He flung a stone at it. Stress coiled tighter in him. He lay flat on his back, sweating, a hand clenched over his genitals.

The arc of serene evening sky and the whisper of gently lapping water calmed him for a while. A shred of common sense told him that the loss of Brychan Cottage was not a matter of life and death. But he could not forget Mrs Vines. He tried to think how he could appease her with some act of service. He remembered that until he was about seventeen she would ask him to do odd jobs for her, such as clearing fallen branches, setting fire to wasp holes, and—she made him wear a bonnet and veil for this—collecting the combs from her beehives. But what could he do now? She had shut herself away from everybody for years.

He could not shake off thought of her. Half-forgotten memories of the past came back. When he was about twelve, how surprised his mother had been when he told her that he had been taken upstairs in Plas Idwal and shown six kittens born that day! Soon after that, Mrs Vines had come down to this bank, where he had sat fishing, and said she wanted him to drown three of the kittens. She had a tub of water ready outside her kitchen door, and she stood watching while he held a wriggling canvas sack under the water with a broom. The three were males, she said. He had to dig a hole close to the greenhouses for the sack.

She never gave him money for any job, only presents from the house—an old magic lantern, coloured slides, dominoes, a box of crayons, even a doll's house. Her big brown eyes would look at him without any sign of temper at all. Once, when she asked him, 'Are you a dunce in school?' and he said, 'Yes, bottom of the class,' he heard her laugh aloud for the first time, and she looked very ·pleased with him. All that, he remembered, was when visitors had stopped going to Plas Idwal, and there was not a servant left; his mother said they wouldn't put up with Mrs Vines' bad ways any more. But people in the town who had worked for her said she was a very clever woman, with letters after her name, and it was likely she would always come out on top in disputes concerning her estate.

Other scraps of her history returned to his memory—things heard from old people who had known her before she shut herself away. Evan Matthews, who used to be her estate keeper and had been a friend of his father's, said that for a time she had lived among African savages, studying their ways with her first husband. Nobody knew how she had got rid of

10

that husband, or the whole truth about her second one. She used to disappear from Plas Idwal for months, but when her father died she never went away from her old home again. But it was when her second husband was no longer seen in Plas Idwal that she shut herself up there, except that once a month she hired a Daimler from the county town and went to buy, so it was said, cases of wine at Drapple's, and stuff for her face at the chemist's. Then even those trips had stopped, and everything was delivered to Plas Idwal by tradesmen's vans or post.

No clue came of a way to appease her. He rose from the river bank. The sunset light was beginning to fade, but he could still see clearly the mansion façade, its twelve bare windows, and the crumbling entrance portico, which was never used now. In sudden compulsion, he strode down to the narrow, weed-filled ditch marking the boundary of Brychan Cottage land. But he drew up at its edge. If he went to see her, he thought, he must prepare what he had to say with a cooler head than he had now.

Besides, to approach the mansion that way was forbidden. She might be watching him through binoculars from one of those windows.

An ambling sound roused him from this torment of in-decision. Fifty yards beyond the river's opposite bank, the 7.40 slow train to the county town was approaching. Its passage over the rough stretches of meadowland brought back a reminder of his mother's bitter grudge against the family at Plas Idwal. The trickery that had been done before the railroad was laid had never meant much to him, though he had heard about it often enough from his mother. Late in the nineteenth century, her father, who couldn't read or write, had been persuaded by Mrs Vines' father to sell to him, at a low price, not only decaying Brychan Cottage but, across the river, a great many acres of useless meadowland included in the cottage demesne. As a bait, a seventy-five-year retaining lease of the cottage and a piece of land to the river bank were granted for a hundred pounds. So there had been some money to stave off further dilapidation of the cottage and to put by for hard times. But in less than two years after the transaction, a railroad loop to a developing port in the west

11

had been laid over that long stretch of useless land across the river. Mrs Vines' father had known of the project and, according to the never-forgotten grudge, cleared a big profit from rail rights. His explanation (alleged by Rufus' mother to be humbug) was that he had wanted to preserve the view from possible ruination by buildings such as gasworks; a few trains every day, including important expresses and freight traffic, did not matter.

Watching, with a belligerent scowl, the 7.40 vanishing into the sunset fume, Rufus remembered that his father used to say that it wasn't Mrs Vines herself who had done the dirty trick. But was the daughter proving herself to be of the same robbing nature now? He could not believe that she intended razing Brychan Cottage to the ground. Did she want to trim it up and sell or rent at a price she knew he could never afford? But she had planty of money already—everybody knew that. Was it only that she wanted him out of sight, the last member of his family, and the last man on the estate?

He strode back to the cottage with the quick step of a man reaching a decision. Yet when he entered the dusky, low-ceilinged living room the paralysis of will threatened him again. He stood gazing round at the age-darkened furniture, the steel and copper accoutrements of the cavernous fireplace, the ornaments, the dim engravings of mountains, castles, and waterfalls as though he viewed them for the first time. He could not light the oil lamp, could not prepare a meal, begin his evening routine. A superstitious dread assailed him. Another presence was in possession here.

He shook the spell off. In the crimson glow remaining at the deep window, he read the letter once more, searching for some hint of a loophole. There seemed none. But awareness of a challenge penetrated his mind. For the first time since the death of his parents an important event was his to deal with alone. He lit the lamp, found a seldom-used stationery compendium, and sat down. He did not get beyond, 'Dear Madam, Surprised to receive your letter. . .' Instinct told him he must wheedle Mrs Vines. But in what way? After half an hour of defeat, he dashed upstairs, ran down naked to the kitchen to wash at the sink, and returned upstairs to rub scented oil into his tough black hair and dress in the new cotton trousers and

12

elegant windcheater of green suède that had cost him more than a week's wages.

Audrey Vines put her binoculars into her tapestry bag when Rufus entered Brychan Cottage and, her uninterested old bulldog at her heels, stepped out to the slope from between a brace of low-sweeping cypress branches. After concealing herself under the massive tree minutes before the noise of Rufus' motor cycle had come, as usual, a few minutes before seven, she had studied his face and followed his prowlings about the garden and river bank for nearly an hour. The clear views of him this evening had been particularly satisfactory. She knew it was a dictionary he had consulted under the pear tree, where he often sat drinking from a large Victorian mug. The furious hurling of a branch in the direction of the cypress had pleased her; his stress when he paced the garden had been as rewarding as his stupefied reading of the deliberately perplexing phraseology of her letter.

'Come along, Mia. *Good* little darling! We are going in now.'

Paused on the slope in musing, the corpulent bitch grunted, blinked, and followed with a faint trace of former briskness in her bandily aged waddle. Audrey Vines climbed without any breathlessness herself, her pertinacious gaze examining the distances to right and left. She came out every evening not only to feed birds but to scrutinize her estate before settling down for the night. There was also the passage of the 7.40 train to see; since her two watches and every clock in the house needed repairs, it gave verification of the exact time, though this, like the bird feeding, was not really of account to her.

It was her glimpses of Rufus that provided her long day with most interest. For some years she had regularly watched him through the powerful Zeiss binoculars from various concealed spots. He renewed an interest in studies begun during long-ago travels in countries far from Wales, and she often jotted her findings into a household-accounts book kept locked in an old portable escritoire. To her eye, the prognathous jaw, broad nose, and gypsy-black hair of this heavy-bodied but personable young man bore distinct atavistic elements.

13

He possessed, too, a primitive bloom, which often lingered for years beyond adolescence with persons of tardy mental development. But this throwback descendant of an ancient race was also, up to a point, a triumph over decadence. Arriving miraculously late in his mother's life, after three others born much earlier to the illiterate woman had died in infancy, this last-moment child had flourished physically, if not in other respects.

Except for the occasions when, as a boy and youth, he used to come to Plas Idwal to do odd jobs and run errands, her deductions had been formed entirely through the limited and intensifying medium of the binoculars. She had come to know all his outdoor habits and activities around the cottage. These were rewarding only occasionally. The days when she failed to see him seemed bleakly deficient of incident. While daylight lasted, he never bathed in the river without her knowledge, though sometimes, among the willows and reeds, he was as elusive as an otter. And winter, of course, kept him indoors a great deal.

'Come, darling. There'll be a visitor for us tonight.'

Mia, her little question-mark tail unexpectedly quivering, glanced up with the vaguely deprecating look of her breed. Audrey Vines had reached the balustraded front terrace. She paused by a broken sundial for a final look round at the spread of tranquil uplands and dim woods afar, the silent river and deserted meadows below, and, lingeringly, at the ancient trees shading her estate. Mild and windless though the evening was, she wore a long, draggled coat of brown-dyed ermine and, pinned securely on skeins of vigorous hair unskilfully home-dyed to auburn tints, a winged hat of tobacco-gold velvet. These, with her thick bistre face powder and assertive eye pencilling, gave her the look of an uncompromisingly womanly woman in an old-style sepia photograph, a woman halted for ever in the dead past. But there was no evidence of waning powers in either her demeanour or step as she continued to the side terrace. A woman of leisure ignoring time's urgencies, she only suggested an unruffled unity with the day's slow descent into twilight.

The outward calm was deceptive. A watchful gleam in her eyes was always there, and the binoculars were carried for a reason additional to her study of Rufus. She was ever on the lookout for trespassers and poachers or tramps on the estate, rare though such were. When, perhaps three or four times a year, she discovered a stray culprit, the mature repose would disappear in a flash, her step accelerate, her throaty voice lash out. Tradesmen arriving legitimately at her kitchen door avoided looking her straight in the eye, and C W Powell, her solicitor, knew exactly how far he could go in sociabilities during his quarterly conferences with her in the kitchen of Plas Idwal. Deep within those dissociated eyes lay an adamantine refusal to acknowledge the existence of any friendly approach. Only her animals could soften that repudiation.

'Poor Mia! We won't stay out so long tomorrow, I promise! Come along.' They had reached the unbalustraded side terrace. 'A flower for us tonight, sweetheart, then we'll go in,' she murmured.

She crossed the cobbled yard behind the mansion. Close to disused greenhouses, inside which overturned flowerpots and abandoned garden tools lay under tangles of grossly overgrown plants sprouting to the broken roofing, there was a single border of wallflowers, primulas, and several well-pruned rosebushes in generous bud. It was the only evidence in all the Plas Idwal domain of her almost defunct passion for flower cultivation. One pure white rose, an early herald of summer plenty, had begun to unfold that mild day; she had noticed it when she came out. Raindrops from a morning shower sprinkled on to her wrist as she plucked this sprightly first bloom, and she smiled as she inhaled the secret odour within. Holding the flower aloft like a trophy, she proceeded to the kitchen entrance with the same composed gait. There was all the time in the world.

Dusk had come into the spacious kitchen. But there was sufficient light for her activities from the curtainless bay window overlooking the yard and the flower border in which, long ago, Mia's much loved predecessor had been buried. Candles were not lit until it was strictly necessary. She fumbled among a jumble of oddments in one of the two gloomy little pantries lying off the kitchen, and came out with a cone-shaped silver vase.

Light pattering sounds came from beyond an open inner

15

door, where an uncarpeted back staircase lay, and five cats came bounding down from the first-floor drawing room. Each a ginger tabby of almost identical aspect, they whisked, mewing, around their mistress, tails up.

'Yes, yes, my darlings,' she said. 'Your saucers in a moment.' She crossed to a sink of blackened stone, humming to herself.

A monster Edwardian cooking range stood derelict in a chimneyed alcove, with three portable oil stoves before it holding a covered frying pan, an iron stewpan, and a tin kettle. Stately dinner crockery and a variety of canisters and tinned foodstuff packed the shelves of a huge dresser built into the back wall. A long table stretching down the centre of the kitchen was even more crowded. It held half a dozen bulging paper satchels, biscuit tins, piles of unwashed plates and saucers, two stacks of *The Geographical Magazine*, the skull of a sheep, heaped vegetable peelings, an old wooden coffee grinder, a leatherette hatbox, a Tunisian birdcage used for storing meat, several rib-boned chocolate boxes crammed with letters, and a traveller's escritoire of rosewood. On the end near the oil stoves, under a three-branched candelabra of heavy Sheffield plate encrusted with carved vine leaves and grapes, a reasonably fresh cloth of fine lace was laid with silver cutlery, a condiment set of polished silver, a crystal wine goblet, and a neatly folded linen napkin. A boudoir chair of gilded wood stood before this end of the table.

When the cold-water tap was turned on at the sink, a rattle sounded afar in the ·house and ended in a groaning cough—a companionable sound, which Mrs Vines much liked. She continued to hum as she placed the rose in the vase, set it below the handsome candelabra, and stepped back to admire the effect. Pulling out a pair of long, jet-headed pins, she took off her opulent velvet hat.

'He's a stupid lout, isn't he, Queenie?' The eldest cat, her favourite, had leaped on the table. 'Thinking he was going to bed that chit down here and breed like rabbits!'

She gave the cats their separate saucers of liver, chopped from cold slices taken from the frying pan. Queenie was served first. The bulldog waited for her dish of beef chunks from the stewpan, and, given them, stood morosely for a minute, as if counting the pieces. Finally, Audrey Vines took for herself a remaining portion of liver and a slice of bread from a loaf on the dresser, and fetched a half bottle of champagne from a capacious oak chest placed between the two pantries. She removed her fur coat before she settled on the frail boudoir chair and shook out her napkin.

Several of these meagre snacks were taken every day, the last just after the 11.15 night express rocked away to the port in the west. Now, her excellent teeth masticating with barely perceptible movements, she ate with fastidious care. The bluish light filtering through the grimy bay window soon thickened, but still she did not light the three candles. Her snack finished, and the last drop of champagne taken with a sweet biscuit, she continued to sit at the table, her oil-stained gown tea of beige chiffon ethereal in the dimness.

She became an unmoving shadow. A disciplined meditation or a religious exercise might have been engaging her. Mia, also an immobile smudge, lay fast asleep on a strip of coconut matting beside the gilt chair. The five cats, tails down, had returned upstairs immediately after their meal, going one after the other as though in strict etiquette, or like a file of replete orphans. Each had a mahogany cradle in the drawing room, constructed to their mistress' specifications by an aged craftsman who had once been employed at Plas Idwal.

She stirred for a minute from the reverie, but her murmuring scarcely disturbed the silence. Turning her head in mechanical habit to where Mia lay, she asked, 'Was it last January the river froze for a fortnight? . . . No, not last winter. But there were gales, weren't there? Floods of rain . . . Which winter did I burn the chairs to keep us warm? That idiotic oilman didn't come. Then the candles and matches gave out, and I used the electricity. One of Queenie's daughters died that winter. It was the year he went to work in a factory.'

Time had long ago ceased to have calendar meaning in her life; a dozen years were as one. But lately she had begun to be obsessed by dread of another severe winter. Winters seemed to have become colder and longer. She dreaded the deeper hibernation they enforced. Springs were intolerably long in coming, postponing the time when her child of nature became visible again, busy under his flowering trees and splashing in the river. His reliable appearances brought back flickers of

17

interest in the world; in comparison, intruders on the estate, the arrival of tradesmen, or the visits of her solicitor were becoming of little consequence.

She lapsed back into silence. The kitchen was almost invisible when, swiftly alert, she turned her head towards the indigo blue of the bay window. A throbbing sound had come from far away. It mounted to a series of kicking spurts, roared, and became a loudly tearing rhythm. She rose from her chair and fumbled for a box of matches on the table. But the rhythmic sound began to dwindle, and her hand remained over the box. The sound floated away.

She sank back on the chair. 'Not now, darling!' she told the drowsily shifting dog. 'Later, later.'

The headlamp beam flashed past the high entrance gates to Plas Idwal, but Rufus did not even glance at them. They were wide open and, he knew, would remain open all night. He had long ceased to wonder about this. Some people said Mrs Vines wanted to trap strangers inside, so that she could enjoy frightening them when they were nabbed, but other townsfolk thought that the gates had been kept open for years because she was always expecting her second husband to come back.

At top speed, his bike could reach the town in less than ten minutes. The fir-darkened road was deserted. No cottage or house bordered it for five miles. A roadside farmstead had become derelict, but in a long vale quietly ascending towards the mountain range some families still continued with reduced sheep farming. Rufus knew them all. His father had worked at one of the farms before the decline in agricultural prosperity set in. From the outskirts of the hilly town he could see an illuminated clock in the Assembly Hall tower. It was half-past nine. He did not slow down. Avoiding the town centre, he tore past the pens of a disused cattle market, a recently built confectionery factory, a nineteenth-century Nonconformist chapel, which had become a furniture depository, then past a row of cottages remaining from days when the town profited from rich milk and tough flannel woven at riverside mills. Farther round the town's lower folds, he turned into an area of diminutive back-to-back dwellings, their fronts ranging direct along narrow pavements.

18

Nobody was visible in these gaslit streets. He stopped at one of the terraces, walked to a door, and, without knocking, turned its brass knob. The door opened into a living room, though a sort of entrance lobby was formed by a chenille curtain and an upturned painted drainpipe used for umbrellas. Voices came from beyond the curtain. But only Gloria's twelve-year-old brother sat in the darkened room, watching television from a plump easy chair. His spectacles flashed up at the interrupting visitor.

'Gone to the pictures with Mum.' The boy's attention returned impatiently to the dramatic serial. 'Won't be back till long after ten.'

Rufus sat down behind the boy and gazed unseeingly at the screen. A feeling of relief came to him. He knew now that he didn't want to show the letter to Gloria tonight, or tell her anything about the lease of Brychan Cottage. Besides, she mustn't read those nasty insults about her in the letter. He asked himself why he had come there, so hastily. Why hadn't he gone to Plas Idwal? Mrs Vines might give way. Then he needn't mention anything at all to Gloria. If he told her about the letter tonight, it would make him look a shifty cheat. She would ask why he hadn't told her about the lease before.

He began to sweat. The close-packed little room was warm and airless. Gloria's two married sisters lived in poky terrace houses just like this one, and he became certain that it was sight of Brychan Cottage and its garden last Sunday that convinced her to marry him. Before Sunday, she had always been a bit off hand, pouting if he said too much about the future. Although she could giggle and squeal a lot, she could wrinkle up her nose, too, and flounce away if any chap tried any fancy stuff on her in the factory recreation room. He saw her little feet skipping and running fast as a deer's.

The torment was coming back. This room, instead of bringing Gloria closer to him, made her seem farther off. He kept seeing her on the run. She was screeching as she ran. That loud screech of hers! He had never really liked it. It made his blood go cold, though a chap in the factory said that screeches like that were only a sign that a girl was a virgin and that they disappeared afterwards. Why was he hearing them now?

19

Then he remembered that one of Mrs Vines' insults was about the screeching.

His fingers trembled when he lit a cigarette. He sat a little while longer telling himself he ought to have gone begging to Plas Idwal and promised to do anything if he could keep the cottage. He would work on the estate evenings and weekends for no money; a lot of jobs needed doing there. He'd offer to pay a good rent for the cottage, too. But what he ought to get before going there, he thought further, was advice from someone who had known Mrs Vines well. He peered at his watch and got up.

'Tell Gloria I thought she'd like to go for a ride on the bike. I won't come back tonight.'

'You'll be seeing her in the factory tomorrow,' the boy pointed out.

It was only a minute up to the town centre. After parking the bike behind the Assembly Hall, Rufus crossed the quiet market square to a timbered old inn at the corner of Einon's Dip. He had remembered that Evan Matthews often went in there on his way to his night job at the reservoir. Sometimes they'd had a quick drink together.

Thursdays were quiet nights in pubs; so far, there were only five customers in the cozily rambling main bar. Instead of his usual beer, he ordered a double whisky, and asked Gwyneth, the elderly barmaid, if Evan Matthews had been in. She said that if he came in at all it would be about that time. Rufus took his glass over to a table beside the fireless inglenook. He didn't know the two fellows playing darts. An English-looking commercial traveller in a bowler sat at a table scribbling in a notebook. Councillor Llew Pryce stood talking in Welsh to Gwyneth at the counter, and, sitting at a table across the bar from himself, the woman called Joanie was reading the local newspaper.

Staring at his unwatered whisky, he tried to decide whether to go to Evan's home in Mostyn Street. No, he'd wait a while here. He wanted more time to think. How could Evan help, after all? A couple of drinks—that's what he needed now. Empty glass in hand, he looked up. Joanie was laying her newspaper down. A blue flower decorated her white felt hat, and there was a bright cherry in her small wineglass.

20

He watched, in a fascination like relief, as she bit the cherry from its stick and chewed with easy enjoyment. She'd be about thirty-five, he judged. She was a Saturday-night regular, but he had seen her in The Drovers on other nights, and she didn't lack company as a rule. He knew of her only from tales and jokes by chaps in the factory. Someone had said she'd come from Bristol, with a man supposed to be her husband, who had disappeared when they'd both worked in the slab-cake factory for a few months.

Joanie looked at him, and picked up her paper. He wondered if she was waiting for someone. If Evan didn't come in, could he talk to her about his trouble, ask her the best way to handle a bad-tempered old money-bags? She looked experienced and good-hearted, a woman with no lumps in her nature. He could show her the letter; being a newcomer to the town, she wouldn't know who Mrs Vines was.

He rose to get another double whisky but couldn't make up his mind to stop at Joanie's table or venture a passing nod. He stayed at the counter finishing his second double, and he was still there when Evan came in. He bought Evan a pint of bitter, a single whisky for himself, and, Joanie forgotten, led Evan to the inglenook table.

'Had a knockout when I got home this evening.' He took the black-edged envelope from a pocket of his windcheater.

Evan Matthews read the letter. A sinewy and well-preserved man, he looked about fifty and was approaching sixty; when Mrs Vines had hired him as estate keeper and herdsman, he had been under forty. He grinned as he handed the letter back, saying, 'She's got you properly skewered, boyo! I warned your dad she'd do it when the lease was up.'

'What's the reason for it? Brychan Cottage isn't unfit for living it, like she says—there's only a bit of dry rot in the floor boards. I've never done her any harm.'

'No harm, except that you're a man now.'

Uncomprehending, Rufus scowled. 'She used to like me. Gave me presents. Is it more money she's after?'

'She isn't after money. Audrey P Vines was open-fisted with cash—I'll say that for her. No, she just hates the lot of us.'

'Men, you mean?'

'The whole bunch of us get her dander up.' Recollection

21

lit Evan's eyes. 'She gave me cracks across the head with a riding crop that she always carried in those days. I'd been working hard at Plas Idwal for five years when I got my lot from her.'

'Cracks across the head?' Rufus said, sidetracked.

'She drew blood. I told your dad about it. He said I ought to prosecute her for assault. But when she did it I felt sorry for her, and she knew it. It made her boil the more.'

'What you'd done?'

'We were in the cowshed. She used to keep a fine herd of Jerseys, and she blamed the death of a calving one on me— began raging that I was clumsy pulling the calf out, which I'd been obliged to do.' Evan shook his head. 'It wasn't *that* got her flaring. But she took advantage of it and gave me three or four lashes with the crop. I just stood looking at her. I could see she wanted me to hit back and have a proper set-to. Of course, I was much younger then, and so was she! But I only said, "You and I must part, Mrs Vines." She lifted that top lip of hers, like a vixen done out of a fowl—I can see her now— and went from the shed without a word. I packed up that day. Same as her second husband had walked out on her a couple of years before—the one that played a violin.'

'You mean . . .' Rufus blurted, after a pause of astonishment. 'You mean, you'd *been* with her?'

Evan chuckled. 'Now, I didn't say that!'

'What's the *matter* with the woman?' Rufus exclaimed. The mystery of Mrs Vines' attack on himself was no clearer.

'There's women that turn themselves into royalty,' Evan said. 'They get it into their heads they rule the world. People who knew little Audrey's father used to say he spoiled her up to the hilt because her mother died young. He only had one child. They travelled a lot together when she was a girl, going into savage parts, and afterwards she always had a taste for places where there's no baptized Christians. I heard that her first husband committed suicide in Nigeria, but nobody knows for certain what happened.' He took up Rufus' empty whisky glass, and pushed back his chair. 'If he did something without her permission, he'd be for the crocodiles.'

'I've had two doubles and a single and I haven't had supper yet,' Rufus protested. But Evan fetched him a single whisky.

When it was placed before him, Rufus stubbornly asked, 'What's the best thing for me to do?'

'Go and see her.' Evan's face had the tenderly amused relish of one who knows that the young male must get a portion of trouble at the hands of women. 'That's what she wants. I know our Audrey.' He glanced again at this slow-thinking son of an old friend. 'Go tonight,' he urged.

'It's late to go tonight,' Rufus mumbled. Sunk in rumination, he added. 'She stays up late. I've seen a light in her kitchen window when I drive back over the rise after I've been out with Gloria.' He swallowed the whisky at a gulp.

'If you want to keep Brychan Cottage, boyo, *act*. Night's better than daytime for seeing her. She'll have had a glass or two. Bottles still go there regularly from Jack Drapple's.'

'You mean, soft-soap her?' Rufus asked with a grimace.

'No, not soft-soap. But give her what she wants.' Evan thought for a moment, and added, a little more clearly, 'When she starts laying into you—and she will, judging by that letter—you have a go at *her*. I wouldn't be surprised she'll respect you for it. Her and me in the cowshed was a different matter—I wasn't after anything from her. Get some clouts in on her, if you can.'

Rufus shook his head slowly. 'She said in the letter it was final,' he said.

'Nothing is final with women, boyo. Especially what they put down in writing. They send letters like that to get a man springing up off his tail. They can't bear us to sit down quietly for long.' Evan finished his beer. It was time to leave for his watchman's job at the new reservoir up at Mynydd Baer, the towering mountain from which showers thrashed down.

'Brychan Cottage belongs to me! Not to that damned old witch!' Rufus had banged the table with his fist. The dart players turned to look; Joanie lowered her paper; the commercial traveller glanced up from his notebook, took off his bowler, and laid it on the table. Gwyneth coughed and thumped a large Toby jug down warningly on the bar counter.

Evan said, 'Try shouting at *her* like that—she won't mind language—but pipe down here. And don't take any more whisky.'

'I'll tell her I won't budge from Brychan Cottage!' Rufus

announced. 'Her father cheated my grandfather over the railway—made a lot of money. She won't try to force me out. She'd be disgraced in the town.'

'Audrey Vines won't care a farthing about disgrace or gossip.' Evan buttoned up his black mackintosh. 'I heard she used to give her second husband shocking dressings-down in front of servants and the visitors that used to go to Plas Idwal in those days. Mr Oswald, he was called. A touch of African tarbrush in him, and had tried playing the violin for a living.' A tone of sly pleasure was in his voice. 'Younger than Audrey Vines. One afternoon in Plas Idwal, she caught him with a skivvy in the girl's bedroom top of the house, and she locked them in there for twenty-four hours. She turned the electricity off at the main, and there the two stayed without food or water all that time.' Evan took from his pocket a tasselled monkey cap of white wool, kept for his journey by motor bike into the mountains. 'If you go to see her tonight, give her my love. Come to Mostyn Street tomorrow to tell me how you got on.'

'What happened when the two were let out of the bedroom?'

'The skivvy was sent flying at once, of course. Mari, the housekeeper, told me that in a day or two Mrs Vines was playing her piano to Mr Oswald's fiddle as usual. Long duets they used to play most evenings, and visitors had to sit and listen. But it wasn't many weeks before Mr Oswald bunked off, in the dead of night. The tale some tell that he is still shut away somewhere in Plas Idwal is bull.' He winked at Rufus.

'I've heard she keeps the gates open all the time to welcome him back,' Rufus persisted, delaying Evan still longer. It was as though he dreaded to be left alone.

'After all these years? Some people like to believe women get love on the brain. But it's true they can go sour when a man they're set on does a skedaddle from them. And when they get like that, they can go round the bend without much pushing.' He rose from the table. 'But I'll say this for our Audrey. After Mr Oswald skedaddled, she shut herself up in Plas Idwal and wasn't too much of a nuisance to people outside. Far as I know, I was the only man who had his claret tapped with that riding crop!' He drained a last swallow from

24

his glass. 'Mind, I wouldn't deny she'd like Mr Oswald to come back, even after all these years! She'd have ways and means of finishing him off.' He patted Rufus' shoulder. 'In the long run it might be best if you lost Brychan Cottage.'

Rufus' jaw set in sudden obstinate sullenness. 'I've told Gloria we're going to live there for ever. I'm going to Plas Idwal tonight.'

When he got up, a minute after Evan had left, it was with a clumsy spring; the table and glasses lurched. But his progress to the bar counter was undeviating. He drank another single whisky, bought a half bottle, which he put inside his elastic-waisted windcheater, and strode from the bar with a newly found hauteur.

She came out of her bedroom above the kitchen rather later than her usual time for going down to prepare her last meal of the day. Carrying a candleholder of Venetian glass shaped like a water lily, she did not descend by the adjacent back staircase tonight but went along a corridor and turned into another, off which lay the front drawing room. Each of the doors she passed, like every other inside the house, was wide open; a bronze statuette of a mounted hussar kept her bedroom door secure against slamming on windy nights.

She had dressed and renewed her make-up by the light of the candle, which was now a dripping stub concealed in the pretty holder. Her wide-skirted evening gown of mauve taffeta had not entirely lost a crisp rustle, and on the mottled flesh of her bosom a ruby pendant shone vivaciously. Rouge, lip salve, and mascara had been applied with a prodigal hand, like the expensive scent that left whiffs in her wake. She arrayed herself in this way now and again—sometimes if she planned to sit far into the night composing letters and always for her solicitor's arrival on the evening of quarter day, when she would give him soup and tinned crab in the kitchen.

She never failed to look into the first-floor drawing room at about eleven o'clock, to bid a good night to the cats. The bull-dog, aware of the custom, had preceded her mistress on this occasion and stood looking in turn at the occupants of five short-legged cradles ranged in a half circle before a gaunt and empty fireplace of grey stone. Pampered Queenie lay fast asleep on her eiderdown cushion; the other tabbies had heard their mistress approaching and sat up, stretching and giving themselves a contented lick. Blue starlight came from four tall windows, whose satin curtains were drawn back tightly into dirt-stiff folds, rigid as marble. In that quiet illumination of candle and starlight, the richly dressed woman moving from cradle to cradle, stroking and cooing a word or two, had a look of feudally assured serenity. Mia watched in pedigreed detachment; even her squashed face achieved a debonair comeliness.

'Queenie, Queenie, won't you say good night to me? Bowen's are sending fish tomorrow! Friday fish! Soles, darling! *Fish fish!*'

Queenie refused to stir from her fat sleep. Presently, her ceremony performed, Audrey Vines descended by the front staircase, candle in hand, Mia stepping with equal care behind her. At the rear of the panelled hall, she passed through an archway, above which hung a Bantu initiatory mask, its orange and purple stripes dimmed under grime. A baize door in the passage beyond was kept open with an earthenware jar full of potatoes and onions. In the kitchen, she lit the three-branched candelabra from her pink-and-white holder, and blew out the stub.

This was always the hour she liked best. The last snack would be prepared with even more leisure than the earlier four or five. Tonight, she opened a tin of sardines, sliced a tomato and a hard-boiled egg, and brought from one of the dank little pantries a jar of olives, a bottle of mayonnaise, and a foil-wrapped triangle of processed cheese. While she buttered slices of bread, the distant rocking of the last train could be heard, its fading rhythm leaving behind all the unruffled calm of a windless night. She arranged half a dozen sponge fingers clockwise on a Chelsea plate, then took a half bottle of champagne from the chest, hesitated, and exchanged it for a full-sized one.

Mia had occupied herself with a prolonged examination and sniffing and scratching of her varicoloured strip of matting; she might have been viewing it for the first time. Noticing that her mistress was seated, she reclined her obdurate bulk on the strip. Presently, she would be given her usual two sponge fingers dipped in champagne. She took no notice when a throbbing sound came from outside or when it grew louder.

'Our visitor, sweetheart. I told you he'd come.'

Audrey Vines, postponing the treat of her favourite brand of sardines until later, dabbed mayonnaise on a slice of egg, ate, and wiped her lips. 'Don't bark!' she commanded. 'There's noise enough as it is.' Becoming languidly alert to the accumulating roar, Mia had got on to her bandy legs. A light flashed across the bay window. The roar ceased abruptly. Audrey Vines took a slice of bread as footsteps approached outside, and Mia, her shred of a tail faintly active, trundled to the door. A bell hanging inside had tinkled.

'Open, open!' Mrs Vines' shout from the table was throaty, but strong and even. 'Open and come in!'

Rufus paused stiffly on the threshold, his face in profile, his eyes glancing obliquely at the candlelit woman sitting at the table's far end. 'I saw your lighted window,' he said. The dog returned to the matting after a sniff of his shoes and a brief upward look of approval.

'Thank God I shall not be hearing the noise of that cursed motor cycle on my land much longer. Shut the door, young man, and sit over there.'

He shut the door and crossed to the seat Mrs Vines had indicated, the same rough bench placed against a wall between the dresser and the inner door on which he used to sit during happier visits long ago. He sat down and forced himself to gaze slowly down the big kitchen, his eyes ranging over the long, crowded table to the woman in her evening gown, to the single, red jewel on her bare chest, and, at last, to her painted face.

Audrey Vines went on with her meal. The silence continued. A visitor might not have been present. Rufus watched her leisurely selection of a slice of tomato and an olive, the careful unwrapping of foil from cheese. Her two diamond rings sparkled in the candlelight. He had never seen her eating, and this evidence of a normal habit both mesmerized and eased him.

'I've come about the letter.'

The words out, he sat up, taut in justification of complaint. But Mrs Vines seemed not to have heard. She sprinkled pepper and salt on the cheese, cut it into small pieces, and looked consideringly at the untouched sardines in their tin, while the disregarded visitor relapsed into silent watching. Three or four minutes passed before she spoke.

'Are you aware that I could institute a police charge against you for bathing completely naked in the river on my estate?'

It stirred him anew to a bolt-upright posture. 'There's nobody to see.'

She turned a speculative, heavy-lidded eye in his direction. 'Then how do I know about it? Do you consider me nobody?' Yet there was no trace of malevolence as she continued. 'You are almost as hairy as an ape. Perhaps you consider that is sufficient covering?' Sedate as a judge in court, she added, 'But your organs are exceptionally pronounced.'

'Other people don't go about with spying glasses.' Anger gave his words a stinging ring.

Turning to the dog, she remarked, 'An impudent defence from the hairy bather!' Mia, waiting patiently for the sponge fingers, blinked, and Audrey Vines, reaching for the tin of sardines, said, 'People in the trains can see.'

'I know the times of the trains.'

'You have bathed like that all the summer. You walk to the river from Brychan Cottage unclothed. You did not do this when your parents were alive.'

'You never sent me a letter about it.'

'I delivered a letter at Brychan Cottage today. *That* covers everything.'

There was another silence. Needing time to reassemble his thoughts, he watched as she carefully manipulated a sardine out of the tin with her pointed fingernails. The fish did not break. She held it aloft by its tail end to let oil drip into the tin, and regally tilted her head back and slowly lowered it whole into her mouth. The coral-red lips softly clamped about the disappearing body, drawing it in with appreciation. She chewed with fastidiously dawdling movements. Lifting another fish, she repeated the performance, her face wholly absorbed in her pleasure.

She was selecting a third sardine before Rufus spoke. 'I want to go on living in Brychan Cottage,' he said, slurring the words. The sardine had disappeared when he continued. 'My family always lived in Brychan Cottage. It belonged to us hundreds of years before your family came to Plas Idwal.'

'You've been drinking,' Audrey Vines said, looking ruminatively over the half-empty plates before her. She did not sound disapproving, but almost amiable. Rufus made no reply. After she had eaten a whole slice of bread, ridding her mouth of sardine taste, she reached for the bottle of champagne. A long time was spent untwisting wire from the cork. Her manipulating hands were gentle in the soft yellow candlelight, and in the quiet of deep country night filling the room she seemed just then an ordinary woman sitting in peace over an ordinary meal, a flower from her garden on the table, a faithful dog lying near her chair.

Making a further effort, he repeated, 'My family always lived in Brychan Cottage.'

'Your disagreeable mother,' Audrey Vines responded, 'allowed a man to take a photograph of Brychan Cottage. I had sent the creature packing when he called here. The photograph appeared in a ridiculous guidebook. Your mother knew I would *not* approve of attracting such flashy attention to my estate. My solicitor showed me the book.'

Unable to deal with this accusation, he fell into headlong pleading. 'I've taken care of the cottage. It's not dirty. I could put new floor boards in downstairs and change the front door. I can cook and do cleaning. The garden is tidy. I'm planning to border the paths with more fruit trees, and—'

'Why did your parents name you Rufus?' she interrupted. 'You are dark as night, though your complexion is pale . . . and pitted like the moon's surface.' The wire was off the cork. 'I wonder were you born hairy-bodied?'

He subsided, baffled. As she eased the cork out, there was the same disregard of him. He jerked when the cork shot in his direction. She seemed to smile as the foam spurted and settled delicately in her crystal glass. She took a sip, and another, and spoke to the saliva-dropping dog.

'Your bikkies in a second. Aren't you a nice quiet little Mia! A pity *he* isn't as quiet, darling.'

'Got a bottle of whisky with me. Can I take a swig?' The request came in a sudden desperate burst.

'You may.'

She watched in turn while he brought the flat, half-sized

29

bottle from inside his windcheater, unscrewed its stopper, and tilted the neck into his mouth. She took further sips of her wine. Absorbed in his own need, Rufus paused for only a moment before returning the neck to his mouth. About half the whisky had been taken when, holding the bottle at the ready between his knees, his eyes met hers across the room's length. She looked away, her lids stiffening. But confidence increased in Rufus.

He repeated, 'I want to live in Brychan Cottage all my life.'

'You wish to live in Brychan Cottage. I wish to raze it to the ground.' A second glass of wine was poured. 'So there we are, young man!' She wetted a sponge finger in her wine and handed it to Mia.

'My mother said the cottage and land belonged to us for ever at one time. Your father cheated us out of . . .' He stopped, realizing his foolishness, and scowled.

'Mia, darling, how you love your drop of champagne!' She dipped another sponge finger; in her obliviousness, she might have been courteously overlooking his slip. 'Not good for your rheumatism, though! Oh, you dribbler!'

He took another swig of whisky—a smaller one. He was sitting in Plas Idwal and must not forget himself so far as to get drunk. Settling back against the wall, he stared in wonder at objects on the long table and ventured to ask, 'What . . . what have you got that skull for? It's a sheep's, isn't it?'

'That? I keep it because it shows pure breeding in its lines and therefore is beautiful. Such sheep are not degenerate, as are so many of their so-called masters. No compulsory education, state welfare services, and social coddling for a sheep!' Rufus' face displayed the blank respect of a modest person hearing academic information beyond his comprehension, and she appended, 'The ewe that lived inside that skull was eaten alive by blowfly maggots. I found her under a hedge below Mynydd Baer.' She finished her second glass, and poured a third.

As though in sociable alliance, he allowed himself another mouthful of whisky. Awareness of his gaffe about her cheating father kept him from returning to the subject of the cottage at once. He was prepared to remain on the bench for hours; she seemed not to mind his visit. His eyes did not stray from her any more; every trivial move she made held his attention now.

30

She reached for a fancy biscuit tin and closely studied the white roses painted on its shiny blue side. He waited. The silence became acceptable. It belonged to the late hour and this house and the mystery of Mrs Vines' ways.

Audrey Vines laid the biscuit tin down unopened, and slowly ran a finger along the lace tablecloth, like a woman preoccupied with arriving at a resolve. 'If you are dissatisfied with the leasehold deeds of Brychan Cottage,' she began, 'I advise you to consult a solicitor. Daniel Lewis welcomes such small business, I believe. You will find his office behind the Assembly Hall. You have been remarkably lackadaisical in this matter . . . No, *not* remarkably, since he is as he is! He should live in a tree.' She had turned to Mia.

'I don't want to go to a solicitor.' After a pause, he mumbled, half sulkily, 'Can't . . . can't we settle it between us?'

She looked up. Their eyes met again. The bright ruby on her chest flashed as she purposelessly moved a dish on the table. But the roused expectancy in Rufus' glistening eyes did not fade. After a moment, he tilted the bottle high into his mouth, and withdrew it with a look of extreme surprise. It was empty.

Audrey Vines drank more wine. Then, rapping the words out, she demanded, 'How much rent are you prepared to pay me for the cottage?'

Rufus gaped in wonder. Had Evan Matthews been right, then, in saying that nothing was final with women? He put the whisky bottle down on the bench and offered the first sum in his mind. 'A pound a week?'

Audrey Vines laughed. It was a hoarse sound, cramped and discordant in her throat. She straightened a leaning candle and spoke with the incisiveness of a nimble businesswoman addressing a foolish client. 'Evidently you know nothing of property values, young man. My estate is one of the most attractive in this part of Wales. A Londoner needing weekend seclusion would pay ten pounds a week for my cottage, with fishing rights.'

It had become 'my cottage'. Rufus pushed a hand into his sweat-damp black hair, and mumbled, 'Best to have a man you know near by you on the estate.'

'For a pound! I fail to see the advantage I reap.'

'Thirty shillings, then? I'm only drawing a clear nine

pounds a week in Nelson's factory.' Without guile, he sped on, 'Haven't got enough training yet to be put on the machines, you see! They've kept me in the packing room with the learners.'

'That I can well believe. Nevertheless, you can afford to buy a motor cycle and flasks of whisky.' She clattered a plate on to another. 'My cottage would be rent-free to the right man. Would you like a couple of sardines with your whisky?'

The abrupt invitation quenched him once more. He lowered his head, scowling, his thighs wide apart. His hands gripped his knees. There was a silence. When he looked up, she was straining her pencilled eyes towards him, as though their sight had become blurred. But now he could not look at her in return. His gaze focused on the three candle flames to the left of her head.

'Well, sardines or not?'

'No,' he answered, almost inaudibly.

'Grind me some coffee, then,' she rapped, pointing to the handle-topped wooden box on the table. 'There are beans in it. Put a little water in the kettle on one of those oil stoves. Matches are here. Coffeepot on the dresser.' She dabbed her lips with her napkin, looked at the stain they left, and refilled her glass.

He could no longer respond in any way to these changes of mood. He neither moved nor spoke. Reality had faded, the kitchen itself became less factual, objects on the table insubstantially remote. Only the woman's face drew and held his eyes. But Audrey Vines seemed not to notice this semi-paralysis; she was allowing a slow-thinking man time to obey her command. She spoke a few words to Mia. She leaned forward to reach for a lacquered box, and took from it a pink cigarette. As she rose to light the gold-tipped cigarette at a candle, he said. 'Brychan Cottage always belonged to my family.'

'He keeps saying that!' she said to Mia, sighing and sitting back. Reflective while she smoked, she had an air of waiting for coffee to be served, a woman retreated into the securities of the distant past, when everybody ran to her bidding.

'What do you want, then?' His voice came from deep in his chest, the words flat and earnest in his need to know.

The mistress of Plas Idwal did not reply for a minute. Her gaze was fixed on the closely woven flower in its silver vase. And a strange transformation came to her lulled face. The

32

lineaments of a girl eased its contours, bringing a smooth texture to the skin, clothing the stark bones with a pastel-like delicacy of fine young flesh. An apparition, perhaps an inhabitant of her reverie, was fugitively in possession.

'I want peace and quiet,' she whispered.

His head had come forward. He saw the extraordinary transformation. Like the dissolving reality of the room, it had the nature of an hallucination. His brows puckering in his efforts to concentrate, to find exactness, he slowly sat back, and asked, 'You want me to stay single? Then I can keep Brychan Cottage?'

In a sudden, total extinction of control, her face became contorted into an angry shape of wrinkled flesh. Her eyes blazed almost sightlessly. She threw the cigarette on the floor and screamed, 'Did you think I was going to allow that slut to live there? Braying and squealing on my estate like a prostitute!' Her loud breathing was that of someone about to vomit.

With the same flat simplicity, he said, 'Gloria is not a prostitute.'

'Gloria! Good God, *Gloria!* How far in idiocy can they go? Why not Cleopatra? I don't care a hair of your stupid head what happens to you and that wretched creature. You are *not* going to get the cottage. I'll burn it to the ground rather than have you and that born prostitute in it!' Her hands began to grasp at plates and cutlery on the table, in a blind semblance of the act of clearing them. 'Stupid lout, coming here! By the autumn there won't be a stone of that cottage left. Not a stone, you hear!'

Her demented goading held such pure hatred that it seemed devoid of connection with him. She had arrived at the fringe of sane consciousness; her gaze fixed on nothing, she was aware only of a dim figure hovering down the room, beyond the throw of candlelight. 'The thirtieth of June, you hear? Or the police will be called to turn you out!'

He had paused for a second at the far end of the table, near the door. His head was averted. Four or five paces away from him lay release into the night. But he proceeded in her direction, advancing as though in deferential shyness, his head still half turned away, a hand sliding along the table. He paused again, took up the coffee grinder, looked at it vaguely, and lowered it to the table. It crashed on the stone floor.

She became aware of the accosting figure. The screaming did not diminish. 'Pick that thing up! You've broken it, clumsy fool. Pick it up!'

He looked round uncertainly, not at her but at the uncurtained bay window giving on to the spaces of night. He did not stoop for the grinder.

'*Pick it up!*' The mounting howl swept away the last hesitation in him. He went towards her unwaveringly.

She sat without a movement until he was close to her. He stopped, and looked down at her. Something like a compelled obedience was in the crouch of his shoulders. Her right hand moved, grasping the tablecloth fringe into a tight fistful. She made no attempt to speak, but an articulation came into the exposed face that was lifted to him. From the glaze of her eyes, from deep in unfathomable misery, came entreaty. He was the chosen one. He alone held the power of deliverance. He saw it, and in that instant of mutual recognition his hand grasped the heavy candelabra and lifted it high. Its three flames blew out in the swiftness of the plunge. There was a din of objects crashing to the floor from the tugged tablecloth. When he rose from beside the fallen chair and put the candelabra down, the whimpering dog followed him in the darkness to the door, as though pleading with this welcome visitor not to go.

He left the motor bike outside the back garden gate of Brychan Cottage, walked along a wicker fence, and, near the river, jumped across the ditch on to Plas Idwal land. Presently, he reached a spot where, long before he was born, the river had been widened and deepened to form an ornamental pool. A rotting summerhouse, impenetrable under wild creeper, overlooked it, and a pair of stone urns marked a short flight of weed-hidden steps. The soft water, which in daytime was as blue as the distant mountain range where lay its source, flowed through in lingering eddies. He had sometimes bathed in this prohibited pool late at night; below Brychan Cottage the river was much less comfortable for swimming.

He undressed without haste, and jumped into the pool with a quick and acrobatically high leap. He swam underwater, rose, and went under again, in complete ablution. When he stood up beside the opposite bank, where the glimmering water reached to his chest, he relaxed his arms along the grassy verge and remained for moments looking at the enormous expanse of starry sky, away from the mansion dimly outlined above the pool.

He was part of the anonymous liberty of the night. This bathe was the completion of an act of mastery. The river was his; returning to its depths, he was assimilated into it. He flowed downstream a little way and, where the water became shallow, sat up. His left hand spread on pebbles below, he leaned negligently there, like a deity of pools and streams risen in search of possibilities in the night. He sat unmoving for several minutes. The supple water running over his loins began to feel much colder. It seemed to clear his mind of tumult. Slowly, he turned his head towards the mansion.

He saw her face in the last flare of the candles, and now he knew why she had tormented him. She had been waiting long for his arrival. The knowledge lodged, certain and tenacious, in his mind. Beyond his wonder at her choice, it brought, too, some easing of the terror threatening him. Further his mind would not go; he retreated from thinking of the woman lying alone in the darkness of that mansion up there. He knew she was dead. Suddenly, he rose, waded to the bank, and strode to where his clothes lay.

His movements took on the neatness and dispatch of a man acting entirely on a residue of memory. He went into Brychan Cottage only to dry and dress himself in the kitchen. When he got to the town, all lamps had been extinguished in the deserted streets. The bike tore into the private hush of an ancient orderliness. He did not turn into the route he had taken earlier that night but drove on at top speed through the market place. Behind the medieval Assembly Hall, down a street of municipal offices and timbered old houses in which legal business was done, a blue lamp shone alight. It jutted clearly from the porch of a stone building, and the solid door below yielded to his push.

Inside, a bald-headed officer sitting at a desk glanced up in mild surprise at this visitor out of the peaceful night, and, since the young man kept silent, asked, 'Well, what can we do for you?'

THE OLD ADAM

Scandals never disturb the placidity of Clawdd, and everybody was put about when Jane Morgan, unwittingly or not, began one by taking a simple bathe on a beautiful summer afternoon. The distressing business was the more out of key because Clawdd, which lies in one of the most secluded valleys of Wales, is noted for its small but old-established theological college. Otherwise, the place has little to recommend it, except the several pure waterfalls and a breed of sheep which, nurtured on moistly succulent pastures, become the tenderest mutton in the land.

Jane, uncumbered by a bathing suit, took the bathe in a pool formed by the river in a glade just below her home, outside the village. Fishing rights in the stretch of river tumbling thereabouts belonged to her pugnacious mother, who rented them by the season to rich anglers coming from elsewhere. But was it true (as one critic suggested that evening in The Hawk Inn) that she had been sent bathing in the pool by her mother as a trap? There was dissent to this. Why shouldn't she enjoy lolling about in out-of-doors water? The criticism was based on the fact that the Morgans couldn't always lay their hands on ready money to pay their bills.

Jane was twenty, and although in her school days, and later, she had been ferocious at all energetic sports, indolence had begun to undo her that summer. After climbing out of the pool she took a long time over drying herself, standing on the daisy-sprinkled bank. Heavy-jowled for her age, and with small grey eyes lapsed too far in, nevertheless she owned a well-off body such as is seen, as a rule, only on a plinth in a museum or, alive in a slip, being chosen for first prize at a seaside fête while the brass band waits to strike up.

Presently she lay down, forgetting that her mother had asked her to pluck a capon killed the day before—a college professor was coming to a meal on Sunday. Her amiable spaniel, a bird or two, and a few droning bees seemed to be her sole companions in enjoyment of the purring sunshine. She was on her mother's enclosed land, and no anglers had arrived that afternoon.

She was not lying there for the sake of health or beauty, either, for in ancient Clawdd, which possesses two valiantly thriving Nonconformist chapels, as well as the esteemed theological college (situated quite near the Morgans' land), the up-to-date manias for sun-therapy and tinting the flesh are not thought about. Innocent of those fads as a nymph of the old dispensation, she dozed off among the daisies.

The spaniel's sudden bark wakened her. She scrambled up and, for a moment, stood posed with wonderfully graceful alertness. The dog, wagging its tail, was ambling to the trunk of a venerable oak which cast shade twelve yards distant up the glade. Jane let out the hallooing cry foxhunters give; then, swift as a released arrow, she charged towards the tree. She did not stop to snatch up her towel. Sun and sleep (so she told Police Sergeant Pryse later) had addled her senses.

A young man fled—foolishly but perhaps naturally—from behind the tree. Jane's cries increased. They were heard by her mother in the old red brick house above. *She* told Sergeant Pryse that she had been in the kitchen making blackberry tart and was unaware of her daughter's habit of bathing in the pool. But for some weeks she and Jane had suspected that an intruder haunted their land, especially at night, and the sergeant had been informed of this already. One morning, indeed, Jane had found a spray of wild cherry blossom—it was too heavy for any bird to have carried—on the window ledge of her bedroom.

Shrieks from an unclothed woman in pursuit are more unnerving than from the clothed. The young man completely lost his head. Or was it that he *wished* to be captured? Instead of fleeing downwards to the left, where the public road to the college lay, he dashed upwards. The delighted spaniel barked, chased and whisked about as if in a game with its own kindred. Jane, a fine sprinter, got the intruder in a couple of minutes.

He had bounded away from a barbed-wire fence enclosing staring sheep in a field rented to a farmer and, just as Mrs Morgan rounded the house, Jane and the spaniel—not that the dog intended seizing him—cornered him where a barn joined the low wall of a disused paddock. Athletic of physique, Jane not only cornered him but leapt and brought him down under her. His head bumped against the stone cobbles.

She scrambled up. 'I know him!' she shouted to her mother, whose own jaw was clamping soundlessly as she drew up. 'He was skulking behind a tree.' A bubble broke at the corner of her mouth. 'I've seen him in chapel!' She looked down at him with the vicious gaze a hunter gives to netted prey. 'His name is Tudor . . . Tudor . . .?'

'Edwards,' supplied the supine young man, in a mumble. He seemed to be in a condition for total submission, perhaps because of the bumping. But his eyes watched her in dark tumult.

Mrs Morgan, understandably, untied her kitchen apron to give her daughter before she found speech. 'If there was a whip—' she panted, looking round at the horseless paddock, long fallen to rack and ruin because of the sloths, dissipations and debts of her recently deceased husband. She turned to the villain, her tone grim as her eye: 'You'll be hearing more about this!'

He lay still on the cobbles, as if shocked to the core. Jane should have run off, the apron not being enough, but she had remained looking down intently at her captive. Her mother gave her a push, and, accompanied by the slavering dog, they left Tudor Edwards where he lay.

He was a native of Clawdd. But he and Jane had never spoken to each other; and in this unseemly way his wooing burst into flower.

Of course, the disagreeable event became common property by that evening, though muddling gossip spread a story, at first, that the culprit was a resident student—some of them came from England—in the college. No one wanted to believe that a son of Clawdd could forget himself so far.

'There's bound to be a goat even in a little college like ours,' remarked Emlyn Prichard, in the saloon bar of The Hawk. The college was not so important as the one in Cardiganshire, but it was more exclusive.

'Students are not proper until they've passed their examinations,' said Blodwen Lewis, who, as barmaid, was the only woman allowed to tread the saloon.

'Perhaps the student just wanted to do a bit of poaching,' Llewellyn Morris ventured.

'Traps,' frowned Ewart Vaughan, who had been fined a pound in his time for landing a salmon, undersized though it was; 'I expect Morgan was put there as a trap.'

Did he mean a trap to catch poachers or to dazzle a student or licensed angler for mother or daughter's own purpose? They were debating this when, at about nine, T D Watkins, owner of the flannel mill and a close friend of Sergeant Pryse, came in and gave the facts.

'No,' he replied to dismayed inquirers on the stools and benches, 'Tudor isn't handcuffed or in a cell. But it's serious. Owing to the college.' It was understood he meant that the incident might put thoughts into the heads of the students.

'Clawdd was here long before the college,' observed Ewart. 'What was Jane doing,' he asked insinuatingly (and was not answered), 'bathing and sleeping like that in the glade? Trees full of leaves don't hide everything—no, not even when they're fig leaves.'

Since Sergeant Pryse didn't come into the inn for his customary refreshment, the affair certainly looked important, and, after ten o'clock closing time, men whose way led past the police station shivered in sympathy for Tudor. Such is the solidarity of old communities. But no one had given credit to the Morgans for their courage in going to the police and thus making public that, private land though she was on, Jane bathed and lay about in that state.

Tudor, who had been hauled out of his mother's cottage three hours earlier, was still inside the police station. He was sipping a cup of tea, an obstinate scowl on his face. Now and again he stroked the back of his head, where a lump had grown to the size of a bantam's egg.

Sergeant Pryse, also with tea, sat irritably making corrections on long sheets of ruled blue paper on his desk. He had wanted to deduct a year from Tudor's exact age. Twenty, and of full stature bodily, nevertheless the face of the accused showed that he had not yet quite emerged from those lunar thickets of youth where incalculable creatures roam bemused, sometimes stamping their hooves in fury.

Pryse suddenly pounced—'Sunday, 1 May, you said it was? Well, 1 May wasn't a Sunday! You're telling me lies.'

'It was a Sunday night,' Tudor maintained. 'I had been looking at her in chapel that evening, and I heard the clock in the college tower strike midnight when I took the ladder out of the Morgans' barn. The moon was full and the blossom was out. It was the first time I had gone there, and I remember thinking, "It's the first day of May."'

'You weren't safe in bed dreaming you did this?' suggested Pryse enticingly.

Tudor shook his head. It was as though, having suffered the pangs of undeclared passion for a long time, he wanted to bellow about them from the housetops. He had told Pryse of behaviour which need not have been applied to that day's offence of loitering on enclosed land and peering from behind a tree while a young lady bathed. In the dead of night, when no other soul was outside the sheets, he had gone many times to the Morgans' house and climbed a ladder to the window of Jane's bedroom. Several reconnoitring visits were made before he discovered which was her room. But all he had done afterwards was sit for a while on the window ledge.

'What did you say your motive was?' the sergeant pressed, returning to this bewildering idiosyncrasy for the third time.

'I just fancied sitting there. The curtains were closed, but I was hoping one night they wouldn't be and Miss Morgan would come to the window and speak to me.'

'To ask if the fine weather was going to change, I expect?' Pryse blew angrily on his tea-damp moustache. 'I wouldn't be surprised,' he said, going beyond his jurisdiction, 'if Mrs Morgan would say you were after her silver, not her daughter. Do you appreciate you could be had up for trying to break in?'

'They haven't got any money. I'll be the one with money after my mother is gone.'

The long interview had got out of hand once or twice. From its start, Pryse, doubtless with Clawdd's prestige as a theological haunt in view, had done his utmost to coax Tudor into admitting that really it was salmon he was after. Poaching for the expensive fish, though liable to prosecution, was a moot offence in the social and moral spheres; people indigenous to the district felt that local wild fish and fowl, if it was possible to consult them about it, would not be so narrowly selective of their captors as was the law. It was merely bad luck when a poacher was nabbed.

'No,' Tudor, adamant on the point, spurned this reiterated blandishment to the end, 'no, I do not know anything about salmon, and I never want to eat it any time of the year.'

'Anyone would think,' Pryse grumbled (and he couldn't be blamed), 'you'd had your gumption knocked out of your head by bumping it on those cobbles.' He looked over the heavily corrected foolscap, and grieved, 'As far as I can tell now, the charge will be breach of the peace. Your Dad wouldn't have liked this.' And after a final version of his statement was read to the accused he signed it and was freed into the moonlit night.

On the telephone, the Rev A C Powys had consented to stand bail for this young member of his flock.

A different ordeal awaited him at home. When he got there, his mother didn't ask him why he had done this extraordinary thing or what was the point of it when he could have approached Jane in a more normal way, especially since the girl attended the same chapel. She laid a poultice on his swelling, then drew a starched cloth off a tray of cold food.

'Now, eat the meat and pickles slowly,' she said, 'or you'll be having nightmares tonight.' She resumed her knitting, sitting in the rocking chair in which her only child used to be sung to sleep.

A small woman with a politely mild face and a voice that rarely darted up into anger, she had never got too big for her boots, though her husband, a builder's repairs man when she married him at eighteen, had later done well for himself in buying up old properties in Marlais, the nearby town. But a policeman—and on such an errand!—had never darkened her threshold before; as she told Mrs Powys later, she would hear for many years the sound of those feet coming to her cottage door. Her knitting was faster than usual.

'Mam,' Tudor said, the meal rapidly finished, 'I'll have to stand up in court next week.'

'I am surprised you have let yourself be gone on Jane Morgan,' she commented. 'There's half a dozen good-minded girls in Clawdd would be glad to know you've clapped eyes on them.'

He pondered, and said, meekly, 'Well, I thought to myself, Jane's like me, the same age and with only a widowed mother and no brothers and sisters. Except she's got no money. The four of us, I thought, could sit here in Clawdd in comfort, with Jane fetching the rents after you're gone.' Every first of the month his mother went off unobtrusively to Marlais and collected the rents of the eight houses which had been expertly renovated by his father.

Although admiring his sentiment, she objected, 'That dressy mother of hers is a proud one, front and back, and Jane's got the same mighty way of walking, in her fine clothes which they can't afford. If you had been a young man from the college, very likely Jane would have taken you into the house to tea when she found you on their land.'

'Yes,' he sighed, after another gloomy pause, 'I ought to have gone to a college and been made a BA.'

Still not showing signs of being very cast down, she said, 'While you were in the police station I thought I ought to go and plead with Mrs Morgan and Jane not to let this business go any further.'

Tudor reared up, like an angry turkey-cock. '*No.*'

She nodded approvingly, briskly stuck her needles into the ball of wool, and said, 'Mind you don't do anything foolish after this. Men have drowned themselves over women. But not men with full-weight heads.'

She knew better than to upbraid him in dire terms. He was not a wild one, but had always gone his own way. Stubborn against his father's wish to educate him for work entailing pomp and circumstance, he had dropped school as soon as the law allowed and begun work as a ploughboy on one of the ancestral local farms, where he had quickly progressed. He was able to judge a cow or ewe at market expertly. With help from her, he could buy a farm of his own presently; there was a plan that they would acquire one owned by an ageing relative in North Wales, far over the mountains. And nothing had seemed to rankle in him until lately.

'I won't be going to chapel tomorrow,' he said, as midnight put an end to the disastrous Saturday.

Supporters and inquisitive natives of Clawdd who were able to attend the court in Marlais travelled the seven miles by bus, cars and bikes; dressed in best clothes, the contingent was of sufficient strength for a distinct odour of camphor balls to fill the eighteenth-century courtroom. Mrs Morgan and her daughter were there, although told they would not be called to witness, since the accused was pleading guilty; both of them wore new hats.

Tudor's case was the last of the morning's ration of district ill-doings, which had included theft of a sheep, assault and battery during a Saturday night brawl in Marlais, and a summons concerning the father of a bastard. 'It is unusual for us to find such a charge as this one from Clawdd,' began the chairman ominously, after Tudor was called to the dock. It was a hint that the good status of the scholastically religious village was in jeopardy.

But of the three magistrates on the bench, one was a woman. She was comfortably stout, wore flashing, very observant glasses, and it soon became clear that she was dubious of the case. That Tudor was pleading guilty shortened the proceedings, but nevertheless, after Sergeant Pryse had related the arrest and admissions of the accused, this Mrs Ellen Jones, JP, bristled.

'Boiled down,' she said, 'what is this charge but the paltry misdemeanour of a lovesick farmhand? Why, not a hundred years ago there was a custom in these parts of a suitor being admitted to a young lady's room from a ladder at night, and such courtships were acceptable to families of the best repute. A young man was trusted in those simple days—but God help him if he betrayed that trust! The accused may have heard of this custom of our respected forefathers and—'

'We are not living a hundred years ago,' interrupted the chairman rudely.

'Terrible things were done in those days. A man could be sent to Australia for stealing a sheep.'

43

'It is our bounden duty,' said his elderly male confrère, 'to distinguish in this case between a genuine need to court and something much more vulgar—' Looking annoyed by someone's loud titter, he corrected himself, 'Something that is very vulgar in comparison.'

The chairman took a long, beady look at the accused. Tudor's mother had insisted that he wear a starched white collar and the black suit—now very tight—bought for his father's funeral. But the effect of respectability was spoiled by his fierce scowl—due, perhaps, to Jane being there to view his public humiliation. A tuft of unruly hair shoved down on his forehead somehow added to the surliness. Yet Mrs Ellen Jones, also giving him a scrutiny, seemed even more impatient that the charge had been brought. She jerked about in her seat. But she had two against her.

'What were your intentions towards Miss Morgan?' the chairman demanded.

'To see her,' Tudor replied, omitting 'sir'.

'We know that,' sniffed the other male beak, cynically. 'Were you aware that she was in the habit of bathing in her private pool?'

'Yes.'

'Ha!' said the two men, almost simultaneously, and the elderly one commented, 'To stare at an unrobed young lady for forty-five minutes from behind a tree in broad daylight shows a very warped mentality, to say the least.'

'This sitting on her window ledge late at night,' Mrs Ellen Jones persisted, encouragingly, '—what were your intentions in that?'

'Only to sit outside her room, Your Worship.'

The chairman barked, '*Not* to go inside, of course, of course! . . . Stand down.'

Mrs Jones pouted at the short-shrift chairman. But she gave way. No doubt the chairman felt this was a case men could judge best. The three consulted together in lowered voices. Then the chairman announced judgement. A very old law—it was the Peeping Tom Act of 1361—was quoted to the extreme detriment of the accused. But on account of his youth and previously unblemished character he was to be let off lightly. 'You are fined fifteen shillings,' the chairman told him, 'and I warn you not to let us see you here again.' The court closed, and the smell of mothballs evaporated.

Opinion in The Hawk Inn that evening was that the charge would have been dismissed if the theological college hadn't been part of Clawdd. Commiseration was expressed by everybody; if Tudor had gone into the inn he would not have been allowed to spend a penny on whatever he fancied. Sergeant Pryse openly remarked, 'I did my best to make him see sense. He could have pleaded to me he had bad eyesight and thought it was a big fish dipping about in that pool.'

The damage was done, however. He had stood in a dock of malefactors; his name had gone down in police records; the case was reported in full in the Marlais weekly newspaper. On the other hand, his behaviour certainly got him Jane's awareness in full measure.

He went about in a watchfully saturnine way, like a man who waits to pick a quarrel with anyone. He bit his nails, shaved less often, didn't take to drinking, and went for morose walks on his own in the evenings, some times carrying his licensed gun for rabbiting. Either the gnawing beetle of love hadn't been killed by the magistrates or else he was belatedly feeling the disgrace of the prosecution. He might have been in that state of thwarted passion which men of other days sometimes tried to forget by disappearing into Indian jungles to shoot tigers.

His mother made efforts to repair him; she baked his favourite dishes and, in a roundabout way, drew his attention to several Clawdd girls who were in the pink of condition. He scowled down his strong-rooted nose and had nothing to say. And on the first Sunday after the court appearance he became difficult just as they were about to leave for chapel.

'I'm going to become an atheist,' he announced, resolutely sitting down.

'There's plenty of those in our chapel,' she said, pulling on lace gloves. 'I wouldn't try to coax you if it wasn't that Mrs Morgan and Jane will sure to be there—and won't they be glad they've driven you from where your dear father was made a deacon the year before he died! Are they to see me sitting alone in our pew like a woman who's lost everybody?'

45

'I can't help staring at Jane right through the sermon,' he lamented.

'Well, stare at her,' she said firmly, and gave him the hymn book they always shared. 'Though what there's left for you to see I can't think.'

Owing to his humming and hawing they were the last to enter the full chapel. Their seats were a good way down, on a raised side-portion where the pews stood crosswise to the middle ones. The ghost of a commotion stirred the air; Jane, sitting in a middle pew, was observed to lower her head. As soon as mother and son were seated, the organ, played by Ewart Vaughan, burst into a Handel piece like a fanfare of trumpets, and, until the Rev A C Powys, DD, opened with his prayer, it was unavoidable that most people couldn't help thinking of Jane lying in a Garden of Eden state beside her pool. It was a brief ordeal endured not only by the characters most concerned.

'Things will be easier for you from now,' his mother comforted him, when they got home. 'Soon everything will be forgotten.'

He pursed his lips. But always afterwards, as on that Sunday, he succeeded in keeping his gaze away from Jane's in the chapel. *Her* seat, though, was so placed that her small, gone-in eyes could rest on her melancholy victim without a turn of her head. And in small country places even the bitterest enemies are likely, sooner or later, to come face to face at a quiet spot. One evening in August, as he neared a humped stone bridge over the river, about a mile from the village, Jane came looming up towards him from the other side. The puce after-tint of sunset had not yet darkened into night, and a sickle moon lay flimsy above the lonely woodlands.

Her spaniel, running ahead, recognized Tudor instantly and offered a saluting leap and lick; he bent to return the greeting with a pat. Jane, in a thin, low-cut dress because of the warmth, halted when she got a step past him on the shady bridge, and turned.

'Tudor Edwards,' she said, 'I forgive you.' She put her head on one side and continued, 'My mother and I ought to have thought twice before going to the police.' He carried his gun, and a limp rabbit was slung over his shoulder; since he said nothing, she asked, chattily, 'Been rabbiting?'

46

He took the rabbit from his shoulder, looked at it in great surprise, and said, 'Why, it was a salmon just before I came on this bridge!'

Jane fingered a string of coral pieces round her tawny throat and found herself able to smile. 'Oh, well,' she said, 'strange things happen every night and day, don't they?' No apparition, her affluent figure stood clear-cut in the twilight. Her thick-featured face was golden from all the sunshine of that good summer.

He gave her a pondering look, blinked, then slowly turned his head as though what his hardened eyes saw caused him agony which must be conquered at all costs. Yet, stammering over it, he asked, 'Going for . . . for a walk?'

Thereafter, to everybody's surprise, he began to meet Jane frequently for courting walks. And again he seemed a changed man. On the free nights he went up to The Hawk and drank more than he should. Extravagance possessed him. He bought chocolates and knick-knacks regularly for Jane, and for himself high-priced neckties, glossy shoes, and a fancy waistcoat of canary yellow. It looked as if the demolished pride of a young man was restored. Yet his drinking in The Hawk did not have the ease and calm of one who had climbed into man's estate.

'Courting Jane Morgan now, are you?' remarked Ewart Vaughan, who had once taught him the elements of the Gospels in the chapel Sunday-school. 'Well, a lady often likes to scratch a man before she finds out that he's fit for her under the skin.'

Tudor stared into his pewter tankard in a way that might have meant bashfulness or the tight refusal of a man who won't speak. A lot of Clawdd business was done in the Gents Saloon of The Hawk, if only in the way of information and discussion, and Walter Leyshon, a clerk in the Marlais water-rates office, said, 'Well, now, Tudor, you'll have to be the boss and tidy up the Morgans' affairs. Three applications for payment of last quarter's water I've sent to Mrs Morgan. She'll be cut off one day and have to fetch her water from that pool where Jane splashes about and frightens the trout away.'

'That's enough!' cried Blodwen Lewis, from behind the bar. She always interfered when the men went too far in

47

comment, abuse or revelation. '*I* don't blame Mrs Morgan and Jane for making the best of themselves,' she said. Presumably she meant their habit of dressing in the height of fashion. She served Tudor with another pint of beer—his sixth—in a censorious way, however. 'Taking it while you can?' she asked.

'A gin for you?' he invited, insisting on buying her a drink although she remarked that he'd want a lot of money for his future. And when Police Sergeant Pryse came in Tudor bought him a drink too, before leaving. It was noticed that he always left The Hawk soon after the Sergeant's time of entrance, as if sight of the law's representative gave him a bitter pain he could not forget.

Clawdd, on the whole, was pleased to hear about the courtship. The Morgans, though extravagantly stiff-necked, were as much true local stock as the Edwardses; it wasn't as if strangers had upset the place by calling in the law to Tudor's conduct. It would be a nice development in logic if his doting offence in the glade should be reduced to something seen through the clean circle of a wedding ring.

But it was not to be expected that an affair which had begun to the portentous tramp of a constable's feet would proceed with the delicate smoothness of a minuet. Tudor's mother expressed her forebodings, though she saw that a man in love—especially one who has suffered prosecution for it—must be allowed his excesses, and she had faith in his good sense asserting itself when the humdrum of married life barred these youthful capers. She spoke up in real indignation only after the occasion of Mrs Morgan's formal visit to the obscure cottage down by Three Saints Well.

The two widows spent half an hour in conclave. Mrs Morgan had called with the bygone manner of a squire's lady bringing bounty to the hard-pressed, despite the knowledge she had acquired of Mrs Edwards' circumstances, possession of which she presently disclosed. Living just the same as when she was married, and still baking her own bread in a hearth oven with a Jehovah among wheatsheaves designed on its iron door, Mrs Edwards had never bought a dress or hat which made other women think.

'I'll be truthful and say he'd not be of my choosing for Jane,' Mrs Morgan began, a few cool politenesses over. 'But times have changed. The bit of trouble in July can be overlooked. I've made inquiries and I'm told your son is an excellent worker in Treharne's farm—'

'I'll be truthful too,' Tudor's mother put in, 'and say we women can't properly understand what a man sees when he looks at us.'

Mrs Morgan appeared about to be contentious. But she proceeded, 'Now, what about his means and prospects? A farmhand doesn't earn much. It's not his intention to stay one all his life?'

'Tudor gets full union rate of pay, and he'll get what I've got when I'm gone.'

'You're only about fifty,' Mrs Morgan quibbled. She paused, then said, 'Mrs Powys, the minister's wife, has mentioned to me that you own eight houses in Marlais. Is your son to inherit these? If so, surely he should be given some of them on marriage? I intend giving Jane a grazing meadow.'

Not a flicker of surprise or resentment showed in Mrs Edwards' face. But she asked, 'You didn't know about my houses until after Tudor was fined in the police court?'

'No,' replied Mrs Morgan, too secure in her social advantage to see a necessity for evasion. 'When Mrs Powys came to tea after the police proceedings it was natural we should talk about you. Facts must be faced. Jane is accustomed to a good house and table.'

Mrs Edwards, after a glance at her visitor's clothes, took deep thought, while Mrs Morgan took admiring stock of the treasure-packed room. There were valuable painted glass plaques and Swansea plates on the walls, the furniture was of old black oak, and there were china effigies, including one of the young Queen Victoria and one of Christmas Evans, the famous divine whose single seeing eye had done the work of forty scarifying orbs. Mrs Morgan, who knew about the value of such items, had been forced to sell most of her own household rarities.

'I've always told Tudor,' his mother said at last, 'that I'll give him the deeds of three houses in Marlais when he gets married. His father wished that. He'll get everything else when I'm gone.'

'Couldn't he be given *four* houses?' demanded Mrs Morgan.

'Half the total number would be sensible and just.'

'His father said three. Three it will be.'

The visitor took the hint not to interfere so calculatingly in the love business of the young, rose, praised the Staffordshire effigies, and departed; she looked more or less satisfied. But Mrs Edwards felt in need of a glass of elderberry wine after the exit; and when Tudor arrived home from work, she fumed, while he sat to a bottle of ginger ale as usual, 'Mrs Morgan has been here. You're not of her choosing, but she brought a pair of scales with her. In one pan she sat her daughter Jane, and three of my houses in the other. But the scales didn't balance and she asked for another house.'

He remained gazing reflectively down at his farm boots, nodded, then heaved himself up. Dismissing her recital of the interview, he said, 'Now, Mam, leave this to me. I'll manage them. You and I will talk about the houses *after* I am married.'

She could make nothing of his smile. Had love made a complete dolt of him? Was it possible that he could transform Jane into a pleasingly obedient married woman? She said nothing more, and at eight o'clock, his black hair perfumed with oil, he went out for his courting walk. She watched him disappear up the lane of trees reaching from the cottage. His gait certainly had the strut of a man who knew what he was about.

When he returned from that particular walk he announced with peculiar affableness, 'Well, we settled a lot tonight, Mam.' The hope faded out of her face as he added, 'Jane thinks it ought to be four houses, not three, and I told her I would try my best to make you say yes.'

'If the Morgans are not careful,' she said, grim in her disappointment, 'there won't be *one* house.'

He nodded, sitting down to a piece of her excellent cold veal pie. Decision seemed to have eased his bones. Smiling at a segment of pie impaled on his fork, he said, 'We have settled for a wedding on 2 October. A Saturday.'

'Tudor,' she allowed herself to shout, 'you've gone off your head. Those two are a pair of greedy foxes.'

He looked at her, and said, 'A man can teach a lesson to a fox.' And he went on, 'Jane wants to go to London for the honeymoon.'

50

She gave up, but protested, 'London!' It might have been Baghdad. 'You ought to go to North Wales and visit my cousin Ellis at his farm. If he likes the shape of things in this wedding he might let you have the farm cheap when he's ready to sell.'

'Jane,' he said, a note of teasing in his voice, 'wants to see shops in London. She doesn't know anything about your cousin Ellis' farm. Time enough for seeing about that later on . . She wants a motor car,' he continued, 'and a refrigerator for when I've bought my own farm. Her mother's got her mind on old Will Mansell's place.'

'There'll be a big mortgage to raise for Will Mansell's farm,' she warned.

'Where there's a will there's a way,' he grinned. 'I'll tell Jane you won't budge from more than three houses.'

She expressed no further important criticism after that night, even accepting the decision for a wedding as soon as October. From a social point of view, perhaps it was best for the July disgrace to be wiped out as soon as possible, and she was comforted by a new realization that he seemed to have a lot of grown-up fight in him now.

'I'm going to be master,' he assured her. 'The Morgans have trod on me once.'

In addition to the three houses she had decided to present the couple with two pairs of linen bedsheets, a tapestry quilt made by eighty-year-old Jessie James, and, as a reminder of the sterner matters in life, the china statue of Christmas Evans.

These articles she sent up, like the true Christian she was, to Mrs Morgan's house on the day before the wedding. Jane wanted him to live there until the gift of the three Marlais houses was turned into cash for the purchase of a farm. He had agreed to this with a jaunty readiness.

It was a fine Saturday for the wedding, the autumn sun clear and warm, and at about one o'clock he said to his mother, 'Some of the men want to give me good wishes in The Hawk. So I'll be off now. See you in the chapel.'

'It's last night the men should have done that,' she expostulated. 'You'll be smelling in the chapel.' She was hurt that he was allowing her to proceed there alone, though the distance was short and no car had been hired.

He promised not to allow the well-wishers to incommode him, praised her silk dress, and went off up the lane of russet trees. Did he need drink and male jests to give him courage after all? But he hadn't been at all jumpy or excited during the morning. At noon, dressed in his expensive new suit, and his fresh-cut hair glistening with oil, he had eaten a substantial meal.

The ceremony had been fixed for two fifteen on the holiday afternoon, to allow as many people as possible to attend. Just after two, closing time in The Hawk until the evening session, a dozen or so men crossed the road to pay respects by attending. The unusual courtship had brought in other people besides formally invited guests; five theological students were there, too, supposedly to see how wedding ceremonies in Nonconformist chapels were conducted. The groom's mother sat alone in her pew. Jane, with her mother and a male escort from Marlais, waited in the vestry for Tudor's arrival. He should have been standing by the vase of white chrysanthemums under the pulpit, and at two twenty-five the Rev A C Powys came out of the vestry, crossed to Mrs Edwards, and asked why her son was late.

'He left home at one o'clock to go up to The Hawk,' she mumbled, very flustered.

There was a tightening of silence among the congregation when, a few minutes later, she was called into the vestry. It had been easy to discover that Tudor hadn't visited The Hawk; and his mother, eyes as agog as everybody's, had barely entered the vestry when Blodwen Lewis, the barmaid, hastened in with her gaping nephew, a boy of ten who was still carrying a glass jar with a huge frog in it.

'I saw Tudor Edwards running on the river bank about half an hour ago,' he blurted, encouraged to it by his aunt. 'He had a bag and went climbing up to Howell's Spout.'

Everybody knew that at two fifteen a bus to Marlais and its railway station passed the Howell's Spout crossroads outside the village.

'His new bag,' declared his mother, at once, 'was in my house when I left. Packed ready for London.'

52

Cross-examination of the boy revealed that it was the same bag. 'Then he must have gone back to the house to fetch it!' deduced the reverend cleverly. He was distracted at the prospect of a nasty vendetta developing between two valued families of his flock.

Jane, sitting on a hard chair in a flounced-out dress of pearly grey, did not swoon. But she gazed fixedly into the air, her strong jaw dropped, this contest lost. Mrs Morgan pranced about on high heels. But, because of the sacred nature of the adjoining edifice, rising tempers had been kept in check. Then the minister returned from announcing to the congregation that the ceremony was postponed.

'Tudor is gone out of his mind and is wandering!' the groom's mother cried, her distress so wholehearted that no one could accuse her of a taunt as she gasped, 'Tell the police!'

'Postponed?' the bride's mother burst out, while the minister poured a glass of water for her silent daughter. 'He'd marry her across my dead body!'

The reverend quickly took out his watch. 'Baptism of the Leyshons' baby is in fifteen minutes,' he said, more peremptorily than was usual with him. 'So now I must get ready in quiet, please.' Outside the chapel people stood babbling in close groups as if some big event, such as declaration of another war, had happened.

Opinion in The Hawk, early that evening, was cautious. No one denounced Tudor, and neither was he praised. Dirty tricks should not be countenanced, but it was vain to sit in judgement on the eternal slipperiness of love. As well sit on the meaning of the vanishing rainbow or a kingfisher's flight down a stream.

Sergeant Pryse said, 'His mother hasn't reported to me that he's missing, and till she does that I don't know anything.' Always a sign that he was speaking as an ordinary man, he laid his helmet on the bar counter. 'People say a fellow can't help coming back to where he's done a deed, but I dare say we won't be seeing Tudor in these parts again. It's been the old Adam coming out in him today. He grew up on that day in court.'

'Old Adam fiddlesticks!' sniffed the listening barmaid, who didn't care much for Pryse. 'It's hard on his poor mother—

53

she'll be there, bearing the brunt. I expect she's collapsing in in her cottage, and if *I* was a policeman I'd be down there trying to find out what I could.'

The absconder's mother wasn't really collapsing. She had found a token of his regard in an envelope on her dressing table when, still panting a little, she had gone upstairs to change into everyday clothes. He never had been a boy to write letters and, in his outsize scrawl, all he said was:

> Dear Mam, I am catching the three o'clock train in Marlais and I will be looking over Cousin Ellis' farm before dark. You see, Mam, I thought to myself how Jane and her mother liked to show off and have things done for all the people of Clawdd to see, same as before the magistrates in court last July. So they can do the same today. Jane asked me for twenty-five pounds to help to buy her clothes for today, and I gave it. So I haven't robbed her—not of money—and she's got the engagement ring costing thirty pounds. She bought a fine dress. I didn't tell you about this because you had been very upset when they wanted four houses, and I was upset too and I began to make up my mind about today then. Jane pretended.

> from Tudor

She sat for a while in reverie. He had known she would not have allowed him to do the act of that day! No good woman would have approved it. Yet she couldn't help admiring its angry rigour now. A young man worth his salt mustn't be a worshipping angel all the time. How stupid of Jane to let herself ask for cash before the permission of marriage! And how that day had been a high-priced one for everybody concerned! She stroked the lovely silk of her own dress.

After giving the Morgans decent time to recover, she put on the costly hat bought for the wedding and went up to their house. Opening the porch door, off which the paint was flaking, Mrs Morgan admitted the silent visitor. 'Where is he?' she demanded, as they went into a room off the gloomy hall. 'I'll track him to the ends of the earth and sue.'

A three-tiered cake, a whole ham, dishes of sandwiches, small pies, and bottles of drink were spread on a white-clothed table.

Tudor's mother looked at these festive things in horror. Why hadn't they been put out of sight?

'The expense I've gone to!' Mrs Morgan continued her bombast. 'But I'll get every penny back!'

Mrs Edwards glanced at a board erected on trestles in a corner; on it were displayed the wedding gifts, which included two clocks not yet going, a set of saucepans, an electric iron and a tea-cosy. 'Your daughter?' she asked, looking about her in the fading light.

'Jane, come down,' Mrs Morgan shouted into the hall. 'His mother's here.'

She came in at a run, wearing a crumpled new dressing gown, as if she had been lying on her bed. 'He's come back?' she cried.

Mrs Edwards shook her head. 'I wouldn't be surprised to hear he's gone to join the Army,' she said.

Jane sank to a chair. 'I'll sue him for breach of promise!'

'Tudor's got no money or property to pay for breach of promise. The business of the three houses was put off till you were settled.' Mrs Edwards took a long breath, turned her back on Mrs Morgan, and addressed Jane. 'I have come to say I am sorry ... But you were hard and foolish in getting the magistrate to fine a man that only wanted to *look* on what had taken his fancy, strange though that was. Tudor is a boy that gets queer notions. I have noticed that when the moon is rising—'

'The moon has got nothing to do with it,' Mrs Morgan cut into what seemed the beginning of a long speech of humble defence. 'The plain fact is that he's a born clod and needs a good thrashing.'

'Then what he's done is best for Jane's future,' Mrs Edwards said, still meek.

Jane's hands seemed to be trying to push an awful outburst back down her shapely bosom. She succeeded, and only exclaimed, 'You've been in league with him, you humbug, and egged him on in what he's done!'

Mrs Edwards looked at Jane's foreshadowing chin, and at the solid face that should have been eased by true love. She shook her head again, as at some erroneous piece of judgement on nature's part, and asked, 'Would I have paid twelve pounds for this silk dress if I knew what he was going to do? And three

55

pounds for this hat?' She crossed to the display of gifts and picked up Christmas Evans. 'Would I have given you *this*, and the sheets and quilt?' She held aloft the effigy of the celebrated divine. 'I swear by Christmas Evans that I did *not* know!'

'Put that ornament back!' commanded Mrs Morgan, stepping to her.

Mrs Edwards held the preacher against her chest. 'He was one of *my* wedding presents,' she said, and suddenly her demeanour became so steely and menacing that Mrs Morgan, as if fearing Christmas Evans would be smashed on her head, shrank back. 'He will be more at home in my cottage,' she added. 'You can keep the linen bedsheets and the seven-guinea quilt, in memory.' She walked out of the house unmolested.

She did not uproot herself from Clawdd for several months, occupied with the business of selling her cottage. And Jane did not sue for breach of promise. With their ferretings into privacies and idyllic things that often take place—at least, in Clawdd—under trees in lonely woodlands or on a sweet river bank, when only bats or an owl are unbiased witnesses, such lawsuits can be undignified as well as costly to pocket and reputation. But she got her reward for this self-discipline. In due course a youngish schoolmaster in Marlais stood beside her under the pulpit. A sound man, he played cricket and football, and tore about ancient Clawdd on a roaring motor-scooter, Jane proudly erect behind him. He was not the sort to relish a girl who forgot delicacy so far as to rush to a public court over a love affair gone wrong.

FEAR

As soon as the boy got into the compartment he felt there was
something queer in it. The only other occupant was a slight,
dusky man who sat in a corner with that air of propriety and
unassertiveness which his race—he looked like an Indian—tend
to display in England. There was also a faint sickly scent. For
years afterwards, whenever he smelled that musk odour again,
the terror of this afternoon came back to him.

He went to the other end of the compartment, sat in the
opposite corner. There were no corridors in these local trains.
The man looked at him and smiled friendlily. The boy
returned the smile briefly, not quite knowing what he was
thinking, only aware of a deep, vague unease. But it would
look so silly to jump out of the compartment now. The train
gave a jerk and began to move.

Then, immediately with the jerk, the man began to utter a
low humming chant, slow but with a definite rhythm. His lips
did not open or even move, yet the hum penetrated above the
noise of the train's wheels. It was in a sort of dreamy rhythm,
enticing, lonely and antique; it suggested monotonous deserts,
an eternal patience, a soothing wisdom. It went on and on.
It was the kind of archaic chant that brings to the mind images
of slowly swaying bodies in some endless ceremony in a barbaric
temple.

Startled, and very alive to this proof of there being something
odd in the compartment, the boy turned from staring out of the
window—already the train was deep in the country among
lonely fields and dark wooded slopes—and forced himself to
glance at the man.

The man was looking at him. They faced each other across
the compartment's length. Something coiled up in the boy. It

was as if his soul took primitive fear and crouched to hide. The man's brown lips became stretched in a mysterious smile, though that humming chant continued, wordlessly swaying out of his mouth. His eyes, dark and unfathomable, never moved from the boy. The musk scent was stronger.

Yet this was not all. The boy could not imagine what other fearful thing lurked in the compartment. But he seemed to sense a secret power of something evilly antipathetic. Did it come from the man's long pinky-brown hands, the sinewy but fleshless hands of a sun-scorched race? Long tribal hands like claws. Or only from the fact that the man was of a far country whose ways were utterly alien to ours? And he continued to smile. A faint and subtle smile, while his eyes surveyed the boy as if he contemplated action. Something had flickered in and out of those shadowy eyes, like a dancing malice.

The boy sat stiffly. Somehow he could not return to his staring out of the window. But he tried not to look at the man again. The humming did not stop. And suddenly it took a higher note, like an unhurried wail, yet keeping within its strict and narrow compass. A liquid exultance wavered in and out of the wail. The noise of the train, the flying fields and woods, even the walls of the compartment, had vanished. There was only this chant, the man who was uttering it, and himself. He did not know that now he could not move his eyes from those of the man.

Abruptly the compartment was plunged into blackness. There was a shrieking rush of air. The train had entered a tunnel. With a sudden jerk the boy crouched down. He coiled into the seat's corner, shuddering, yet with every sense electrically alive now.

Then, above the roar of the air and the hurling grind of the train, that hum rose, dominantly establishing its insidious power. It called, it unhurriedly exhorted obedience, it soothed. Again it seemed to obliterate the louder, harsher noises. Spent and defeated, helplessly awaiting whatever menace lay in the darkness, the boy crouched. He knew the man's eyes were gazing towards him; he thought he saw their gleam triumphantly piercing the darkness. What was this strange presence of evil in the air, stronger now in the dark?

Suddenly crashing into the compartment, the hard blue and

white daylight was like a blow. The train had gained speed in the tunnel and now hurled on through the light with the same agonizing impetus, as if it would rush on for ever. Spent in the dread which had almost cancelled out his senses, the boy stared dully at the man. Still he seemed to hear the humming, though actually it had ceased. He saw the man's lips part in a full enticing smile, he saw teeth dazzlingly white between the dusky lips.

'You not like dark tunnel?' The smile continued seductively; once more the flecks of light danced wickedly in his eyes. 'Come!' He beckoned with a long wrinkled finger.

The boy did not move.

'You like pomegranates?' He rose and took from the luggage-rack a brown wicker basket. It was the kind of basket in which a large cat would be sent on a journey. 'Come!' he smiled friendlily and, as the boy still did not move, he crossed over and sat down beside him, but leaving a polite distance.

The staring boy did not flinch.

'Pomegranates from the East! English boy like, eh?' There seemed a collaboration in his intimate voice; he too was a boy going to share fruit with his friend. 'Nice pomegranates,' he smiled with good-humour. There was also something stupid in his manner, a fatuous mysteriousness.

The basket lay on his knees. He began to hum again. The boy watched, still without movement, cold and abstract in his non-apprehension of this friendliness. Bur he was aware of the sickly perfume beside him and, more pronounced than ever, of an insidious presence that was utterly alien. That evil power lay in his immediate vicinity. The man looked at him again and, still humming, drew a rod and lifted the basket's lid.

There was no glow of magically gleaming fruits, no yellow-and-rose-tinted rinds enclosing honeycombs of luscious seeds. But from the basket's depth rose the head of a snake. It rose slowly to the enchantment of the hum. It rose from its sleepy coil, rearing its long brownish-gold throat dreamily, the head swaying out in languor towards the man's lips. Its eyes seemed to look blindly at nothing. It was a cobra.

Something happened to the boy. An old warning of the muscles and the vulnerable flesh. He leapt and flung himself headlong across the compartment. He was not aware that he gave a sharp shriek. He curled against the opposite seat's back, his knees pressing into the cushion. But, half turning, his eyes could not tear themselves from that reared head.

And it was with other senses that he knew most deeply he had evoked rage. The cobra was writhing in disturbed anger, shooting its head in his direction. He saw wakened pin-point eyes of black malice. More fearful was the dilation of the throat, its skin swelling evilly into a hood in which shone two palpitating sparks. In some cell of his being he knew that the hood was swelling in destructive fury. He became very still.

The man did not stop humming. But now his narrowed eyes were focused in glittering concentration on the snake. And into that hum had crept a new note of tenacious decision. It was a pitting of subtle power against the snake's wishes and it was also an appeasement. A man was addressing a snake. He was offering a snake tribute and acknowledgement of its right to anger; he was honeyed and soothing. At the same time he did not relax an announcement of being master. There was courtesy towards one of the supreme powers of the animal kingdom, but also there was the ancient pride of man's supremacy.

And the snake was pacified. Its strange reared collar of skin sank back into its neck; its head ceased to lunge towards the boy. The humming slackened into a dreamy lullaby. Narrowly intent now, the man's eyes did not move. The length of tawny body slowly sank back. Its skin had a dull glisten, the glisten of an unhealthy torpidity. Now the snake looked effete, shorn of its venomous power. The drugged head sank. Unhurriedly the man closed the basket and slipped its rod secure.

He turned angrily to the boy; he made a contemptuous sound, like a hiss. 'I show you cobra and you jump and shout, heh! Make him angry!' There was more rebuke than real rage in his exclamations. But also his brown face was puckered in a kind of childish stupidity; he might have been another boy of twelve.

'I give you free performance with cobra, and you jump and scream like little girl.' The indignation died out of his eyes; they became focused in a more adult perception. 'I sing to keep cobra quiet in train,' he explained. 'Cobra not like train.'

The boy had not stirred. 'You not like cobra?' the man

60

asked in injured surprise. 'Nice snake now, no poison! But not liking you jump and shout.'

There was no reply or movement; centuries and continents lay between him and the boy's still repudiation. The man gazed at him in silence and added worriedly: 'You going to fair in Newport? You see me? Ali the Snake Charmer. You come in free and see me make cobra dance—'

But the train was drawing into the station. It was not the boy's station. He made a sudden blind leap away from the man, opened the door, saw it was not on the platform side, but jumped. There was a shout from someone. He ran up the track, he dived under some wire railings. He ran with amazingly quick short leaps up a field—like a hare that knows its life is precarious among the colossal dangers of the open world and has suddenly sensed one of them.

I WILL KEEP HER COMPANY

When he achieved the feat of getting down the stairs to the icy living room, it was the peculiar silence there that impressed him. It had not been so noticeable upstairs, where all night he had had company, of a kind. Down in this room, the familiar morning sounds he had known for sixty years—all the crockery, pots and pans, and fire-grate noises of married life at break of day, his wife's brisk soprano not least among them— were abolished as though they had never existed.

It was the snow that had brought this silence, of course. How many days had it been falling—four, five? He couldn't remember. Still dazed and stiff from his long vigil in a chair upstairs, he hobbled slowly to the window. Sight of the magnificent white spread brought, as always, astonishment. Who would have thought such a vast quantity waited above? Almighty in its power to obliterate the known works of man, especially his carefully mapped highways and byways, the weight of odourless substance was like a reminder that he was of no more account than an ant. But only a few last flakes were falling now, the small aster shapes drifting with dry languor on the hefty waves covering the long front garden.

'They'll be here today,' he said aloud, wakened a little more by the dazzle. The sound of his voice was strange to him, like an echo of it coming back from a chasm. His head turning automatically towards the open door leading to the hallway, he broke the silence again, unwilling to let it settle. 'Been snowing again all night, Maria. But it's stopping now. They'll come today. The roads have been blocked. Hasn't been a fall like it for years.'

His frosting breath plumed the air. He turned back to the window and continued to peer out for a while. A drift swelled to above the sill, and there was no imprint of the robins and tits that regularly landed before the window in the mornings, for breakfast crumbs. Neither was there a sign of the garden gate into the lane, nor a glimpse of the village, two miles distant down the valley, which could be seen from this height on green days. But the mountains, ramparts against howling Atlantic gales, were visible in glitteringly bleached outline against a pale-blue sky. Savage guardians of interior Wales, even their lowering black clouds and whipping rains were vanquished today. They looked innocent in their unbroken white.

His mind woke still more. The manacled landscape gave him, for the moment, a feeling of security. This snow was a protection, not a catastrophe. He did not want the overdue visitors to arrive, did not want to exercise himself again in resistance to their arguments for his future welfare. Not yet. He thought of his six damson trees, which he had introduced into the orchard a few years before and reared with such care. Last summer, there had been a nice little profit from the baskets of downy fruit. Was he to be forced away from his grown-up darlings now? Just one more season of gathering, and, afterwards, he would be ready to decide about the future . . .

Then, remembering something else, he lamented, 'They'll come, they'll come!' They had such a special reason for making the journey. And this marooning snow would give even more urgency to their arguments regarding himself. He strained his keen old countryman's eyes down the anonymous white distances. *Could* they come? Could anyone break a way through those miles of deep snow, where nothing shuffled, crawled, or even flew? The whole world had halted. They would not come today. There would be one more day of peace.

Mesmerized at the window, he recalled another supreme time of snow, long ago, before he was married. He and two other farm workers had gone in search of Ambrose Owen's sheep. An old ram was found in a drift, stiff and upright on his legs, glassy eyes staring at nothing, curls of wool turned to a cockleshell hardness that could be chipped from the fleece. Farther away in the drift, nine wise ewes lay huddled against each other, and these were carried upside down by the legs to the farmhouse kitchen, where they thawed into life. But Ambrose, like that man in the Bible with a prodigal son, had

63

broken down and shed tears over his lost ram that had foolishly wandered from the herd. The elderly farmer was in a low condition himself at the time, refusing to be taken to hospital, wanting to kick the bucket not only in his own home but downstairs in his fireside chair. Quite right too.

He returned from the window at last, drew a crimson flannel shawl from his sparsely-haired head, and rearranged it carefully over his narrow shoulders. He wore two cardigans and trousers of thick homespun, but the cold penetrated to his bones. Still unwilling to begin the day's ritual of living down in this room, he stood gazing vaguely from the cinder-strewn fireplace to the furniture, his eyes lingering on the beautifully polished rosewood table at which, with seldom a cross word exchanged (so it seemed now), he had shared good breakfasts for a lifetime. Was it because of the unnatural silence, with not the whirr of a single bird outside, that all the familiar contents of the room seemed withdrawn from ownership? They looked stranded.

Remembrance came to him of the room having this same hush of unbelonging when he and Maria had first walked into it, with the idea of buying the place, a freehold stone cottage and its four acres, for ninety-five sovereigns, cash down. They were courting at the time, and the property was cheap because of its isolation; no one had lived there for years. The orchard, still well-stocked, had decided him, and Maria, who could depend on herself and a husband for all the talking company she needed, agreed because of the tremendous views of mountain range and sky from this closed end of the valley. What a walker she had been! Never wanted even a bike, did not want to keep livestock, and was content with the one child that came very soon after the rushed purchase of the cottage. But, disregarding gossip, she had liked to go down to church in the village, where she sang psalms louder than any other woman there.

He had huddled closer into the shawl. Since he would not be staying long down here, was it worth while lighting a fire? Then he realized that if the visitors found means of coming, it would be prudent to let them see he could cope with the household jobs. First, the grate to be raked and a fire laid; wood and coal to be fetched from outside. But he couldn't

64

hurry. His scalp was beginning to prickle and contract, and he drew the shawl over his head again. Feeling was already gone from his feet when he reached the shadowy kitchen lying off the living room, fumblingly pulled the back door open, and faced a wall of pure white.

The entire door space was blocked, sealing access to the shed in which, besides wood and coal, oil for the cooking stove was stored. He had forgotten that the wall had been there the day before. Snow had drifted down the mountain slope and piled as far as the back window upstairs even then; it came back to him that he had drawn the kitchen window curtains to hide that weight of tombstone white against the panes. 'Marble,' he said now, curiously running a finger over the crisply hardened surface. He shut the door, relieved that one item in the morning jobs was settled; it would be impossible to reach the shed from the front of the cottage.

Pondering in the dowdy light of the kitchen, he looked at the empty glass oil-feeder of the cooking stove, at the empty kettle, at an earthenware pitcher, which he knew was empty, too. He remembered that the water butt against the outside front wall had been frozen solid for days before the snow began. And even if he had the strength to dig a path to the well in the orchard, very likely that would be frozen. Would snow melt inside the house? But a little water remained in an ewer upstairs. And wasn't there still some of the milk that the district nurse had brought? He found the jug in the slate-shelved larder, and tilted it; the inch-deep, semi-congealed liquid moved. He replaced the jug with a wrinkling nose, and peered at three tins of soup that also had been brought by Nurse Baldock.

Sight of the tins gave him a feeling of nausea. The last time the nurse had come—*which* day was it?—a smell like ammonia had hung about her. And her pink rubber gloves, her apron with its row of safety pins and a tape measure dangling over it, had badly depressed him. A kind woman, though, except for her deciding what was the best way for a man to live. The sort that treated all men as little boys. She had a voice that wouldn't let go of a person, but being a woman, a soft wheedling could come into it when she chose. Thank God the snow had bogged her down.

65

He reached for a flat box, opened it, and saw a few biscuits. Maria always liked the lid picture of Caernarvon Castle, which they'd visited one summer day; he looked at it now with a reminiscent chuckle. His movements became automatically exact, yet vague and random. He found a tin tray inscribed 'Ringer's Tobacco' and placed on it the box, a plate and, forgetting there was no milk left upstairs, a clean cup and saucer. This done, he suddenly sat down on a hard chair and closed his eyes.

He did not know how long he remained there. Tapping sounds roused him; he jerked from the chair with galvanized strength. Agitation gave his shouts an unreasonable cantankerousness as he reached the living room. 'They've come! Open the door, can't you? It's not locked.'

He opened the front door. There was nobody. The snow reached up to his waist, and the stretch of it down the garden slope bore not a mark. Only an elephant could come to this door. Had he dreamed the arrival? Or had a starving bird tapped its beak on the window? The dread eased. He shut the door with both his shaking hands, and stood listening in the small hallway. 'They haven't come!' he shouted up the stairs, wanting to hear his voice smashing the silence. 'But they will, they will! They are bringing my pension money from the post office. Dr Howells took my book with him.' Self-reminder of this ordinary matter helped to banish the dread, and the pain in his chest dwindled.

Pausing in the living room, he remembered that it was actually Nurse Baldock who had taken his book and put it in that important black bag of hers. She had arrived that day with Dr Howells in his car, instead of on her bike. The snow had begun to fall, but she said it wouldn't be much—only a sprinkling. And Dr Howells had told him not to worry and that everything would be put in hand. But even the doctor, who should have had a man's understanding, had argued about the future, and coaxed like Nurse Baldock. Then *she* had said she'd bring Vicar Pryce on her next visit. People fussing! But he couldn't lock the door against them yet. It was necessary for them to come just once again. He would pretend to listen to them, especially the vicar, and when they had gone he would lock the door, light a fire, and sit down to think of the future in his own way.

His eyes strayed about the room again. He looked at the table with its green-shaded oil lamp, at the dresser with its display of brilliant plates and lustre jugs, at the comfortable low chairs, the bright rugs, the scroll-backed sofa from which Maria had directed his activities for the week before she was obliged to take to her bed at last. After the shock of the fancied arrival, the objects in the room no longer seemed withdrawn from ownership. They would yield him security and ease, for a long while yet. And the cooking stove in the kitchen, the pans, brooms, and brushes—they had belonged solely to Maria's energetic hands, but after a lifetime with her he knew exactly how she dealt with them. Any man with three-penn'orth of sense could live here independently as a lord. Resolve lay tucked away in his mind. Today, with this cold stunning his senses, not much could be done. He must wait. His eyes reached the mantelpiece clock; lifting the shawl from his ears, he stared closer at the age-yellowed face. *That* was why the silence had been so strange! Was even a clock affected by the cold? Surely he had wound it last night, as usual; surely he had come downstairs? The old-fashioned clopping sound, steady as horse hoofs ambling on a quiet country road, had never stopped before. The defection bothering him more than the lack of means for a fire and oil for the stove, he reached for the mahogany-framed clock, his numb fingers moving over it to take a firm grip. It fell into the stoneflagged hearth. There was a tinkle of broken glass.

'Ah,' he shouted guiltily, 'the clock's broken, Maria! Slipped out of my hand!'

He gazed at it in a stupor. But the accident finally decided him. Down in this room the last bits of feeling were ebbing from him. There was warmth and company upstairs. He stumbled into the kitchen, lifted the tin tray in both hands without feeling its substance, and reached the hallway. Negotiation of the stairs took even more time than his descent had. As in the kitchen, it was the propulsion of old habit that got him up the flight he had climbed thousands of times. The tray fell out of his hands when he reached a squeaking stair just below the landing. This did not matter; he even liked the lively explosion of noise. 'It's only that advertisement tray the shop gave you one Christmas!' he called out, not mentioning the crocks and biscuit box which had crashed to the bottom. He did not attempt to retrieve anything. All he wanted was warmth.

In the clear white light of a front room he stood for some moments looking intently at the weather-browned face of the small woman lying on a four-poster bed. Her eyes were compactly shut. Yet her face bore an expression of prim vigour; still she looked alert in her withdrawal. No harsh glitter of light from the window reached her, but he drew a stiff fold of the gay-patterned linen bed curtains that, as if in readiness for this immurement, had been washed, starched, and ironed by her three weeks before. Then he set about his own task. The crimson shawl still bonneted his head.

His hands plucked at the flannel blankets and larger shawls lying scattered on the floor around a wheelbacked armchair close to the bed. Forcing grip into his fingers, he draped these coverings methodically over the sides and back of the chair, sat down, and swathed his legs and body in the overlapping folds. It all took a long time, and for a while it brought back the pain in his chest, compelling him to stop. Finally, he succeeded in drawing portions of two other shawls over his head and shoulders, so that he was completely encased in draperies. There had been good warmth in this cocoon last night. The everlasting flannel was woven in a mill down the valley, from the prized wool of local mountain sheep. Properly washed in rain water, it yielded warmth for a hundred years or more. There were old valley people who had been born and had gone in the same pair of handed-down family blankets.

Secure in the shelter, he waited patiently for warmth to come. When it began to arrive, and the pain went, his mind flickered into activity again. It was of the prancing mountain ponies he thought first, the wild auburn ponies that were so resentful of capture. He had always admired them. But what did their lucky freedom mean now? *They* had no roof over their heads, and where could they find victuals? Had they lost their bearings up in their fastnesses? Were they charging in demented panic through the endless snow, plunging into crevices, starvation robbing them of instinct and sense? Then there were the foxes. He remembered hearing that during that drastic time of snow when he rescued Ambrose Owen's sheep, a maddened fox had dashed into the vicarage kitchen when a servant opened the back door. It snatched in its teeth a valuable Abyssinian cat lying fast asleep on the hearth rug, and streaked out before the petrified woman could scream.

A little more warmth came. He crouched into it with a sigh. Soon it brought a sense of summer pleasures. A long meadow dotted with buttercups and daisies shimmered before him, and a golden-haired boy ran excitedly over the bright grass to a young white goat tied to an iron stake. Part of the meadow was filled with booths of striped canvas, and a roundabout of painted horses galloped to barrel-organ music. It was that Whitsuntide fete when he had won the raffled goat on a sixpenny ticket—the only time he had won anything all his life. Maria had no feeling for goats, especially rams, but she had let their boy lead the snowy-haired beast home. Richard had looked after it all its sturdy years and, at its hiring, got for himself the fees of its natural purpose in life—five shillings a time, in those far-off days.

The father chuckled. He relaxed further in the dark chair. His hands resting lightly on his knees, he prepared for sleep. It was slow in taking him, and when, drowsily, he heard a whirring sound he gave it no particular attention. But he stirred slightly and opened his eyes. The noise approached closer. It began to circle, now faint, then loud, now dwindling. He did not recognize it. It made him think of a swarm of chirping grasshoppers, then of the harsh clonking of roused geese. Neutral towards all disturbance from outside, he nestled deeper into the warmth bred of the last thin heat of his blood, and when a louder noise shattered the peace of his cocoon he still did not move, though his eyes jerked wide open once more.

The helicopter circled twice above the half-buried cottage. Its clacking sounded more urgent as it descended and began to pass as low as the upstairs windows at the front and back. The noise became a rasp of impatience, as if the machine were annoyed that no reply came to this equivalent of a knocking on the door, that no attention was paid to the victory of this arrival. A face peered down from a curved grey pane; the head of another figure dodged behind, moving to both the side panels.

Indecision seemed to govern this hovering above the massed billows of snow. After the cottage had been circled three times, the machine edged nearer the front wall, and a square box wrapped in orange-coloured oilskin tumbled out, fell accurately before the door, and lay visible in a hole of snow. The machine rose; its rotor blades whirled for seconds above the cottage before it mounted higher. It diminished into the pale afternoon light, flying down the valley towards immaculate mountains that had never known a visit from such a strange bird.

Evening brought an unearthly blue to the sculptured distances. Night scarcely thickened the darkness; the whiteness could be seen for miles. Only the flashing of clear-cut stars broke the long stillness of the valley. No more snow fell. But the cold hardened during the low hours, and at dawn, though a red glow lay in the sun's disc on Moelwyn's crest, light came with grudging slowness, and there was no promise of thaw all morning. But, soon after the sun had passed the zenith, another noise smashed into the keep of silence at the valley's closed end.

Grinding and snorting, a vehicle slowly burrowed into the snow. It left in its wake, like a gigantic horned snail, a silvery track, on which crawled a plain grey motor van. Ahead, the climbing plough was not once defeated by its pioneering work, thrusting past shrouded hedges on either side of it, its grunting front mechanism churning up the snow and shooting it out of a curved-over horn on to bushes at the left. The attendant grey van stopped now and then, allowing a measure of distance to accumulate on the smooth track.

The van had three occupants. Two of them, sitting on the driver's cushioned bench, were philosophically patient of this laborious journeying. The third, who was Nurse Baldock, squatted on the floor inside the small van, her legs stretched towards the driver's seat and her shoulders against the back door. She was a substantial woman, and the ungainly fur coat she wore gave her the dimensions of a mature bear. She tried not to be restless. But as the instigator of this rescuing operation, she kept looking at her watch, and she failed to curb herself all the time. The two men in front had not been disposed for talk.

'I hope that thing up there won't break down,' she said presently. 'It's a Canadian snowplough—so I was told on the phone. The Council bought it only last year.'

'It took them a deuce of a time to get one after we had that nasty snowfall in 1947,' remarked the driver, a middle-aged man in a sombre vicuna overcoat and a bowler hat. 'A chap and his young lady were found buried in their car halfway up Moelwyn when we had *that* lot—been there a week, if you remember, Vicar. Thank God these bad falls don't come often.'

'Councils seldom look far outside their town hall chamber after election,' mumbled Vicar Pryce, who had been picked up in Ogwen village twenty minutes earlier. Under his round black hat only his eyes and bleak nose were visible from wrappings of scarves. It was very cold in the utilitarian van, lent for this emergency expedition by a tradesman of the market town at the valley's mouth; the road from there to Ogwen had been cleared the day before.

'Well, our Council has got hold of a helicopter this time, too,' Nurse Baldock reminded them, not approving of criticism of her employers from anyone. 'Soon as I heard they had hired one to drop bundles of hay to stranded cattle and mountain ponies, I said to myself, "Man first, then the beasts," and flew to my phone. I'm fond of old John Evans, though he's so wilful. I arranged to have tins of food, fruit juice, milk, a small bottle of brandy, fresh pork sausages, and bread put in the box, besides a plastic container of cooker oil and a message from me.'

'Couldn't you have gone in the helicopter?' the driver asked, rather inattentively.

'What, and got dropped out into the snow with the box?' The nurse's bulk wobbled with impatience. 'If the machine couldn't land anywhere on those deep slopes of snow, how could I get down, I ask you?'

'I thought they could drop a person on a rope.' The driver sounded propitiatory now. For him, as for most people, the district nurse was less a woman than a portent of inescapable forces lying in wait for everybody.

'Delivery of necessities was the point,' she said dismissingly, and, really for Vicar Pryce's wrapped ears, continued, 'After getting the helicopter man's report yesterday, I was on the phone to the Town Hall for half an hour. I insisted that they let me have the snowplough today—I *fought* for it. It was booked for this and that, they said, but I had my way in the end.'

71

'Last night was bitter,' Vicar Pryce said, following a silence. 'I got up at 3 am and piled a sheepskin floor rug on my bed.'

'Bitter it *was*,' agreed Nurse Baldock. 'We single people feel it the more.' Neither of the men offered a comment, and, with another look at her watch, she pursued, 'Of course, the helicopter man's report needn't mean a lot. Who could blame Evans if he stayed snuggled in bed all day? And at his age, he could sleep through any noise.'

'One would think a helicopter's clatter would bring him out of any sleep, Nurse,' the Vicar remarked.

'I think he's a bit deaf,' she replied, rejecting the doubt. 'In any case, I don't suppose he'd know what the noise meant.' The van stopped, and she decided, 'We'll have our coffee now.'

She managed to spread quite a picnic snack on the flat top of a long, calico-covered object lying beside her, on which she wouldn't sit. There were cheese and egg sandwiches, pieces of sultana cake, plates, mugs, sugar and a large Thermos flask. A heavy can of paraffin propped her back, and, in addition to the satchel of picnic stuff, she had brought her official leather bag, well known in the valley. Nurse Baldock's thoroughness was as dreaded by many as was sight of her black bag. After determined efforts over several years, she had recently been awarded a social science diploma, and now, at forty-five, she hoped for a more important position than that of a bicycle-borne district nurse.

This rescuing mission today would help prove her mettle, and Vicar Pryce, to whom she had insisted on yielding the seat in front, would be a valuable witness of her zeal.

'I'll keep enough for the young man in the snowplough,' she said, pouring coffee. 'He ought not to stop now. The quicker we get there the better.'

'Makes one think of places in the moon,' the driver remarked, gazing out at the waxen countryside.

Sipping coffee, she resumed, 'I have eight patients in Ogwen just now, and really I ought not to be spending all this time on a man who's got nothing the matter with him except old age and obstinacy. Two confinements due any day now.' The men drank and ate, and she added, 'What a time for births! There's Mavis Thomas, for instance—she's not exactly entitled to one, is she, Vicar? But at least that man she lives with keeps her house on Sheep's Gap warm, and her water hasn't frozen.'

'Nobody except a choirboy turned up for matins last Sunday,' the meditative vicar said. 'So I cancelled all services that day.'

Nurse Baldock finished a piece of cake. 'I heard yesterday that a married woman living up on Sheep's Gap was chased by two starving ponies that found a way down from the mountains. You know how they won't go near human beings as a rule, but when this woman came out of her farmhouse in her gumboots they stampeded from behind a barn; with their teeth grinding and eyes flaring. She ran back screaming into the house just in time.'

'Perhaps she was carrying a bucket of pig feed and they smelt it,' the driver suggested, handing back his mug.

Undeterred, Nurse Baldock gave a feminine shiver. 'I keep an eye open for them on my rounds. We might be back in the days of wolves.' The van resumed its amble on the pearly track as she proceeded.

'But these are modern times. Old Evans would never dream he would get a helicopter for his benefit, to say nothing of that great ugly thing in front, *and* us. There's real Christianity for you! This affair will cost the Council quite a sum. It will go on the rates, of course.'

'John and Maria Evans,' Vicar Pryce said, rewrapping his ears in the scarves, 'were always faithful parishioners of mine when they were able to get down to the village. I remember their son Richard, too. A good tenor in the choir. Emigrated to New Zealand and has children of his own there, I understand.'

'Well, Vicar,' Nurse Baldock said, packing the crocks into the satchel between her knees, 'I hope you'll do your very best to persuade Evans to leave with us today and go to Pistyll Mawr Home. Heaven knows, I did all I could to coax him when I was at the cottage with Dr Howells the other day.'

'It will be a business,' he mumbled.

She pursed her lips. 'He told me it was healthy up there in his cottage, and that he and his wife had always liked the views. "Views!" I said, "Views won't feed and nurse you if you fall ill. Come now, facts must be faced." Then he said something about his damson trees. I told him Pistyll Mawr had fruit trees in plenty.'

The driver, who lived in the market town, spoke. 'Don't the new cases take offence at being forced to have a bath as soon as they enter the doors of Pistyll Mawr?'

'So you've heard that one, have you? Why, what's wrong with a bath? Is it a crime?' Nurse Baldock had bridled. 'I am able to tell you there's a woman in Pistyll Mawr who *brags* about her baths there—says that for the first time in her life she feels like a well-off lady, with a maid to sponge her back and hand her a towel. You're out of date, sir, with your "take offence".'

'Aren't there separate quarters for men and women, even if they're married?' he persisted.

'As if very elderly people are bothered by what you mean! Besides, they can flirt in the garden if they want. But old people have too much dignity for such nonsense.'

'I dare say there are one or two exceptions.'

'Ah, I agree there.' Nurse Baldock pulled gauntlet gloves over her mittens. 'The aged! They're our biggest problem. The things that come my way from some of them! One has to have nerves of iron, and it doesn't do to let one's eyes fill. Why must people trouble themselves so much about the young? My blood boils when I see all the rubbishy fuss made about the youngsters by newspapers and busybodies of the lay public. Sight of the word "teenagers" makes me want to throw up. Leave the young alone, I say! They've got all the treasures of the world on their backs, and once they're out of school they don't put much expense on the rates.'

After this tirade no one spoke for a time. As the van crawled nearer the valley's majestic closure, Nurse Baldock herself seemed to become oppressed by the solemn desolation outside. Not a boulder or streak of path showed on Moelwyn's swollen heights. Yet, close at hand, there were charming snow effects. The van rounded a turn of the lane, and breaks in the hedges on either side revealed birch glades, their spectral depths glittering as though from the light of ceremonial chandeliers. All the crystalline birches were struck into eternal stillness— fragile, rime-heavy boughs sweeping downward, white hairs of mourning. Not a bird, rabbit, or beetle could stir in those frozen grottoes, and the blue harebell or the pink convolvulus never ring out in them again.

'Up here doesn't seem to belong to us,' Vicar Pryce said, when the van halted again. 'It's the white. If only we could see just one little robin hopping about the branches! The last time I came this way, I saw pheasants crossing the road, and then they rose. Such colour! It was soon after Easter, and the wind-flowers and primroses were out.'

'We might be travelling in a wheelbarrow,' sighed Nurse Baldock, as the van moved. She looked at her watch, then into her official bag, and said, 'I've got Evans' old-age pension money. Because of his wife's taking to her bed, he worried about not being able to leave the cottage. I told him, "You're lucky you've got someone like me to look after you, but it's not my bounden task to collect your pension money, Council-employed though I am. Things can't go on like this, my dear sir, come now."'

'You've been kind to him,' the Vicar acknowledged at last.

'It's the State that is kind,' she said stoutly. 'We can say there's no such thing as neglect or old-fashioned poverty for the elderly now. But in my opinion the lay public has begun to take our welfare schemes too much for granted. The other day, I was able to get a wig free of charge for a certain madam living not a hundred miles from this spot, and when I turned up with it on my bike she complained it wasn't the right brown shade and she couldn't wear it—a woman who is not able to step outside her door and is seventy-eight!'

'The aged tend to cling to their little cussednesses,' Vicar Pryce mumbled, in a lacklustre way.

'Yes, indeed.' They were nearing their destination now, and Nurse Baldock, tenacity unabated, seized her last opportunity. 'But do press the real advantages of Pistyll Mawr Home to Evans, Vicar. We are grateful when the Church does its share in these cases. After all, my concern is with the body.' This earned no reply, and she said, 'Germs! It's too icy for them to be active just now, but with the thaw there'll be a fine crop of bronchials and influenzas, mark my words! And I don't relish coming all this way to attend to Evans if he's struck down, probably through not taking proper nourishment.' There was a further silence, and she added, 'On the other hand, these outlying cases ought to convince the Health Department that I must be given a car—don't you agree, Vicar?'

'I wonder you have not had one already. Dr Howells should—'

A few yards ahead, the plough had stopped. Its driver leaned out of his cabin and yelled, 'Can't see a gate!'

'I'll find it,' Nurse Baldock declared.

The vicar and van driver helped to ease her out of the back doors. She shook her glut of warm skirts down, and clumped forward in her gumboots. A snow-caked roof and chimney could be seen above a billowing white slope. Scanning the contours of a buried hedge, the nurse pointed. 'The gate is there. I used to lean my bike against that tree.' It was another lamenting birch, the crystal-entwined branches drooped to the snow.

The plough driver, an amiable-looking young man in an elegant alpine sweater, brought out three shovels. Nurse Baldock scolded him for not having four. Valiantly, when he stopped for coffee and sandwiches, she did a stint, and also used the Vicar's shovel while he rested. They had shouted towards the cottage. There was no response and, gradually, they ceased to talk. It took them half an hour to clear a way up the garden. They saw the oilskin-wrapped box as they neared the door. The nurse, her square face professionally rid of comment now, had already fetched her bag.

It was even colder in the stone house than outside. Nurse Baldock, the first to enter, returned from a swift trot into the living room and kitchen to the men clustered in the little hall-way. She stepped to the staircase. All-seeing as an investigating policewoman, she was nevertheless respecting the social decencies. Also, despite the sight of broken crockery, a biscuit box, and a tray scattered below the stairs, she was refusing to face defeat yet. 'John Ormond Evans,' she called up, 'are you there?' Her voice had the challenging ring sometimes used for encouraging the declining back to the world of health, and after a moment of silence, she added, with an unexpected note of entreaty, 'The vicar is here!' The three men, like awkward intruders in a private place, stood listening. Nurse Baldock braced herself. 'Come up with me,' she whispered.

76

Even the plough driver followed her. But when the flannel wrappings were stripped away, John Ormond Evans sat gazing out at them from his chair as though in mild surprise at this intrusion into his comfortable retreat. His deep-sunk blue eyes were frostily clear under arched white brows. He looked like one awakened from restorative slumber, an expression of judicious independence fixed on his spare face. His hands rested on his knees, like a Pharaoh's.

Nurse Baldock caught in her breath with a hissing sound. The two older men, who had remained hatted and gloved in the icy room, stood dumbly arrested. It was the ruddy-cheeked young man who suddenly put out a bare, instinctive hand and, with a movement of extraordinary delicacy, tried to close the blue eyes. He failed.

'I closed my father's eyes,' he stammered, drawing away in bashful apology for his strange temerity.

'Frozen,' pronounced Vicar Pryce, removing his round black hat. He seemed about to offer a few valedictory words.

Nurse Baldock pulled herself together. She swallowed, and said, 'Lack of nourishment, too!' She took off a gauntlet glove, thrust fingers round one of the thin wrists for a token feel, and then stepped back. 'Well, here's a problem! Are we to take him back with us?'

Vicar Pryce turned to look at the woman lying on the curtain-hung bed. Perhaps because his senses were blurred by the cold, he murmured, 'She's very small—smaller than I remember her. Couldn't he go in the coffin with her for the journey back?'

'No,' said Nurse Baldock promptly. 'He couldn't be straightened here.'

The van driver, an auxiliary assistant in busy times to Messrs Eccles, the market-town undertakers, confirmed, 'Set, set.'

'As he was in his ways!' burst from Nurse Baldock in her chagrin. 'This needn't have happened if he had come with me, as I wanted six days ago! Did he sit there all night deliberately?'

It was decided to take him. The coffin, three days late in delivery, was fetched from the van by the driver and the young man. Maria Evans, aged eighty-three, and prepared for this journey by the nurse six days before, by no means filled its depth and length. Gone naturally, of old age, and kept fresh by the cold, she looked ready to rise punctiliously to meet the face of the Almighty with the same hale energy as she had met each washing day on earth. Her shawl-draped husband, almost equally small, was borne out after her in his sitting posture.

Nurse Baldock, with the Vicar for witness, locked up the house. Already it had an air of not belonging to anyone. 'We must tell the police we found the clock lying broken in the hearth,' she said. 'There'll be an inquest, of course.'

John Evans, head resting against the van's side, travelled sitting on his wife's coffin; Vicar Pryce considered it unseemly for him to be laid on the floor. The helicopter box of necessities and the heavy can of oil, placed on either side of him, held him secure. Nurse Baldock chose to travel with the young man in the draughty cabin of his plough. Huddled in her fur coat, and looking badly in need of her own hearth, she remained sunk in morose silence now.

The plough, no longer spouting snow, trundled in the van's rear. 'Pretty in there!' the driver ventured to say, in due course. They were passing the spectral birch glades. A bluish shade had come to the depths.

Nurse Baldock stirred. Peering out, she all but spat. 'Damned, damned snow! All my work wasted! Arguments on the phone, a helicopter, and this plough! The cost! I shall have to appear before the Health Committee.'

'I expect they'll give you credit for all you've done for the old fellow,' said the driver, also a Council employee.

She was beyond comforting just then. 'Old people won't *listen!* When I said to him six days ago, "Come with me, there's nothing you can do for her now," he answered, "Not yet. I will keep her company." I could have taken him at once to Pistyll Mawr Home. It was plain he couldn't look after himself. One of those unwise men who let themselves be spoilt by their wives.'

'Well, they're not parted now,' the young man said.

'The point is, if he had come with me he would be enjoying a round of buttered toast in Pistyll Mawr at this very moment. I blame myself for not trying hard enough. But how was I to know all this damn snow was coming?'

'A lot of old people don't like going to Pistyll Mawr Home, do they?'

'What's wrong with Pistyll Mawr? Hetty Jarvis, the matron, has a heart of gold. What's more, now I've got my social science diploma, I'm applying for her position when she retires next year.'

'Good luck to you.' The driver blew on his hands. Already, the speedier van had disappeared into the whiteness.

'The lay public,' Nurse Baldock sighed, looking mollified, '*will* cling to its prejudices.' And half to herself, she went on, 'Hetty Jarvis complained to me that she hasn't got anything like enough inmates to keep her staff occupied. "Baldock," she said to me, "I'm depending on you," and I phoned her only this week to say I had found someone for her, a sober and clean man I would gamble had many years before him if he was properly cared for.'

'Ah,' murmured the driver. He lit a cigarette, at which his preoccupied passenger—after all, they were in a kind of funeral —frowned.

'People should see the beeswaxed parquet floors in Pistyll Mawr,' she pursued. 'When the hydrangeas are in bloom along the drive, our Queen herself couldn't wish for a better approach to her home. The Bishop called it a noble sanctuary in his opening-day speech. And so it is!'

'I've heard the Kingdom of Heaven is like that,' the young man remarked idly. 'People have got to be pushed in.'

Nurse Baldock turned to look at his round face, to which had come, perhaps because of the day's rigours, the faint purple hue of a ripening fig. 'You might think differently later on, my boy,' she commented in a measured way. 'I can tell you there comes a time when few of us are able to stand alone. You saw today what resulted for one who made the wrong choice.'

'Oh, I don't know. I expect he knew what he was doing, down inside him.'

She sighed again, apparently patient of ignorance and youthful lack of feeling. 'I was fond of old Evans,' she said.

'Anyone can see it,' he allowed.

She remained silent for a long while. The costly defeat continued to weigh on her until the plough had lumbered on to the flat of the valley's bed. There, she looked at her watch and began to bustle up from melancholy. 'Five hours on this one case!' she fidgeted. 'I ought to have gone back in the van. I'm due a at case up on Sheep's Gap.'

'Another old one?'

'No, thank God. An illegitimate maternity. Not the first one for her either! And I've got another in the row of cottages down by the little waterfall—a legitimate.' The satisfaction of a life-giving smack on the bottom seemed to resound in her perked-up voice. 'We need them more than ever in nasty times like these, don't we? Providing a house is warm and well stocked for the welcome. Can't you make this thing go faster?'

'I'm at top speed. It's not built for maternities of any kind.'

Nurse Baldock sniffed. She sat more benevolently, however, and offered from the official black bag a packet of barley-sugar sweets. The village lay less than a mile distant. But it was some time before there was a sign of natural life out in the white purity. The smudged outline of a church tower and clustering houses had come into view when the delighted young man exclaimed, 'Look!' Arriving from nowhere, a hare had jumped on to the smooth track. His jump lacked a hare's usual celerity. He seemed bewildered, and sat up for an instant, ears tensed to the noise breaking the silence of these chaotic acres, a palpitating eye cast back in assessment of the oncoming plough. Then his forepaws gave a quick play of movement, like shadow-boxing, and he sprang forward on the track with renewed vitality. Twice he stopped to look, as though in need of affiliation with the plough's motion. But, beyond a bridge over the frozen river, he took a flying leap and, paws barely touching the hardened snow and scut whisking, escaped out of sight.

A VISIT TO
EGGESWICK CASTLE

As was their custom when they moved for the summer months to their country house, eighty miles from London, Mr and Mrs Chalmers made the cook and the housemaid travel first-class on the train, while they themselves, in obedience to their protesting principles (and perhaps as a hair-shirt for their well-off condition), went in the crowded third.

Dorinda Chalmers would say, to such friends as were surprised by this eccentricity: 'Bertie and I are active in our socialism, not mere theorists. Besides, the domestics have the physical work to do when they arrive at Sallows, after a restful journey.' Experienced in social work since her remote girlhood, she yet never paused to wonder if the domestics might feel ill at ease in their first-class splendour.

Cook, in particular, always thought worriedly of the elderly master and mistress getting crushed, hot, and grubby down the train among the riff-raff; faithful to the Chalmerses for a dozen years now, she still hadn't accustomed herself to this topsy-turvy example of their democratic views, although, a meat eater herself, she had rapidly adapted her talents to their strict vegetarianism.

And this year, again, there was a new housemaid—how they came and went!—and, as usual, she had to placate the girl about the summer move. 'Socialists they might be, Marjorie,' she whispered as they settled in the train, 'but in my opinion it's carrying things too far to make us travel first-class. Never mind, I do promise you that Sallows is a lovely house and the countryside the sweetest in England.'

There was only one other passenger in their compartment, an ignoring old gentleman buried under *The Times*, but after sitting *sotto voce* on the edge of the plump upholstery for the first mile or two, they kept entirely without a twitter for the rest of the journey.

Marjorie, indeed, brooded with an unwonted intensity of silence. Cook, knowing from bitter experience how London-born housemaids tended to be incommoded by isolated country parts, did not like her aspect at all. Herself of the old régime and always loyal to the family she chose to serve, she had felt uncertain of Marjorie since the girl arrived out of the foggy unknown during the winter in London.

The democratic mistress, saying she relied on her eye for character, never asked for references. But, of course, Marjorie belonged to the new, flighty brigade—girls who rankled against sleeping in at their jobs, whose corners were not good, who, off-hand with milkmen and window-cleaners, flopped down on sofas with film magazines. From the first, too, Cook had been suspicious of a sultry 'something' lurking in Marjorie's ox-blood eye, and also of her obscure allusions to a Mr Grigson, to whom she was denying wedlock because he drank.

'I *don't* like first-class,' the girl observed pettishly when they emerged from the ordeal at Aldridge station. 'Not a soul to talk to! Often one can pick up a lively acquaintance in the thirds.'

Cook, peering down the platform for the mistress' famous cream cloak, made the best of the unwelcome luxury: 'A woman can depend on respect in the firsts.'

Her cloak—Mrs Chalmers possessed three, of identical cut and shade—flowing from a glittering silver chain at her throat, the mistress swept up to them, while Mr Chalmers, tall, pale green, and as distinguished-looking as a saint, supervised the luggage with the welcoming station-master (to whom he had long ago predicted the nationalization of the railways) and two obsequious porters. It was like royalty arriving. The mistress presented Cook with a key.

'You and Marjorie can go on before us. Take either of the two cars waiting outside. . . . We had such an absorbing conversation in our compartment with an Urban Council rodent operator,' she said. 'In the old days, he would have been called a rat-catcher. He told us a great deal about his work and views. Were you comfortable?'

'Yes, ma'am,' Cook said, and added, a little censoriously:

'Marjorie complained of the lack of company.'

'Oh, but both of you are rested? . . . Marjorie'—the mistress turned to the morose, shoe-gazing girl—'some day this ridiculous class distinction on the railways will be abolished and we shall all travel together happily. We are already a good step towards it with the nationalisation of the lines, and if the Labour Government returns to power next election—' There on the platform she gave quite an oration, until her husband himself released them. He reminded her that before proceeding to Sallows they were paying a call on their bank manager in Aldridge.

'You'd think,' Marjorie grumbled, in the sumptuous hired limousine, 'they'd have a car of their own, with a house in the country.' She had surveyed without enthusiasm the picturesque Aldridge street the car glided through.

'They believe in not having too much that's different from what we have,' Cook said, sounding woolly in this herself.

Now they were out in the lanes among the uninhabited fields, Marjorie began to look alarmed, and even hunted. It was fourteen miles to Sallows, and as the landscape took on a more and more lonely appearance, with the road going through deserted beech-woods ('Forests!' she muttered) of budding green, she let out a little whimper. Suddenly, when the car took a sharp turn, she sat back in a dumpy, gasping heap. 'Ah!' she panted.

Cook said warily: 'Don't you like the countryside? It's pretty. You've gone quite pale!'

Marjorie, as suddenly, sat bolt upright, her protuberant eyes fixed on the glass partition separating them from the driver. 'Have I?' she said. 'I dare say I *have* gone pale!' she added, in a smart, back-answering manner. 'So would you. You see, I'm expecting a little one at the end of September.'

'My God!' Cook, despite her previous forebodings, herself went pale. 'And we're in the country! Till the middle of October!' It was late May.

'I don't care where I am,' Marjorie asserted, still bolt upright and breathing hard. 'It's Mr Grigson.'

'*Now*,' Cook declared, quickly recovering, 'you'll have to marry him, drink or not.'

'He's married. I never seen him touch a drop of drink. I lied to you.'

Cook momentarily edged away from it all; she couldn't abide a liar. 'Well, it's a whole bottle of pickles for you to be in, isn't it!' she said, in due course and with beady satire. Then 'Who's to tell the mistress?'

'I give her satisfaction, don't I?' Marjorie demanded, more herself now the revelation was completed. She always had difficulty in making a direct answer to any question.

No one had ever said that Bessie Allen had a hard heart, and as they drew up to the rose-brick old house, in its charming flower gardens, she announced: 'Well, I'll tell the mistress, and do the best I can for you.'

'No, I'll tell her.' Marjorie spoke with truculence. 'When we're settled in.'

'Best let me do it,' Cook fought.

'Mrs Allen,' Marjorie said proudly, 'it's *my* affair. See?'

That day, and on many other days, they had quite a battle over the necessity of informing Mrs Chalmers. But Marjorie refused to be overcome, and Cook saw that she was of those who always postpone unpleasantness until tomorrow. Nor would she discuss her paramour with any realism, and Mr Grigson remained veiled in thick married-man mists. She even giggled a little hysterically when Cook tried to pin her down to some definite action against the culprit. To offset all this, however, she uncomplainingly accepted the loneliness of the countryside, and, as if her bout of wickedness had improved her character, she worked remarkably well in the house, which wasn't too large.

'I never knew the country could be so good for the nerves,' she declared, always ready to leap when Mrs Chalmers rang the bell.

It wasn't rung often. Master was writing his book out in the garden study, with Mistress helping him. Visitors came to stay most week-ends, but they were talking ones, of serious and tidy disposition, all of them elderly and socialistically considerate of domestic legs.

Then, one morning in the fourth week at Sallows, Cook remarked: 'It's beginning to speak for itself. Even the mistress will notice soon, though the master never will.'

'The mistress can see I'm a good maid,' Marjorie, aware that Cook had something else waiting under her tongue, reiterated.

Cook shook out the contents of a Nut Health Food package into a mixing bowl and said: 'Their daughter is coming down next week-end. She's going to have a baby, too. The mistress told me this morning. Of course, *she* is entitled to one.'

Marjorie, as if abruptly deflated of all power, sat down. 'Ah!' she breathed. 'Ah!'

'The daughter's having hers round about your time, too, I think. So you'll have a rival.'

'I'm an orphan,' Marjorie panted. 'I'll tell Mistress today.'

'Get ready what you're going to say about Mr Grigson,' Cook advised, relenting. 'If you want any help from them, you must blame *him*.'

'Tell them, you mean, I didn't know he was married till too late?'

'Say what you like,' Cook replied, pursily withdrawing. 'Sometimes I believe you've got a mind besides your other things.'

Mrs Chalmers, as her housemaid stood before her with dropped head and made confession, was delighted; she had expected to be given notice when Marjorie requested a private interview. 'Remarkable!' she said. 'This is the second time I have been told such happy news today. I am to be a grand-mother early in October, Marjorie.'

'Soon after my time,' Marjorie whimpered, head drooping lower, the unfortunate one in contrast with the other.

Dorinda Chalmers had not been a public-speaking woman and a Fabian for nearly half a century without learning, she thought, the art of being firmly authoritative while retaining her warm human interior. Confronted with disaster in the lower classes (she had worked for years, early in the century, at one of the idealists' settlements in the East End of London), she always wanted to comfort first, before dwelling on a concrete remedy. 'Now, my dear girl,' she said, 'don't cry. Has the father any plans about it?'

'He broke my heart,' Marjorie sobbed. 'Mr Grigson by name. I found out that he's married.'

At this, Mrs Chalmers bridled up into full alertness. One of her earliest campaigns had been of the feminist persuasion; it was rather old hat now, but a whiff of it was still not offensive to her. An uneducated young woman had been downtrodden in the way that still gave meaning to the ancient crusade. 'Has this man left you entirely to your own resources?' she asked.

Marjorie uttered a sound that seemed an affirmative neigh. 'I'm an orphan,' she added further.

'You poor girl. No doubt that is why you felt the urge to motherhood at all costs. But are you still enamoured of this man?'

The victim managed a straight reply: 'I won't ever see him again.'

'Then we must see what we can do for you,' declared Mrs Chalmers, always an admirer of decisiveness. 'You are fortunate,' she went on, the public-speaking clatter beginning to mount into her voice, 'that we are now living in what is termed—imprecisely as yet, I admit—the Welfare State. This includes a sensible attitude towards unmarried mothers. There is every provision for your category. I can remember, Marjorie, when it was very different! Nowadays you will not want for advice, the finest treatment, and even money.' Always at her best in opportunities for her organizing ability, she was in full and pleasurable flow. 'The State apart, the master and I will not let you down, Marjorie. I would like to arrange your lying-in and convalescence. Meanwhile, of course, you will remain in our employment.' As Marjorie, the emotional crisis of confession over, lifted her head at last, the mistress proceeded: 'But surely you wish to sue the father? If so, we will take legal advice for you.'

'I couldn't face a court, madam,' whimpered Marjorie, becoming agitated again. 'I couldn't, I couldn't.'

'Is this Mr Grigson a scoundrel?'

'I don't want to break up his home.'

'Pride is often a mistake, Marjorie. Don't you think this man should be taught a lesson? Demands on their pocket is the thing that teaches them! Probably you could obtain cash by merely *threatening* proceedings.'

'Mr Grigson is a respectable man,' the girl wept.

Mrs Chalmers, controlling her indignation under these tears, resumed: 'Come, we don't want to make a tragedy of it. With the State so helpful, the moral stigma of your condition is entirely a personal affair nowadays; certainly the retributive element has been abolished and—' Her attention arrested by the apathy settling in the housemaid's face, she pulled herself up. 'Cook knows about this? She is not upset with you?' It was the working class that displayed the most drastic feelings in such a matter.

'Cook has been a married woman,' Marjorie replied obscurely.

'And she has lived in my household a good many years!' the mistress clarified Cook's apparently sensible attitude. 'Now, my dear girl, go and lie down. You are overwrought.'

She stepped briskly into the garden, to tell Bertie without delay. In the country, so little happened. And to ensure that Marjorie obtained all those benefits for which pioneers such as she and Bertie had preached and fought, she could go into action again. Although such old fellow-campaigners as remained were ready enough to visit comfortable Sallows, and the flow of talk never lapsed, she faced the fact that they all were stagnant back-numbers now. The fate of pioneers! And she and Bertie were pioneers who had never achieved fame or notoriety. Vigour unimpaired, she felt not a day over fifty.

On Saturday afternoon, she pecked at her daughter's cheek in the porch, demanding: 'Why didn't you tell us before this week?' Grace, looking in her usual state of decorative torpor, murmured something non-committal, and her mother bustled on: 'There is a pleasing coincidence. Marjorie told me on the day you telephoned that she is expecting a child, too—and more or less at your time.'

'Marjorie?' Grace said, typically blank.

'The housemaid. You visit us so very infrequently that you haven't noticed her. An illegitimate case.' By the time they had crossed the rose garden to Bertie's study, Dorinda had given an account of her plan to avail Marjorie of all State succour.

Bertie craned his long neck at his daughter, greeting her with the arch breeziness that with him took the place of parental pride.

'You bring great news,' he chuckled. 'Sly little puss, keeping it all to yourself till now!'

'David thought his family name ought to be preserved.' Grace sank into the softest chair. 'So I hope it's a boy.'

'Ah, these glamorous titles!' Bertie, shaking his greenishly leonine head, made a rhetorical platform gesture with his hands.

'They'll be totally obsolete in due course,' his wife pronounced. 'Besides, in this case, is there any money to support the glamour?' Sir Leonard, Grace's father-in-law, had nothing but a mouldy manor-house, its acres let out to the local agricultural authority at a nominal rent; the house itself would be the next to go, and probably would become a school or hostel.

'Where *is* your husband, Grace?' she continued, putting her feet up on a stool of blue velvet. It was always 'your husband'.

Vaguely stroking her cascade of fox-coloured hair, which she wore in an uninhibited style testifying to her studio *milieu*, Grace looked somewhat vanquished already. 'David? Painting in Greece.'

'How long has he been there?' The wasp hum was more definite in Dorinda's voice now.

'Three weeks. I told him to get out of the way until I was normal shape again.'

Was she a trifle furtive? That Bohemian world of revolutionary sex freedom that she inhabited! Already, at thirty, she had had two husbands, the divorce from the first decided upon as lightly as an order to the grocer. Her mother, at moments willing to be just, sometimes asked herself if this freedom was a logical development of the feminist rebellion of an earlier era. Was this wayward daughter, despite her inertia, truly the offspring of the fighting energy that was Dorinda Chalmers?

'Well,' she said, looking somewhat halted, 'I suppose he'll be back for the accouchement?'

'I don't see what use he can be with that.' Grace's strange lapis-lazuli eyes fixed themselves speculatively on her mother. 'A painter needs freedom to move about, and you know—don't you—I have the objection of a cow to travelling.'

'Ha, ha!' chuckled her father.

Dorinda, unamused, often suspected that Grace, always

sitting about in sluggish reveries that had no hint of planning, secretly laughed at her long-viewing mother. Even as a child, her attitude at home had been one of orientally passive resistance. 'It's most odd that she's always so lazy!' Mrs Chalmers frequently remarked of this disappointing daughter, born as late as possible, for which surprising event her mother had been compelled to forgo attendance at a Fabian summer school frequented by the Webbs.

'Why doesn't the Arts Council do something for your husband?' She spoke in a brisk forestalling manner, suspecting, and rightly, that Grace had made the journey to Sallows in the hope of borrowing money yet again. 'It is State-financed. But there! If he can afford to travel about Greece—'

'But without me, Mother.' Grace, looking a degree more vanquished, added: 'Perhaps his next exhibition will earn enough to buy a few diapers.'

Dorinda, dismissing this frivolity, resumed the inquiry. 'Are you living alone in that Chelsea flat?'

'I go to the cinema a lot.' Unexpectedly, the examinee began to laugh, with running gurgles and queer convulsive movements of her indolent flesh, so that even her limbs seemed to exclude mirth. 'To the comics, mostly. I even journey out to the surburbs. . . . Oh, I saw such a funny one yesterday.' Her laughter reached boisterous force, as she attempted to engage their attention in a description of some farce.

The hysteria was, of course, a symptom of her condition. After allowing it to subside, Dorinda went on: 'Did your husband get the commission for the theatrical designs?' Grace had 'borrowed' a hundred pounds on this probability.

'No.' A giving-up-the-ghost tone succeeded her mirth. 'The people thought his sketches too fantastic.'

'I'm not surprised.' His mother-in-law had been to one exhibition of his work and considered the afternoon thoroughly misspent. The catalogue introduction had suggested that his revolutionary work represented the chaos and destruction of life today . . . Chaos and destruction! When one of the greatest experiments of modern times, the Socialist State, was in creation before the eyes of these artists and their preposterous women, whose faces, judging by her glimpses of them at David's 'private view', were depraved from inferior intoxicants and, worse, loose living. 'Revolutionary', indeed! These people contaminated the word.

She reverted dutifully to the chief matter in hand. 'Where will you have the child?'

'Oh . . . In the flat, I suppose.'

'Since we are organizing Marjorie's accouchement, your father and I thought you should take advantage of it. Perhaps you could go into the same maternity home—you might have a companion in Marjorie, should your times coincide. You've kept up the National Insurance stamps, of course?'

Her daughter might have been as remote from National Insurance as a woman on the moon. 'I believe we have the card for them,' she murmured glassily.

'Well, as your husband sees fit to remain wandering about Greece at such a time, we had certainly better organize this affair for you. You would go into the same maternity home as Marjorie?'

Grace seemed roused at last. Her Modigliani-type neck, which was not so long as her father's, flexed slightly. 'Oh, there's plenty of time, Mother!' she protested. 'Why fuss?'

'Grace can look after herself,' her father crowed, belatedly interfering. 'Ha, these modern young women, they know everything, Dorrie.'

'Very well.' Dorinda spoke as if it were her last word, dismissing the matter from her aid. 'You may as well take advantage of State benefits in these things,' she added, however. 'People pay for them with the stamps, and I am informed the service is of the best, from the cradle to the grave.'

'Their funerals are not like those that used to be known as paupers' funerals?' Grace asked.

'In the Welfare State'—her mother took a firm stand, lifting the house telephone to ring for tea—'there is no such person as a pauper.'

Grace, waiting for tea, relapsed into the silence usual with her in these rare home visits. Odour of countless roses came through the open lattices. The room seemed the tranquil haven of a well-used life; it was bright with Morris chintz, hand-thrown pottery, folk-weave rugs, crowded with books, busts, and browned old photographs autographed by Fabian celebrities, including the Webbs, Shaw and Henry Salt, and

90

Labour Party politicians of fiery early vintage.

When Marjorie came in, Grace took a trance-like glance at her, which was returned with a behaved primness.

'I'm not sure if Marjorie ought to carry a heavy tea-tray across the garden,' Dorinda said after her protégée had retired.

'She looked as strong as a horse to me,' Grace made an effort into consciousness. 'How are the "Memoirs" getting on, Father?'

'I have to jog his memory so much,' Dorinda replied for him. 'It's really half my book.'

Ownership of Sallows was hers, too, in addition to the other securities. Bertie's inherited money, imprudently invested, had become negligible since World War I. But otherwise they were socialistically united, and had never seriously crossed swords since they first met, in an East End Settlement, shortly after Bertie came down from Oxford in a Ruskin blaze of idealism.

'I want him to bring this Marjorie business into the last chapter of the "Memoirs",' Dorinda resumed, eating a buttered muffin. 'The things that will be done for her will show that the Socialist State is not founded on humbug.'

'The question arises'—Bertie attempted to start a debate— 'do State benefits help the *emotional* condition of this poor girl ill-treated by a married man? What do you think, Grace?'

But Grace, cast again into reverie, only shook her head. She had given up hope of a loan; a week-end had to be got through; her parents were evangelistic teetotallers, and there was never even a bottle of brandy for possible, though unlikely, collapses of the retired old warriors who frequented the house. Her mother's heart had become an institute, and she had done nothing to earn admittance there.

Settling to supper in the kitchen that evening, Marjorie said to Cook, with satisfaction: 'That daughter has been a wild one. I can tell! But she's got caught now, and she don't welcome it. I tell you what, Mrs Allen—it's because she's the child of vegetarians. Man and his woman was meant to eat meat, like you and me do; that's how we get the strength to take things as they come. Mark my words, she'll get a difficult time, and it's not her fault, poor thing, daughter of a woman that only eats monkey food.'

91

Bessie Allen was just old enough to realise the value of the hard fights the mistress and her like had waged for both the poor and her sex. 'If you are referring to the mistress,' she said majestically, 'you have cause to be thankful for what monkey food, as you call it, has done.'

Marjorie frowned at the scolding. 'I don't dispute the mistress is kind.'

'Many a one,' continued Cook, who was finding Marjorie's new, conceited manner very trying, 'would have sent you packing out of the house. Then you *would* be obliged to find your Mr Grigson, since you've got no savings.'

'*Wrong*,' Marjorie retaliated. 'The mistress told me the Government supports and encourages a woman in my position, to keep the birth-rate up.' And to show that she was offended she refused a second helping of Cook's delicious steak pie. Mrs Chalmers was forced to allow meat in the kitchen.

As the summer proceeded, Marjorie got more and more above herself. The mistress asked Cook not to overburden the jilted girl. Free National Health bottles of orange juice and vitamin capsules arrived regularly from a clinic in the county town to which Mrs Chalmers had taken Marjorie in a car for an interview. There had been, too, a visit to a lady in the town's Moral Welfare Centre, where both practical and psychological advice were given to the unfortunate girl, though Marjorie still refused, in the most adamantine fashion, to allow any stalking down of Mr Grigson. In addition, Mrs Chalmers obtained information about a wonderful rest home for after the event.

'I hope to get you into it, Marjorie,' she said. 'It's run for such cases as yours and is a Labour Government experiment. The idea is that you can adjust yourself there to the psychological damage you may have sustained in your misfortune—if one may call it that. I don't think you are a neurotic type, but why shouldn't you take advantage of a rest in Eggeswick Castle? The National Insurance covers everything; there won't be a penny to pay.' Returned from the drawing room after being told of this likely treat, Marjorie announced importantly: 'I'll be going to Eggeswick Castle for three weeks' rest. Damage has been done to me.'

Cook only pursed her lips. But her choler, much as she tried to control it, was growing. She considered the mistress' zeal misplaced. Marjorie was giving herself, more and more, the most irritating duchess airs—perhaps not surprisingly, since she had not to lift a hand in self-labour over her plight, except to swallow fruit juice and capsules.

The weather, too, became torrid, and one August afternoon, when Marjorie refused to clean the cutlery, saying the heat 'daunted' her, a kitchen fracas developed. In its crescendo, Cook, at last, crystallized her dissatisfaction. She brought out, with rising colour: 'And it's my belief that there's *no* Mr Grigson. Married *or* single!'

Marjorie gave her a long look of devilish subtlety before replying: 'And there you're right, for once.'

'Then who is he?' Cook demanded.

Marjorie thrust out her head. 'Go on!' she taunted. 'Go on, run to the mistress and tell her I don't know who he is! It won't make any difference.' She showed signs, nevertheless, of a reduction in her belligerent supremacy. 'I took the name out of a newspaper—Mr Grigson, of Berkeley Square. The paper had his photo, and I liked the size and look of him.' She added defiantly: 'So there *is* a Mr Grigson.'

Verified in her suspicion though she was, Cook collapsed in horror. The drama was of that unkempt order about which nothing can be done, except, in this case, an ultimatum that either she or the housemaid must terminate service to the household. If Marjorie hadn't herself collapsed into violent tears, prior to obediently laying out the cutlery, this drastic solution would have ensued. Cook had to admit to herself that the mistress' high code would still not have allowed her to cast Marjorie away, and it seemed she had the nation behind her.

'I'll keep my mouth shut,' she pronounced, in a tone of washing her hands of it all. 'I dare say the Government has got lovely mansions where evil liars, and worse, can go to have breakfast in bed under eiderdowns.'

'The mistress,' Marjorie said, perking up a little, 'said that the Government feels shame because of the nasty way unmarried mothers were treated in the old days. She's an education, the mistress is.'

Mrs Chalmers, indeed, went further in kindness. So that Marjorie could obtain final metropolitan advantages, she closed Sallows a fortnight earlier than was her custom. The two domestics travelled to London first-class, as usual, while their employers went third. And from the house in Hampstead the mistress went into action the day after arrival, accompanying Marjorie to a clinic.

On other days she inspected, in her cream cloak and with her sharp eye of a regally experienced hen, three maternity homes, greatly impressing the staffs and, of course, obtaining priority of attention. In the one she chose, tea was given her up in the Matron's parlour while Marjorie remained below on an examination table.

An important point remained undecided. The mistress took it up. 'Now, Marjorie, we must decide what is to become of the child.'

Marjorie, immediately hanging her head, whimpered: 'I won't tell Mr Grigson. I'd rather die.'

'The State will be a better father than that man!' Mrs Chalmers said, with asperity. 'I have inquired most thoroughly about the Homes for these children, and during your lying-in I intend to inspect one or two that are near London.'

'Foundling places!' grieved Marjorie, who had confided to horrified Cook her hope that the Chalmerses would adopt the child. 'Orphanages!'

'Oh, nonsense. It's old-fashioned to associate these Homes with delinquency.' Mrs Chalmers took up a document from her desk and, scanning it, continued: 'There is no need to be depressed. You are by no means a lonely pariah. I have some facts here. One in ten of the births in Great Britain in 1945 was illegitimate; there were sixty-five thousand in all. The numbers in subsequent years are somewhat lower, but not at all disheartening for you. Your child won't feel out of place in our little country.'

Marjorie pleaded: 'If it is a girl, can I name her after you, and after the master if it is a boy?'

Mrs Chalmers, remarkably, looked at a loss, but struck a lame mean in her indecision. 'There is no copyright in names. It would be delightful.'

At dinner, when she told Bertie of this compliment, he said:

'To tell you the truth, Dorrie, I will be relieved when we're rid of this problem child and it's safely shut up in a Home far from London.'

'There speaks a man! You sit upstairs in comfort while I run charitably all over London.'

'Did you succeed in getting Grace on the telephone today?' he asked, a trifle pointedly.

'Yes,' Dorinda blew. 'At last! Why is she never at home in that Chelsea flat, and why doesn't she come to see us? She said her husband is still in Greece. I couldn't get anything sensible from her about her arrangements. She thinks she has three or four weeks to go yet—imagine it, *thinks*! So typical.'

Marjorie, her time announced by a series of breakfast grunts, went off to the maternity home with such lack of dismay that Cook wondered if it was the first occsaion. In conclave with the matron, Mrs Chalmers had bespoken for her protégée the services of the best gynaecologist on the visiting National Health Service staff. So it was not surprising that a fine, sturdy girl was born in entire safety later in the day. Matron herself telephoned the news to Mrs Chalmers, who broke into her husband's sanctum upstairs.

'Yes, yes, Dorrie,' he said, somewhat testy at the interruption. 'This birth was expected, wasn't it?'

'The sex wasn't.' Mrs Chalmers descended to the kitchen, where Cook controlledly expressed the appropriate remarks of gratification. 'She'll settle down now,' the mistress averred. 'You and I know too well, Mrs Allen, how difficult it is to find housemaids that will sleep in and go to Sallows.'

'We must *hope* she'll settle, ma'am,' Cook toook leave to amend. 'Her nature is on the turn, and it might be to sweet or sour.'

'It could easily have been to sour in the old days, Mrs Allen. But now she has seen what is being done for her by the Welfare State . . . And there are her three weeks at Eggeswick Castle to come, too. She'll be a welcome guest in a historic residence where ten years ago she might well have been a kitchenmaid. One could call this a National baby.'

Cook said: 'Well, we have National teeth, spectacles, wigs and whatnot—and few of us know where they really come from, do we?'

A little flurried by the rage she sensed in Cook, usually so discreet, Mrs Chalmers pursued: I think I deserve an outing to Eggeswick next week, don't you? Perhaps the following week you'd like a trip there yourself?'

It was three hours by slow train from London, and then a hired car from Eggeswick station, but the castle was well worth the journey.

The first glimpse of the harmonious pile, stone-blue in the mild early October sunshine, soothed the heart with a sense of unruffled eternalness. But a more personal and up-to-date pleasure was to come.

Once the fortress of thieving medieval barons, and for subsequent centuries the jewel-box home of a Tory-fisted aristocratic line, now under the portcullis of the entrance tower a new, beautifully streamlined ambulance car preceded Mrs Chalmers' old country taxi, and in a window of one of the fairy-tale turrets above the russet bailey she caught sight of a snowy-capped nurse looking at a thermometer. Later, during her tour of the entire castle, she panted up to the battlements, where, catching the high, sweet breeze, long ropes of State diapers dried quickly above the rusty cannon balls still left there for antiquarian display.

Erring girls might well find a repairing peace here. They could be seen scattered about the greenswards of the outer domain in ruminating couples and trios. After a long, surprisingly inefficient delay in the reception hall, Mrs Chalmers, hothouse peaches and grapes under her cream cloak, found her own protégée in converse with two other patients in a small flower garden.

'Oh, madam!' Marjorie began to rise rather languidly from the bright cushions and rugs of her chaise-longue, placed on the edge of a sunken lily-leafed pond. Her companions, pretty though sharp-faced, sat on other cushions. The trio made a delightful picture. Foolish nymphs learning wisdom, they were feeding the goldfish.

'No, no, don't get up, Marjorie. What a superb view you have from here!' Mrs Chalmers waved the satchel of fruit at the tranquil landscape. 'A perfect retreat for convalescents. It moves me to think that ten years ago you—no, don't go, dear

96

girls.' The visitor, never losing an opportunity to address the proletariat, detained the other two.

'Dorrie,' Marjorie broke into the oration when a chance offered, making her mistress start at this use of her name, 'is in the nursery, madam. I'll take you up.' Her companions had begun to fidget.

She led the way into the castle like a tactful chatelaine, and preceded the visitor up the great stone staircase, which was odorous of disinfectant. A giggling girl chased another down a dark corridor. The former armoury contained some three dozen occupied cribs, each with a tied-on label. Tiny Dorinda was fast asleep. Mrs Chalmers cooed dutifully at the anonymous little face, but was much more kindled by the majestic dimensions of this spick-and-span nursery.

'Marjorie,' she declared, 'I think we can congratulate ourselves. I must drop a note to the Minister of Health.'

'We have hobbies and lectures,' Marjorie said primly. She lowered her voice out of the nurse's hearing. 'But to tell you the truth, madam, some of the girls here are too far gone for lectures. Jail is what I would give them. They must *enjoy* nastiness. One of them has stolen my gold locket—what I had Mr Grigson's head in, cut out of a photo, and was keeping for Dorrie as all she'd have of her father.' Ox-blood eyes wide with anxious appeal, she added: 'But don't tell Matron, if you see her. The other girls would make mincemeat of me for carrying tales.'

Mrs Chalmers smiled confederately. 'I won't tell. We must take the rough with the smooth, dear girl. Never mind about the locket. After all, you could have Mr Grigson's head in reality, if you chose.'

'I'd rather die,' Marjorie said. 'Besides, I've heard he's emigrated to New Zealand.'

Taking full advantage of the trip, Mrs Chalmers interviewed Matron and was conducted by her over the castle—even to the dungeons, of evil despot's repute but now the properly ventilated larders of State-provided victuals. Matron refused to be drawn on the political and social inferences of the work under her jurisdiction but admitted that patients often were re-habilitated in the castle. Mrs Chalmers became severe when this lady let slip the word 'delinquents'. 'Surely,' she protested, 'the patients are *victims*, and it is the *causers* of their neurotic condition that are the delinquents?'

For some reason, as happened sometimes in her public life, she did not hit it off with this official. But, leaving the castle, she signed the visitors' book with the remark 'Admirable! I am deeply moved by the Eggeswick experiment and congratulate everybody concerned, including myself.'

She arrived back in London just before midnight. Because of hunger—a vegetarian could seldom get proper food in the carnivorous by-paths of the country—she felt dispirited. As she let herself into the house at Hampstead, her thoughts on a cheese-and-mushroom soufflé, Cook came bustling up from the kitchen in a state of dire excitement.

'Oh, ma'am!' she gasped. 'The master has gone off to St Stephen's Hospital in the East End. Your daughter is there— had her baby suddenly.' She heaved in the distress of having more to tell.

'St Stephen's!' It was a well-known hospital deep in the docks district. 'She's not in danger?'

'Oh dear, no. I haven't got the rights of it properly, but the news on the phone was that she had her baby in some cinema in those parts, and an ambulance took her to St Stephen's. A boy it is, I think Master said, when he hurried off.'

Revived to a bounce, Mrs Chalmers got to the telephone. The night superintendent of St Stephen's, who seemed not at all surprised by the extraordinary venue of the birth, verified that the mother had been sitting in a cinema. But the actual birth had taken place in the manager's office while an ambulance was being called. Luckily, a local doctor had been in the audience. The mother was quite comfortable, the baby doing well, and Mr Chalmers had left for home a few minutes ago.

When Dorinda heard the taxi drive up, she bore down on her husband in the hall, crying out: 'Bertie! What has that madcap been up to?'

He hung up his umbrella with a sigh. 'The newspaper reporters have got hold of it, Dorrie. But Grace doesn't seem to mind. She said it would be good publicity for her husband's work.'

'Whatever was she doing in the East End at such a time?' Dorinda bridled impatiently.

'It seems,' he began, 'Grace has a mania for some film comedians called the Marx Brothers and goes after them wherever their pictures are shown. She took a bus to the East End and admits that she felt she ought not to go.' He coughed deprecatingly. 'The film, apparently, was particularly hilarious. She had made no plans at all for the accouchement,' he added, 'and hadn't been to any clinic or registered with a doctor under the National Health Service.'

Dorinda sat down heavily. 'A daughter of ours, Bertie! What will Sir Leonard say? In an East End cinema!'

'Grace doesn't seem at all put out,' he repeated. 'She said something about having a child in the old-fashioned way, without fuss and a lot of State interference and licking of stamps.'

'The old-fashioned way!' Mrs Chalmers could not subdue a snort. 'Without fuss! In a cinema!'

And the next morning, prominent in one of their two newspapers, was an item: HEIR TO BARONETAGE BORN IN EAST END CINEMA. It stated, with biographical details, that the wife of the well-known young painter had been watching a revival of *Animal Crackers*. A stevedore's wife had given birth three months before in this cinema, situated in a teeming district, and Mr Slocombe, the manager, hoped for the honour of becoming godfather to this second child, too. The Chalmers' other paper, the less radical-toned *Times*, ignored the outlandish event, fortunately.

Flinging her cream cloak on after breakfast, Dorinda pronounced: 'There's only one word for her—"decadent". If she were of a lower class, she'd be called "delinquent".'

'Oh, come, come,' Bertie protested. He added delicately: 'Grace told me last night that it was quite human in St Stephen's, but I felt she needed money. I noticed she was wearing a very coarse-looking night-gown. It had an institute cut.'

'Nothing but *sluttishness*, all her life.' Dorinda, rummaging in her desk for her cheque-book, added: 'She deserves to go to Eggeswick. The matron there would soon know how to deal with her.'

NIGHTGOWN

She had married Walt after a summer courtship during which they had walked together in a silence like aversion.

Coming of a family of colliers, too, the smell of the hulking young man tramping to her when she stepped out of an evening was the sole smell of men. He would have the faintly scowling look which presently she, too, acquired. He half resented having to go about this business, but still his feet impelled him to her street corner and made him wait until, closed-faced and glancing sideways threateningly, she came out of her father's house. They walked wordless on the grit beside the railway track, his mouth open as though in a perpetual yawn. For courting she had always worn a new lilac dress out of a proper draper's shop. This dress was her last fling in that line.

She got married in it, and they took one of the seven-and-six-penny slices of the long blocks of concreted stone whipping round a slope and called Bryn Hyfryd—that is, Pleasant Hill. Like her father, Walt was a pub collier, not chapel.

The big sons had arrived with unchanged regularity, each of the same heavy poundage. When the sex of the fifth was told her, she turned her face sullenly to the wall and did not look at him for some time. And he was her last. She was to have no companionable daughter after all, to dote on when the men were in the pit. As the sons grew, the house became so obstreperously male that she began to lose nearly all feminine attributes and was apt to wear a man's cap and her sons' shoes, socks, and mufflers to run out to the shop. Her expression became tight as a fist, her jaw jutted out like her men's, and like them she only used her voice when it was necessary, though sometimes she would clang out at them with a criticism they did not understand. They would only scowl the family scowl.

For a while she had turned in her shut-up way to Trevor, her last-born. She wanted him to be small and delicate—she had imagined he was of different mould from his brothers—and she had dim ideas of his putting his hand to something more elegant than a pick in the pits. He grew into the tall, gruff image of his brothers. Yet still, when the time came for him to leave school at fourteen, she had bestirred herself, cornering him and speaking in her sullen way:

'Trevor, you don't want to go to that dirty old pit, do you? Plenty of other things to do. One white face let me have coming home to me now.'

He had set up a hostile bellow at once. 'I'm going to the pit. Dad's going to ask his haulier for me.' He stared at her in fear. 'To the pits I'm going. You let me alone.' He dreaded her hard but seeking approaches; his brothers would poke jeering fun at him, asking him if his napkins were pinned on all right, it was as if they tried to destroy her need of him, snatching him away.

She had even attempted to wring help from her husband: 'Walt, why can't Trevor be something else? What do I want with six men in the pit? One collier's more work in the house than four clean-job men.'

'Give me a shilling, 'ooman,' he said, crossing his red-spotted white muffler, 'and don't talk daft.' And off he went to The Miskin Arms.

So one bitter January morning she had seen her last-born leave the house with her other men, pit trousers on his lengthening legs and a gleaming new jack and food tin under his arm. From that day he had ranged up inextricably with his brothers, sitting down with them at four o'clock to bacon and potatoes, even the same quantity of everything, and never derided by them again. She accepted his loss, as she was bound to do, though her jutting jaw seemed more bony, thrust out like a lonely hand into the world's air.

They were all on the day's shift in the pits, and in a way she had good luck, for not one met with any accidents to speak of, they worked regular, and had no fancies to stay at home because of a pain in big toe or ear lobe, like some lazybones. So there ought to have been good money in the house. But there wasn't.

They ate most of it, with the rest for drinking. Bacon was their chief passion, and it must be of the best cut. In the shop, where she was never free of debt, nearly every day she would ask for three pounds of thick rashers when others would ask for one, and if Mr Griffiths would drop a hint, looking significantly at his thick ledger, saying: 'Three pounds, Mrs Rees, *again?*' her reply was always: 'I've got big men to feed.' As if that was sufficient explanation for all debt and she could do nothing about it; there were big, strapping men in the world and they had to be fed.

Except with one neighbour, she made no kind of real contact with anyone outside her home. And not much inside it. Of the middle height and bonily skimped of body, she seemed extinguished by the assembly of big males she had put into the world off her big husband. Peering out surly from under the poke of her man's cap, she never went beyond the main street of the vale, though as a child she had been once to the seaside, in a buff straw hat ringed with daisies.

Gathered in their pit-dirt for the important four-o'clock meal, with bath pans and hot foods steaming in the fireplace, the little kitchen was crowded as the Black Hole of Calcutta. None of the sons, not even the eldest, looked like marrying, though sometimes, like a shoving parent bird, she would try to push them out of the nest. One or two of them set up brief associations with girls which never seemed to come properly to anything. They were of the kind that never marry until the entertainments of youth, such as football, whippet-racing, and beer, have palled at last. She would complain to her next-door-up neighbour that she had no room to put down even a thimble.

This neighbour, Mrs Lewis—the other neighbours set her bristling—was her only friend in the place, though the two never entered each other's house. In low voices they conversed over the back wall, exchanging all the eternal woes of women in words of cold, knowledgeable judgement that God Himself could have learnt from. To Mrs Lewis' remark that Trevor, her last, going to work in the pits ought to set her on her feet now, she said automatically, but sighing for once: 'I've got big men to feed.'

That fact was the core of her world. Trevor's money, even when he began to earn a man's wage, was of no advantage. Still she was in debt at the shop. The six men were profitless; the demands of their insides made them white elephants.

102

So now, at fifty, still she could not sit down soft for an hour and dream of a day by the seaside with herself in a clean new dress at last and a draper's-shop hat fresh as a rose.

But often in the morning she skulked to London House, the draper's on the corner of the main road, and stopped for a moment to peer sideways into the window where two wax women, one fair and one dark, stood dressed in all the latest and smiling a pink, healthy smile. Looking beautiful beyond compare, these two ladies were now more living to her than her old dream of a loving daughter. They had no big men to feed and, poised in their eternal shade, smiled leisurely above their furs and silk blouses. It was her treat to see them, as she stood glancing out from under Enoch's thrown-away cap, her toe-sprouting shoes unlaced and her skirt of drab flannel hanging scarecrow. Every other week they wore something new. The days when Mr Roberts the draper changed their outfits, the sight of the new wonders remained in her eyes until the men arrived home from the pit.

Then one morning she was startled to find the fair wax lady attired in a wonderful white silk nightgown, flowing down over the legs most richly and trimmed with lace at bosom and cuffs. That anyone could wear such luxuriance in bed struck her at first like a blow in the face. Besides, it was a shock to see the grand lady standing there undressed, as you might say in public. But, staring into the window, she was suddenly thrilled.

She went home feeling this new luxury round her like a sweet, clean silence. Where no men were.

At four o'clock they all clattered in, Walt and her five swart sons, flinging down food tins and jacks. The piled heaps of bacon and potatoes were ready. On the scrubbed table were six large plates, cutlery, mugs and a loaf, a handful of lumpy salt chucked down in the middle. They ate their meal before washing, in their pit-dirt, and the six black faces, red mouths and white eyes gleaming, could be differentiated only by a mother.

Jaw stuck out, she worked about the table, shifting on to each plate four thick slices of bacon, a stream of sizzling fat, ladles of potatoes and tinned tomatoes. They poked their knives into the heap of salt, scattered it over the plate, and began. Lap of tongue around food was their only noise for a while. She poured the thick black tea out of a battered enamel pot big enough for a palace or a workhouse.

At last a football match was mentioned, and what somebody said last night in The Miskin taproom about that little whippet. She got the tarts ready, full-sized plates of them, and they slogged at these; the six plates were left naked in a trice. Oddments followed: cheese, cake, and jams. They only stopped eating when she stopped producing.

She said, unexpectedly: 'Shouldn't be surprised if you'd all sit there till doomsday, 'long as I went on bringing food without stoppage.'

'Aye,' said Ivor. 'What about a tin of peaches?'

Yet not one of them, not even her middle-aged husband, had a protuberant belly or any other signs of large eating. Work in the pit kept them sinewy and their sizes as nature intended. Similarly, they could have drunk beer from buckets, like horses, without looking it. Everything three or four times the nice quantities eaten by most people, but no luxuries except that the sons never spread jam thinly on bread like millionaires' sons but in fat dabs, and sometimes they demanded pineapple chunks for breakfast as if they were kings or something. She wondered sometimes that they did not grind up the jam pots, too, in their strong white shiny teeth; but Trevor, the youngest, had the right to lick the pots, and thrust down his tongue almost to the bottom.

At once, after the meal, the table was shoved back. She dragged in the wooden tub before the fire. The pans were simmering on hobs and fire. Her husband always washed first, taking the clean water. He slung his pit clothes to the corner, belched, and stepped into the tub. He did not seem in a hurry this afternoon. He stood and rubbed up his curls—still black and crisp after fifty years—and bulged the muscle of his black right arm. 'Look there,' he said, 'you pups, if a muscle like that you got at my age, men you can call yourselves.'

Ranged about the kitchen, waiting for their bath turn with cigarette stuck to red-licked lower lip, the five sons looked variously derisive, secure in their own bone and muscle. But they said nothing; the father had a certain power, lordly in his maturity. He stood there naked, handsome, and well-endowed; he stood musing for a bit, liking the hot water round his feet and

104

calves. But his wife, out and in with towels, shirts, and buckets, had heard his remark. With the impatience that had seemed to writhe about her ever since they had clattered in, she cried: 'What are you standing there for showing off, you big ram! Wash yourself, man, and get away with you.'

He took no notice. One after the other the sons stripped; after the third bath the water was changed, being then thick and heavy as mud. They washed each other's back, and she scuttled in and out, like a dark, irritated crab this afternoon, her angry voice nipping at them. When Ieuan, the eldest and six foot two, from where he was standing in the tub spat across into a pan of fresh water on the fire, in a sudden fury she snatched up the dirty coal-shovel and gave him a ringing smack on his washed behind. Yet the water was only intended for the dirt-crusted tub. He scowled; she shouted: 'You blackguard, you keep your spit for public-house floors.'

After she had gone into the scullery, Trevor, waiting his turn, grunted: 'What's the matter with the old woman today?' Ieuan stepped out of the tub. The shovel blow might have been the tickle of a feather. But Trevor advised him: 'Better wash your best face again; that shovel's left marks.'

From six o'clock onwards one by one they left the house, all, including Walt, in a navy-blue serge suit, muffler, cap, and yellowish-brown shoes, their faces glistening pale from soap. They strutted away on their long, easy legs to their various entertainments, though with their heads somehow down in a kind of ducking. Their tallness made it a bit awkward for themselves in some of the places down in the pits.

Left alone with the piles of crusted pit clothes, all waiting to be washed or dried of their sweat, she stood taking a cup of tea and nibbling a piece of bread, looking out of the window. Except on Sundays her men seldom saw her take a meal, though even on Sunday she never ate bacon. There was a month or two of summer when she appeared to enjoy a real plate of something, for she liked kidney beans and would eat a whole plateful, standing with her back to the room and looking out of the window towards the distant mountain brows under the sky, as if she was thinking of Heaven. Her fourth son Emlyn said to her once: 'Your Sunday feed lasts you all the week, does it? Or a good guzzle you have when we're in the pit?'

She stood thinking till her head hurt. The day died on the mountain-tops. Where was the money coming from, with them everlastingly pushing expensive bacon into their red mouths? The clock ticked.

Suddenly, taking a coin from a secret place and pulling on a cap, she hurried out. A spot burning in her cheeks, she shot into the corner draper's just as he was about to close, and, putting out her jaw, panted to old Roberts: 'What's the price of that silk nightgown on the lady in the window?'

After a glance at the collier's wife in man's cap and skirt rough as an old mat, Roberts said crossly: 'A price you can't afford, so there!' But when she seemed to mean business he told her it was seventy bob and elevenpence and he hoped that the pit manager's wife or the doctor's would fancy it.

She said defiantly: 'You sell it to me. A bob or more a week I'll pay you, and you keep it till I've finished the amount. Take it out of the window now at once and lay it by. Go on now, fetch it out.'

'What's the matter with you!' he shouted testily, as though he was enraged as well as astonished at her wanting a silk nightgown. 'What d'you want it for?'

'Fetch it out,' she threatened, 'or my husband Walt Rees I'll send to you quick.' The family of big, fighting males was well known in the streets. After some more palaver Roberts agreed to accept her instalments and, appeased, she insisted on waiting until he had undraped the wax lady in the window. With a bony, trembling finger she felt the soft white silk for a second and hurried out of the shop.

How she managed to pay for the nightgown in less than a year was a mystery, for she had never a penny to spare, and a silver coin in the house in the middle of the week was rare as a Christian in England. But regularly she shot into the draper's and opened her grey fist to Roberts. Sometimes she demanded to see the nightgown, frightened that he might have sold it for quick money to someone else, though Roberts would shout at her: 'What's the matter with you? Packed up safe it is.'

One day she braved his wrath and asked if she could take it away, promising faithful to keep up the payments. But he exclaimed: 'Be off! Enough tradesmen here been ruined by credi:. Buying silk nightgowns indeed! What next?'

She wanted the nightgown in the house; she was fearful it would never be hers in time. Her instinct told her to be swift. So she hastened, robbing still further her own stomach and in tiny lots even trying to rob the men's, though they would scowl and grumble if even the rind was off their bacon. But at last, when March winds blew down off the mountains so that she had to wrap round her scraggy chest the gaunt shawl in which her five lusty babies had been nursed, she paid the last instalment. Her chin and cheeks blue in excitement, she took the parcel home when the men were in the pit.

Locking the door, she washed her hands, opened the parcel, and sat with the silk delicately in her hands, sitting quiet for half an hour at last, her eyes come out in a gleam from her dark face, brilliant. Then she hid the parcel down under household things in a drawer which the men never used.

A week or two later, when she was asking for the usual three pounds of bacon at the shop, Mr Griffith said to her, stern: 'What about the old debts, now then? Pity you don't pay up, instead of buying silk nightgowns. Cotton is good enough for my missus to sleep in, and you lolling in silk, and don't pay for all your bacon and other things. Pineapple chunks every day. Hoo!' And he glared.

'Nightgown isn't for *my* back,' she snapped. 'A wedding present for a relation it is.' But she was a bit winded that the draper had betrayed her secret to his fellow tradesman.

He grumbled: 'Don't know what you do with all you take out of my shop. Bacon every day enough to feed a funeral, and tins of fruit and salmons by the dozen. Eat for fun, do you?'

'I've got big men to feed.' She scowled, as usual.

Yet she seemed less saturnine as she sweated over the fireplace and now never once exclaimed in irritation at some clumsiness of the men. Even when, nearly at Easter, she began to go bad, no complaint came from her, and of course the men did not notice, for still their bacon was always ready and the tarts as many, their bath water hot, and evening shirts ironed.

On Easter Bank Holiday, when she stopped working for a while because the men had gone to whippet races over in Maerdy Valley, she had time to think of her pains. She felt as if the wheels of several coal wagons had gone over her body,

107

though there were no feeling at all in her legs. When the men arrived home at midnight, boozed up, there were hot faggots for them, basting pans savoury full, and their pit clothes were all ready for the morning. She attended on them in a slower fashion, her face closed and her body shorter, because her legs had gone bowed. But they never noticed, jabbering of the whippets.

Mrs Lewis next door said she ought to stay in bed for a week. She replied that the men had to be fed.

A fortnight later, just before they arrived home from the pit and the kitchen was hot as a furnace, her legs kicked themselves in the air, the full frying-pan in her hand went flying, and when they came in they found her black-faced on the floor with the rashers of bacon all about her. She died in the night as the district nurse was wetting her lips with water. Walt, who was sleeping in a chair downstairs, went up too late to say farewell.

Because the house was upside down as a result, with the men not fed properly, none of them went to work in the morning. At nine o'clock Mrs Lewis next door, for the first time after thirty years back-wall friendship with the deceased, stepped momentously into the house. But she had received her instructions weeks ago. After a while she called down from upstairs to the men sitting uneasy in the kitchen: 'Come up; she is ready now.'

They slunk up in procession, six big men, with their heads ducked, disturbed out of the rhythm of their daily life of work, food, and pub. And entering the room for the last view, they stared in surprise.

A stranger lay on the bed ready for her coffin. A splendid, shiny, white silk nightgown flowing down over her feet, with rich lace frilling bosom and hands, she lay like a lady taking a rest, clean and comfortable. So much they stared, it might have been an angel shining there. But her face jutted stern, bidding no approach to the contented peace she had found.

The father said, cocking his head respectfully: 'There's a fine 'ooman she looks. Better than when I married her!'

'A grand nightshirt,' mumbled Enoch. 'That nurse brought it in her bag?'

'A shroud they call it,' said Emlyn.

'In with the medical benefits it is,' said his father soberly. 'Don't they dock us enough every week from our wages?'

108

After gazing for a minute longer at the white apparition, lying there so majestically unknown, they filed downstairs. There Mrs Lewis awaited them. 'Haven't you got no 'ooman relation to come in and look after you?' she demanded.

The father shook his head, scowling in effort to concentrate on a new problem. Big, black-curled, and still vigorous, he sat among his five strapping sons who, like him, smelt of the warm, dark energy of life. He said: 'A new missus I shall have to be looking for. Who is there about, Mrs Lewis, that is respectable and can cook for us and see to our washings? My boys I got to think about. A nice little widow or something you know of that would marry a steady working chap? A good home is waiting for her by here, though a long day it'll be before I find one that can feed and clean us like the one above; *she* worked regular as a clock, fair play to her.'

'I don't know as I would recommend any 'ooman,' said Mrs Lewis with rising colour.

'Pity you're not a widow! Ah well, I must ask the landlady of The Miskin if she knows of one,' he said, concentrated.

GENTS ONLY

While he was busy burying a woman one June afternoon, Lewis the Hearse's wife left him for ever, going by the three o'clock train and joining her paramour at Stickell junction, where they were seen by Matt Morgan waiting for their connection. She left a letter for her husband, a plate of tart for his tea, and that sense of awful desolation a gone person can leave in a house.

What was in that letter no one ever knew, not even Lewis' sister Bloddie, who—for the news was up all the hillsides of Crwtch the same evening—came flying down from her farm up where the old BC tomb had been found. But from that afternoon Lewis was a changed man. Not that he had been a specially bright bit of spring sunshine before, though he was quite a decent-looking man in his way. His manner betokened a sombre nature which was not entirely due to his calling. Because of his reasonable prices and his craftsmanship in coffins, all the people of Crwtch respected him.

'A servant you'll have to take,' Bloddie declared shrilly, and her bosom heaved like the Bay of Biscay because he wouldn't show her the letter. 'Forever running down here I can't be. . . . The house she left clean. I will say.' She looked at the uneaten tart—for Lewis' wife was Crwtch's best tart maker—jealously. 'If that tart you don't want I can take it.'

Lewis lifted his brooding head at last. 'Take it!' he barked, so fierce that she jumped back. 'And your own carcass too.'

But what Crwtch never expected was the decision he came to the very next day. He tore down from outside his house the wooden tablet announcing his name and profession and in its place screwed a new one just painted in the work shed behind the house.

This announced: *J. J. Lewis, Gent's Undertaker.* Seeing

him screw it up, Daniels Long Time, captain of the amateur Fire Brigade and so called because people said his engine was always a long time coming when needed, stopped and asked: 'What is it meaning, Lewis?'

Shaking his screwdriver, Lewis barked: 'My last woman I buried yesterday. From now on, men's funerals only.' And he went in, slamming the door.

No one could believe it. For days it was the talk at every hearth, in every shop and pub in Crwtch. Everybody waited for the next woman to go. A man died and Lewis buried him as usual, very reasonable and the coffin up to standard. Except for this funeral Lewis had not appeared out of doors, not even to go to chapel. His sister Bloddie said he cleaned and cooked for himself, ordering things by his apprentice, Shenkin. At this funeral everybody looked at him inquisitively but could collect nothing but a bleak decision in the uprightness of his body walking behind his lovely crystal hearse.

Then Polly Red Rose went of old age. Licensee of the best pub in Crwtch (now carried on by her son), Polly was respected by both sexes and all creeds. Surely Lewis, who had often enjoyed a glass of the Red Rose beer, would not say no to burying her? The son knocked at Lewis' door. But before he could take off his black bowler and step inside, Lewis said clearly, not angry, but firm as a rock:

'No use coming in. See the plate outside? Gents only, or boys, and no exceptions, sorry to say. Good day.'

Now, there was not another undertaker within fifteen miles of Crwtch, the one in Stickell, a stranger. And not only would he charge extra for travelling his contrivance thirty miles in all, but it was known that his carriages were shabby, being more used in a town the size of Stickell. Everybody knew how Lewis' coffins (to say nothing of his moderate charges) were not only good value but would surely last longer than anybody else's. And so, when the women of Crwtch began to boil against this reflection on their sex and solicited their men to do something about it, even the men more or less began to agree.

'If I was a man,' Mrs Hopcyns the Boot declared to her husband, right in front of a woman customer buying boots, 'horse-whip him I would.'

'Sore he is,' Hopcyns the Boot said mildly. 'Give him a bit

of time to get over the Mrs leaving him like that. Come round he will in a year or two.'

'Anybody would think,' said the customer, kicking off a boot and flushed from bending, 'that men don't mind about it. Forced to bury Polly Red Rose he ought to have been.'

'How?' enquired Hopcyns. 'No law there is about it. Same as I am not bound to sell you a pair of boots!'

'Catching it is, is it!' simmered the customer. In Crwtch there was only one of all trades, except farming, so there was no competition for customers.

The first outcome of all the agitation, however, was that the Big Men of Horeb chapel went in deputation to Lewis. They wore their formal Sunday black, watch-chains, and umbrellas, and in array they looked impressive. Lewis received them readily enough in his parlour, where were the samples of wood, metals, and glass wreaths. But he did not sit down like them, and, before they could speak, he launched like a judge having the last word:

'Lord of himself a man is. Private his soul. Between me and my destiny it is what I have decided in the matter of my funerals. But this I will say: Not only to vex the women of Crwtch is my intention; vex the women of the whole word I would. Yet small of mind is that. This is my true reason—women will see there is a man at last who will not sit down under their carryings-on and shamelessness. A good example I have begun, in a time gone loose and no respect for the vows of the marriage day. No more now. I have decided.'

The Big Men looked at each other, and it was plain there was no stout movement to contradict Lewis or attempt coaxing. At last one said, however: 'But Lewis, Lewis, come now. Surely similar all are in death, and in a hearse there are no trousers or petticoats, properly speaking. The same shroud of Heaven covers all.'

Another, who had a crinkled little old face like an old apple in the loft, added: 'Yes, persons only in the cemetery and not men and women. No carryings-on *there*; the only place safe from such it is. Every door marked "Private", and no back door either. Agree with you I would, Lewis, if the cemetery was a place of this and that; only right it would be for you to say no to taking women there. But surely it is not?'

112

'Obliged I am for the visit,' said Lewis, far away. 'Just now I am starching white collars.' Indeed, starch was whitening his fingers, and he had the air of one with many household tasks to do.

No doubt at all a door was shut fast in his soul. For him no more the peaches and the blossoms of women in the world. The Big Men filed out in the sunshine and adjourned to the vestry of Horeb to consider the manner of their report to their wives. . . . But Crwtch's protest did not stop there. The following week those ten of the business-men who call themselves the Chamber of Trade, meeting once a month in The Red Rose, sought conference with Lewis.

Though, as before, resolutely calm, Lewis made sharp interruption of their mild wheedling: 'Look now, this you must do. Put a big advertisement in the newspaper—"Chance for Undertaker in Well-off Small Town. Present Undertaker Gents Only. Apply to Crwtch Chamber of Trade". See?'

Reproachful, one of the members protested in sorrow: 'A stranger in *your* business is not welcome, Lewis, and well you do know it. Surprised at you I am.' And he added significantly: 'Ointment for bruises there are always, and many in pretty boxes.'

Lewis knew what the member meant. Under the special circumstances he would not become a social outcast if he took a fancy to someone and brought her under his roof, though in Crwtch this was the most abhorrent sin of all. But he said cynically:

'Ointments cost money, and down by half is my business. And will be for ever.'

After the failure of the Chamber of Trade, the Society of Merched y Te itself made attempts. This society of teetotal women formed to spread the ideal of temperance was—no one knew why—of powerful influence in Crwtch and nobody willingly incurred its displeasure. The mother of one of its members having died, the daughter made great groan of the awful cost of the funeral by the undertaker at Stickell, with the coffin looking like one from a factory. The Merched, twenty strong, assembled one August afternoon and marched in procession to Lewis' house. But, apprised of their intention by his spy, Shenkin the apprentice, Lewis had not only locked and barred his door but had nailed a notice on it: '*J. J. Lewis. In Business to Men Only. No Others Admitted. By Order, J. J. Lewis.*'

It is plain that women of affairs, particularly when in concourse, would not be daunted by such a notice. They knocked, they rapped and banged, called through the letter-box and rattled it with fancy umbrellas, tactless as any reforming society can be. There was no reply. Presently the noise was such—it was a hot day and tempers were rising—that a crowd of about two hundred collected, and from his cottage PC Evans the Spike telephoned the Sergeant in Stickell, putting on his helmet first. The Sergeant said that no man is obliged to open the door of his house to the public and that the crowd must be dispersed if it was creating a nuisance. Perspiring, Evans the Spike stepped out, went back for his baton, and then, after plunging into the crowd and enquiring the meaning of this uproar, gave the Sergeant's decision and posted himself in Lewis' doorway.

'Truth of the matter is,' called one of the Merched indignantly, 'supporting the sly old fish the men are. . . . A letter will be written!' she finished with great ominousness.

But it was Bloddie who moved in the affair with better craft. She became incensed that her brother persisted in deliberately throwing away good business. Some years younger than he was, she hoped to benefit one day from the tidy little fortune he could be making.

It was during a visit to her friend's farm over the hill one afternoon that she saw light—in the person of her friend's orphan niece who had just come from the mining valleys to work at the farm. About twenty, Lottie's lovely head shone fresh as a buttercup, and all her presence breathed strong of an obedient nature waiting to devote itself entire to a person. Though dainty-looking she had no nerves and was strong as an ox. Better still, there was a smile behind the naughty blue of her eye, and even better still, she had deficiencies—she did not like hard work, and her lazy mind seemed vacant and only waiting for the one thing to come along and keep her comfortable.

Bloddie conferred with her old friend, who had taken Lottie to live with her because there was no one else to take her. 'Aye,' agreed the aunt at once, 'sweeten him up she could, no doubt. Welcome you are to her, Bloddie.'

'Look how he used to be,' Bloddie remembered, fired, 'as a young man! No 'ooman in Crwtch was safe from him. . . . A man with extremes in his nature he is, evident,' she added, putting her finger on his character accurately.

But how to get Lottie into Lewis' notice was the problem. Bloddie lay in bed of nights brooding. She was the only woman—for a sister is not a woman—who was allowed into her brother's house, and even she was treated with short shrift though he accepted the bit of green stuff or bacon she brought down from the farm. Then one morning she rose and said clearly to herself: 'A new shock often kills an old one.'

Thereafter she took to calling on Lewis frequently, always with presents for his meals, and even daring to follow him into the work shed that abutted on the back lane and talking to him while he made a coffin. Subtly she got to know this and that from his short grunts. One day, splashing the varnish down on a beautiful cut coffin—for Crwtch men still remained faithful to him and his moderate charges—he growled: 'No good you keep coming here, Bloddie. Shenkin the apprentice can do my business for the house. Tomorrow, going by the first train to Stickell he is to buy wallpaper and a chicken in the market.'

'Wallpapering the parlour are you?' she said idly. 'Coffin for Josh Jones that is? A nice wood.'

'Going to him it is the day after tomorrow,' Lewis grunted, and drew the final brush with great delicacy along the lid.

'Would you bury *me*, Johnnie?' she ventured, very sisterly.

'No,' he said.

But later he gave her a cup of tea (the first since his wife had run away, never to be heard of again), and she took it as a good omen of relenting and melting. She dared to stay until quite late that night and went out to the work shed again to fetch the bag of shopping she had left there. 'There,' she said, turning the key of the back kitchen door for him, 'all locked up and everything done for you! Surely a woman in the house is a price above rubies?' She had even washed up and polished the grate.

'You be off now,' he growled, reading a trade paper. 'Your views don't carry weight with me.'

The next morning, a mild October morning very sweet in the

nose, Bloddie let herself and the girl Lottie into Lewis' back-lane door as dawn was breaking. She had left the door unlocked the night before. Lottie was giggling and very ready for the prank, being bored with the lonely farm. They crept into the work shed and Bloddie lit a candle. The lid of Josh Jones' coffin lay ajar on the beautiful varnished casket resting on the trestles.

'There!' said Bloddie. 'And if you do your piece proper a man with money you might marry. Starved he is.'

She moved the lid and helped Lottie into the coffin. She arranged the bright, cool yellow hair and the clean-ironed pink muslin dress that showed legs plain, and in the narrow frame the shapely girl looked like Heaven come to earth. Even Bloddie herself, lifting the candle, exclaimed in wonder: 'Beautiful enough to eat you look, a wedding cake! . . . Now what are you going to say?'

Lottie, her long lashes beating her cheeks, repeated in a pleading voice: 'An orphan I am and looking for someone to take care of me. Cruel everybody has been to me. Last night I ran away from the gipsies and came in by here. Die I want to, for the world I cannot stand no more.' And she smiled a tearful and pleading smile—for the simplest girl can make a good actress when needed—and lifted her arms like swan necks. 'My father's face you got, only younger. Kiss me and let me rest by here.'

'Champion!' said Bloddie admiringly. 'Now take patience, for a long time he might be. A big piece of work you might do for Crwtch, and earn a fortune for yourself too.' She arranged the lid over the coffin as before, leaving a slit of space open, and put out the candle.

'Cosy it is,' Lottie sighed. 'There's nice the wood smells!'

But when Bloddie had gone and an hour passed without Lewis arriving, Lottie, of indolent nature and having been up early, fell fast asleep. The work shed was dark. It had only a small cob-webbed window in the shade of a tree, where a rising wind began to mutter and creak in growing noise.

Bloddie did not go back to the farm as she intended. She went to call on a friend in Mary Ann Street who cut dresses for her, and what with a cup of tea and one thing and another, time passed. Her friend made broth and afterwards they went to visit Mrs Leyshon, who was confined of a son. In the afternoon Bloddie looked at a clock.

'Jawch, I must go now,' she said, suddenly feeling excited. She bought a currant loaf in the baker's and then made quick for her brother's house. 'There's pale you are looking!' her friend said in parting. 'Not well you are feeling?' But Bloddie did not know if she felt well or not.

Lewis, in his shirt-sleeves, answered the door to her timid knock. He stood aside with nothing special in the grudging cast of his face.

'Well,' she said, expectant. 'Things well with you today? Down to do a bit of shopping I am.' In the living room she laid the currant loaf on the table. There was no sign of Lottie anywhere. 'A loaf of currant bread for you, Johnnie.'

There was conversation on several small matters, Lewis grunting as usual, and she tidying the hearth, her eyes restless and her ears cocked to the ceiling. 'Oh, Johnnie,' she burst at last out of her dry throat, 'faint I am for a cup of tea.'

'Get yourself one,' he said, surly. 'I got work in the shed. That Shenkin haven't come back from Stickell yet.' And he went out to the back.

She drank the tea quick for strength. And her queer excitement could be held no more. She went out to the back, down the slice of weedy garden, and peered into the open door of the dusky shed. A dribbling lit candle was stuck on a chest of tools, with Lewis sitting beside it polishing a brass name plate. On the trestle Josh Jones' coffin lay with the lid closed tight over it. Bloddie, stooping, twisted into the shed. Her knees were bending.

'Oh, Johnnie . . .' she began, quavering, in a small going voice.

In the candle-light his shiny little eyes looked up, occupied. 'What now?' he grunted, and went back to his polishing. 'You go and have your tea.'

Breathing hard, she crept across to the coffin. Her hand came out stealthily and made to lift the lid. It would not move. The six big ornamental screws were brassy in the candle-light. 'Johnnie,' she whispered, bending and feeling her head go round, 'what you screwed down the lid for?'

'Ready to go to Josh Jones tomorrow, of course. Lids don't jump about in my hearse.'

She gave the coffin a violent push. But it did not budge. Sure enough it was full as an egg. Beating the lid with her hands, she shrieked: 'You looked inside before screwing it down? . . . Oh, Johnnie!' she wailed.

'What's the matter with you, woman!' he barked. 'Look inside for what? The coffin's been screwed down since first thing this morning. You've been drinking!'

'Lottie is in there!' she screamed. 'Niece of Ceridwen.'

'I don't know any Lottie,' he shouted, irritable. 'That's enough now. I won't have you coming here in the drink.'

Babbling, and her fat little fists without real strength, she began turning the screws. He called out to her to leave his coffin alone, but, still polishing the brass plate, he did not rise from his bench. Six screws she had to loosen. She flung off the lid.

The coffin was empty except for Lewis' big black ledger and many bricks. She spun round with a snarl.

'Oh, wicked old fox that you are, oh—' And this and that.

He rose tremendous, the shining plate in an arm, like Moses. 'Out of my house with you, out now and till Doomsday!'

Sobbing in rage and fright, she ran up the garden, he at her heels. But she called up the criticism of hell on him, and he on her. In the living-room her eye caught the currant loaf. She snatched it up and took it with her through the front door, which slammed behind her for the last time.

Up at the farm she found Lottie in bed not only with a cold but with fright. Fed and comforted, however, the girl dried her tears. 'I went to sleep,' she related, 'and I was woke up by candle grease dropping hot on my face. Red his whiskers were by the candle! I said what you said, but he shouted at me: "A good mind I got to lock you up in this coffin till I call the policeman for a burglar! You be off back to the gipsies. Supply free nights' lodging for trollops I don't. . . ." And he wouldn't help me out of the coffin and wouldn't touch me at all. I lost my head and said where I was from, too. . . .'

Afterwards the aunt tried to console her friend. 'Let the old rascal go, Bloddie. A man he is no more. Cut off the old dolt is.'

'Pew!' breathed Bloddie, stertorous, 'but I thought poor Lottie had been coffined right enough.'

'Never mind,' said Ceridwen; 'not so frivolous and empty-headed it might make her.'

It was the last attempt to make Lewis Gents Only (as he came to be called) relent from his hard vow. He remained faithful to it until he retired from business and went to live in Swansea. All women continued to be buried by the Stickell undertaker, but the man who bought Lewis' business and stock in hand of course changed this. It must be said that though mention of Lewis always made Crwtch women bridle, when he left he went in dignity and with the good wishes and respect of most men. He had that upright look of a man who knows his own mind and abides by its decisions, and in his face independence mingled solemnly with the natural pride of a craftsman. His history is still discussed in the parlour bar of The Red Rose; and it is often the starting point of a deep debate—was he justified or not in refusing to undertake women?

A HUMAN CONDITION

Having done the errand at the Post Office, which he had timed with a beautiful precision that he imagined completely hoodwinked those left at home, Mr Arnold crossed the Market Square just as the doors of The Spreadeagle Inn were opened.

This morning he was in lamentable condition. He felt he would never get through the day without aid. Never, never, never. Deep inside him was a curious dead sensation of which he was frightened. It lay in the pit of his stomach like some coiled serpent fast asleep, and he was fearful that at any moment the thing would waken and writhe up in unholy destructive fury. And ultimately *he* would be destroyed. Not his critics, today collected in dark possession of his home.

He sailed into the pub with his ample, slightly rolling strut, a man of substance handsomely ripe of body and face, his attire as conservative as a psalm to godliness; no one could say Mr Arnold neglected his person. Of the town's few pubs The Spreadeagle was his favourite haunt. It was cosily shut in on itself and dark with shadows; it had low, black-beamed ceilings, copper gleams, honest smells, and morose windows hostile to light. In the hall a torpid spaniel bitch looked at him with the heavily drooping eyes of a *passée* actress; she knew Mr Arnold, and there was no necessity for even a languid wag of her tail. Always the first customer, he stepped into the bar parlour with his usual opening-time briskness. But Mrs Watson, polishing glasses behind the bar, looked at him with a start. 'Well!' she seemed about to exclaim, but only pursed her lips.

'A whisky,' he said; 'a double.'

'A double?' Something was concealed in her tone.

'Yes, for God's sake.' The false briskness was suddenly deflated. 'And pour another for me while you're about it.'

'*No*, Mr Arnold,' she said, flat; 'no. Not *two* doubles. . . . It isn't right,' she bridled; 'not today. Good heavens! Don't forget you've got to be there sober at two o'clock. *No*, Mr Arnold.'

'Hell!' he muttered. He looked over his shoulder with child-blue eyes round in fear. 'Where's Alec?' A man would understand, must surely understand, what that day really meant, Women were incalculable in the domain of the affections, could run so drastically from the extremes of loving solicitude to the bleakest savagery. 'Where's Alec?' he peered.

'Gone to London for the day,' his wife said. 'Gone to buy me a budgerigar.'

'Gone to London,' he mumbled, preoccupied.

'They can chirp ever so sweet,' she said tightly, 'and intelligent, my goodness!—my sister had one that would hop on the table when she was making cake and stone the raisins for her.'

'What?' He started from his glassy preoccupation.

'The budgerigar she had. With its beak. Intelligent, my stars! . . . I've known many a human being,' she added forbiddingly, 'that could do with their brains and feelings.'

Both The Malt Shovel and The Bleeding Horse, which were on his way home, were only beer houses. No licence for spirits. But there was plenty of time. He would climb to Cuckoo Ridge, up to The Self Defence. Its landlord, whose wife had been in an asylum for years, would understand. There was The Unicorn too, nearer, but repellent with its horrible modern cocktail bar, its café look, and its dirty waiters.

Mrs Watson, solicited with flattery and whining, allowed him a single whisky more. She asked him what would be said in the town if she allowed him to have all he wanted on that morning of all mornings. He left the house with dignity, part of him preoccupied with feeling offended, but the greater part obeying a huge desolate urge to complete the scarcely begun journey into that powerful state where he would feel secure, a captain of his fate, if a melancholy one. He had never been able to take to drinking at home. Besides, Susan never encouraged it. Never a bottle of whisky in the house.

In the shopping street, those people who knew Mr Arnold—and they were many, for by now he was a local celebrity—looked at him with their cheerfulness, due to the brilliant day, wiped momentarily from their faces. But he encouraged no one to pass a few words with him; time must not be wasted. He took a side turning and began to climb among loaded apple and pear trees spread over garden walls. The whole fragrantly warm little town was fat with sunlight, fruit, and flowers. Mr Arnold began to pant and lean on his expensive malacca stick.

Above, on the bright emerald slopes with their small well-groomed fields, cows stood like shiny china ornaments. The short local train from London puffed a plume of snowy cotton-wool. It was toy countryside, and Mr Arnold felt obliged to admire its prettiness; it had been Susan's idea to live here on his retirement from his highly successful career in the City lanes near Tower Bridge, where scores of important men knew him. He liked to feel that London was still near, he liked to see, on Sundays and Bank Holidays, clumps of pallid cockney youths and girls in cycling knickers dotting those slopes like mushrooms. The high air, clear as mineral-waters, was supposed to be good for one. Susan said it eased her chest, and she had become a leading voice in the Women's Institute. ... Ah, Susan, Susan! Her husband panted in sore distress, climbing.

On Cuckoo Ridge the landlord of The Self Defence greeted him, after a slight pause, courteously. But Mr Arnold saw at once that he was in the know. Rapidly he asked for a second double. The landlord, a stout, placid man in braces, looked at him. Perhaps he saw a man in agony of spirit; he served the drink. Mr Arnold thought he felt deep sympathy flowing from this man whose own wife had been shut away from him for several years already. He asked for a third double.

The landlord mournfully shook his head. 'Best not, Mr Arnold.'

'One more,' panted Mr Arnold. 'Only one. I've got a day in front of me.' In the pit of his stomach was a stirring of fear, as if the sleeping coil shuddered. 'Never be able to face it,' he whimpered.

The landlord shook his head in slow, heavy decision. 'There's the circumstances to consider,' he said.

Mr Arnold attempted a hollow truculence. 'My money's as good as anyone's—'

'Now, sir,' said the landlord distantly, 'best be on your way.' And, solemnly: 'You've got a job to do, Mr Arnold.'

Mr Arnold walked out with deliberate steadiness. A clock had struck twelve-thirty. It would have to be The Unicorn, and time was pressing now. Actually he had already taken his morning allowance, but today ... today. ... He descended from the Ridge with a careful step, crossed the watercress beds into the London road, and looked sourly at the gimcrack modern façade of The Unicorn, a rebuilt house done up for motoring whipper-snappers and their silly grinning dolls. He went in like an aggressive magistrate with power to deprive the place of its licence. But he cast himself into a bony scarlet-and-nickel chair with a groan, wiping his brow. A white presence slid up to his chair.

'Double whisky,' he said.

'Yes, Mr Arnold,' said the waiter.

He cocked up his eye sharply. Known here too! In a blurred way, the grave young face looking down at him was familiar. Ha, it was Henry, who used to come with his father to do the garden! Quickly Mr Arnold assumed the censorious glare of a boss of substance. 'And mind it's genuine Scotch, Henry,' he said. He did not like the boy's solicitous look as he withdrew to the blonde cimena star serving behind the jazzy zigzagged corner counter. He took out his big presentation gold watch and looked at it importantly. Was there a pausing at the bar, a whispering? Surely he, who had been a guest at Lord Mayors' banquets in the Mansion House, was not going to be dictated to in a shoddy hole like this? Henry brought the double. 'Get me another, my boy,' Mr Arnold said. Henry hesitated, but withdrew; came back—'Sir,' he said awkwardly, 'sir, there's no more except this single. Our supplies haven't arrived; they'll be here by tonight.'

Was everybody his enemy that day? Was there a plot against him? After that long walk, to be allowed only this! Mr Arnold pushed back his chair, made an effort to collect his forces for dire protest. But somehow—was it because of guilt or the heat? —they would not assemble. He could only gaze fixedly at Henry in silent reproach, anger, and, finally, entreaty. 'Very sorry, sir,' mumbled Henry from far away. 'Can I call up the garage for a taxi, sir?'

'A taxi? Certainly not.'

He swallowed the single, tipped lavishly, rose like an

offended emperor, sat down, and rose again, thunderous yet dignified.

'Your stick, Mr Arnold.' Henry handed it.

He needed it now. Outside, his eyes could focus neither on the shifting ground nor the burning pansy-coloured sky. The soft amateur hills ran into each other like blobs of water-colours imperfectly handled. But he would walk, he would walk. Anything rather than be in the house before it was quite essential. Not with *them* there. . . . The town hall clock, its notes gently without chiding, struck the quarter after one. Yet those chimes were like knells bringing grief. Grief, grief. A sensation of burning grief, physical and staggering, pierced him. He sat gasping on the low roadside wall. The day was no longer brilliant, crackling with sun. The desolation of what awaited his presence swept down on him in gusts of black depression. God above, he could never face it. Not without—. He rose with remarkable celerity.

Fool, fool! Why had he forgotten The Adam and Eve? He walked rapidly, a man refreshed, stick striking the road almost evenly. . . . But outside The Adam and Eve, a sixteenth-century house sagging in a dark medieval alley hidden in the town, he paused to arrange himself into the aspect of a man with a grip on himself, and he rolled into the pub with a lordly assurance.

The poky, cool bar parlour was deserted except for a cat enormously asleep on the counter. Mr Arnold called: 'Hey! Customer here!' He banged the counter with his stick. No one appeared. Not a sound shifted into the stagnant air. He gave the cat a sharp dig with his stick; it did not stir or open an eye. He shouted, thumped the counter. A dead petal of plaster fell from the ceiling. But no one came. The silence closed impervious over his shouts of anguish. No one passed in the shadowed alley outside. His stick rang frenziedly on the counter. He had the feeling he was in a dream in which a ghostly, senseless frustration dogs one's every move. The cat slept. The hands of a dusty old clock remained neatly and for ever together at twelve o'clock. The bottles on the shelves looked as if they were never opened. He jabbed at the cat again; it did not move out of its primeval sleep.

Mr Arnold whimpered. He lurched over to the door in the crooked bellied-out wall and lifted the old-fashioned latch. But the door wouldn't open. Had it been locked behind him? Was he being imprisoned? 'Who's there?' he screamed, banging his stick furiously against the rickety panel. The after-silence did not budge. He tore madly at the latch. Suddenly the door flew open; it had jammed in the ancient frame. Raging, Mr Arnold stamped down the passage, threw back another door.

A dazzle of pink interior light struck into his eyes. He stepped into a hot living room with a huge window and an opened door leading to a garden blazing with snapdragons, roses, and holly-hocks. A blue-gowned woman, immensely fat, was pegging out washing over the gush of flowers. Mr Arnold all but sobbed with relief. 'Customer!' he yelled.

'Be there in a minute,' she called affably. 'It's a beautiful dry-ing day.'

'Got a train to catch,' he bellowed. 'I want a double Scotch.'

'All right, all right.' Smooth and brown-faced as an egg, and with a dewlap of Turkish chins, she indolently left her basket, saying: 'No need to be crotchety. Where there's one train there's another; they've got the extra summer service now to London. I'm going up myself on Thursday; my daughter's going to be examined. . . . Why, it's Mr Arnold!' She paused, in pastoral caution. 'Are they taking her by train, then? I didn't know.' As if this settled her doubt, she hurried into the bar.

Mr Arnold said nothing. He drank the double in two gulps and asked for another, saying quickly: 'Then I've got to hurry.' The woman talked of her daughter with soft, unstressed tact. He paused uncertainly after the second double.

'No, Mr Arnold,' she decided for him, 'I can't give you any more.'

'Mrs Busby,' he said grandly, grasping his stick as for a march, 'I know when to stop.'

'Gents always do.' She nodded approval. 'God bless you.'

Now he felt translated into the desired sphere, where he could survey his kingdom without lamentations. Power radiated in him. As in the old days of his office fame, he could have settled a ledger page of complicated figures in a twinkling. And that men-acing dead weight in the pit of his stomach had vanished. He felt himself walking erect and proud through the luncheon-quiet town. He required no one's compassion. This heady brilliance lasted him all the way home. And he would not be late; a fixed stare at his watch testified to that. He congratulated himself on the efficient way he had handled his time. *They* would not be able to rebuke him for being late, on this day of all days.

Yet sight of his well-kept villa at the edge of the town struck a note in his soul like a buried knell. The garden, green-lawned and arched with trellises of roses, was trim beyond reproach—the packet he spent on it every year! And the house was cleanly white as a wedding cake. But quite suddenly now he felt that its walls and contents, its deeds and insurance policies, no longer interested or concerned him. At the gate he paused in panic. Was this the first faint rising of the horror he thought was obliterated from his being? . . . But almost at once this fear became blurred. His stick decisively tapping the crazy paving, he rolled up under the arches of roses with an air of having unfortunate business to transact.

The white-porched door was wide open. He entered bustlingly. Out of the drawing-room came Miriam, his elder sister-in-law; the woman in charge now, and his enemy. She looked at him and shrank. 'We waited lunch as long as we could,' she said, in her hard, gritty way. Her husband hovered behind her, thick horn glasses observant. 'I wanted George to go into the town and look for you—' she said hopelessly.

'Food!' Mr Arnold said, in high rebuke. 'You didn't expect me to eat lunch *today*!'

They all advanced out of the drawing-room into the hall, looking at him sideways. Ellen, the younger sister-in-law, and her husband, the dentist's assistant; their grown-up daughter; and Miriam's adolescent son. Alert but careful, visitors and yet that day not visitors, they were all dressed up and important, as if they were going to be photographed. Mr Arnold stretched his hat to a peg on the stand but miscalculated its position—'Cursed thing,' he remarked solemnly to the fallen hat. He sat heavily in the hard oak hall chair and wiped his brow. 'In good time,' he observed. 'Five minutes yet . . . What . . . What you all standing there for?' He jerked up his head despotically. He saw tears streaming down Ellen's face before she turned and, hurrying into the drawing-room, moaned: 'I shall be ashamed to go. He's ruined the day. Something must be done. Henry—'

126

she motioned to her husband. But Miriam, stark and glaring, stood like judgment.

'They're coming,' called her son, who had gone to the open door and was keeping a watch on the lane.

'Two o'clock!' said Mr Arnold in a solemn but strangely forlorn voice. 'Two o'clock!' Still collapsed in the chair, he groaned; his glassy eyes rolled, then stonily looked forth like tortoise eyes.

Henry and Ellen came back and whispered to Miriam's husband; they advanced briskly to Mr Arnold. 'Look, old boy,' George attempted male understanding. 'We think you'd better not go with us. We will see to everything. Take it easy and have a rest.' Enticingly he laid his hand under Mr Arnold's armpit, while Henry gripped the other arm. 'They're here; come upstairs,' he coaxed. The two sisters watched in pale, angry withdrawal.

Mr Arnold, shaking away the possessive hands, rose from the chair tremendously. 'What!' he panted. 'Better not go!' Masterfully he drew himself up. 'Me! *Me!*'

'*You are drunk,*' pronounced Miriam in icy rage. 'You are blind drunk. It's shameful.' Ellen wilted with a bitter sob against the wall.

Mr Arnold's eyes bulged. Their devilish shine enveloped Miriam with a terrible contempt, restrained for many years. 'This,' said Mr Arnold, '*this* is no time for insults. The pack of you can clear out now if you like. *I will go alone,*' he said defiantly.

'Now look here—' George began, conciliatory but aghast.

At that moment four men loomed at the open doorway. Four tall men, sleek and black-garbed, leanly efficient of aspect. With everyone in the hall black-clothed, too, the fair summer day seemed turned to shadow. The drawing room clock struck two dainty *pings*. At the sound the four men entered, admirably prompt. There was something purifying in their sinewy impersonality. 'Upstairs,' Mr Arnold, steady as a stout column, told them, 'in the back room.' The black quartet filed up the staircase. Out of the kitchen came Mrs Wills, her apron removed, and stood apart with her kind cook's fist under an eye.

'Have you decided to risk it?' Henry muttered to the women, while Mr Arnold reached down with glacial but careful dignity for his black hat. There was whispering, a furtive watching of him.

Down the staircase came the four men with the coffin tilted on their shoulders. The seven mourners stood back. Mr Arnold's face was stonily set again. He followed the quartet out with a stern and stiff gait. George and Henry, watchful, went close behind him. After them, in ceremonious orderliness, the others. But the two sisters, under their fashionably crisp black hats bought especially for the journey, crept forward with heads bowed very low, asking pardon of the world for this disgrace.

Mr Arnold negotiated half the length of the crazy paving with masterful ease. Then he began to sway. A hand grasped the trellis of an arch, and a shower of pink and white petals fell on his head and shoulders; his hat dropped out of his hand. The two men took his elbows, and now he submitted to their aid. Ellen sobbed anew; and Miriam moaned: 'We can only hope people will think it's grief.' Then she hissed frantically: 'Brush those petals off him, George; he looks as if he's getting married.'

The hearse contained its burden, the three limousines behind were elegant. 'Four wreaths,' said the supported Mr Arnold, hanging out his head like a bull. While the impersonal mutes went back to the house, the mourners disposed themselves in the cars. Though the two sisters had planned to occupy the first car with Mr Arnold, their husbands went in with him instead. 'There, take it easy, old boy,' said George, over-friendly now. Mr Arnold was well off and a triumphant example of industrious rectitude in the City.

'Eh? . . . eh?' said Mr Arnold vacantly. And, sunk between the two men into luxurious cushions, he straightway went into a doze. The car began its two-mile journey with a silent, soft glide.

'We mustn't let him go right off,' Henry worried. 'Hey! Mr Arnold, hey!'

Mr Arnold opened his eyes ferociously. 'The best wife a man ever had,' he groaned. 'Susan, Susan!' he called wildly. The driver turned his head for a moment. 'Ha, shameful, am I! . . . That woman hasn't got the intelligence of a . . . of a . . . budgerigar! And no more Christian feeling than a trout. Who'd have thought she and Susan were sisters! . . . And that other one,' he grunted, 'what's her name . . . Ellen, always grizzling and telling Susan she was hard up and her husband kept her short—pah! ... A depressing lot,' summed up Mr Arnold, staring rigidly into space. Then again he called in loud anguish: 'Susan, Susan, what will I do now?'

Beads of perspiration stood on Henry's forehead. But George remained cool; despite the abuse of his wife, he even sounded affectionate—'Never mind, old chap,' he comforted the bereaved, 'it'll be over soon. But keep awake, don't let down the whole family.'

'What family?' asked Mr Arnold. 'Got none.' And, sunk down and torpid, he seemed a secret being gathered eternally in loneliness. The two other men glanced at each other. 'Susan,' whispered Mr Arnold, chin on chest, 'Susan . . . God above!' he wailed again, 'what will I do now?' They were going through the full shopping street; people stopped to look, with arrested eyes. 'The only one of the bunch to keep her sweetness,' muttered Mr Arnold. 'Coming here in their showy hats!' he chuckled. 'But they couldn't make a man feel proud like Susan did. That time I took her to the Mansion House banquet—' But wild grief engulfed him anew. 'Susan, Susan,' he called, 'what'll I do now?'

'Here, pull yourself together,' Henry protested sharply at last, and, perhaps feeling Mr Arnold had gone far enough in insults, 'We're coming to the cemetery.'

Mr Arnold heaved into physical alertness for the ordeal. In a minute or two the car slid to a delicate standstill. Inside the cemetery gates was a group of half-a-dozen women, representatives of the institute for which Susan had organized many an event. Out of the lodge came the surpliced vicar, prayer-book in hand. Henry got out first and, red-faced, offered a hand to Mr Arnold, who ignored it and alighted without mishap. But for an awful moment the widower's legs seemed boneless. Then he drew himself up nobly, stood rock-like in ruminative strength, while the coffin was drawn out and borne ahead.

The two sisters stood in helplessness, hiding their faces, but peering like rabbits. The procession began to form. The vicar turned the pages of his book in mild abstraction. George and Henry sidled up beside Mr Arnold. 'I'll walk alone,' hissed Mr Arnold, and he reminded them fiercely that Miriam and Ellen were entitled to follow immediately behind him. He insisted on that being arranged. The institute women, who seemed unaware of anything unusual, took their places in the rear. The cortège moved.

The cemetery was cut out of a steepish slope, and the newly acquired section was at the top. It was quite a climb for elderly mourners; a discussion had waged in the local paper about the lack of foresight in not making a carriage road through the place. Mr Arnold, close behind the coffin and without his well-known stick, negotiated the climb with an occasional lapsing of his knees, a straightening of his back, or a rigid turning and jerking of his head, like a man doing physical exercises. But he achieved it victoriously. Behind him Ellen wept and Miriam stared in blank fear.

It was not until all were assembled before the graveside and the service had begun that Mr Arnold began to display signs of collapse. He vaguely swayed; his head lolled. George and Henry took a step nearer him. The abstract vicar droned unseeing; the institute women remained tactful behind the chief mourners. The attendants took up the roped coffin; it disappeared; a handful of earth was thrown in after it. Presently the vicar's voice stopped. George and Henry took Mr Arnold's elbows to assist him for the last look.

'Leave me alone,' Mr Arnold muttered, drawing his elbows angrily away. What had these to do with him! He advanced with renewed dignity to the brink of the grave. Looked in as if into an abyss of black tremendous loneliness. Stood there staring down in concentrated intentness, prolonged, fascinated. The vicar waited in faint surprise at the mourner's lengthy scrutiny.

George and Henry darted forward. Too late. While a single hysterical woman's cry shot up, Mr Arnold shot down, falling clumsily, arms flapping out, his disappearing face looking briefly astonished, the mouth wide open and showing all his artificial teeth. There was a moment's hesitation of unbelieving dismay. Then the bustling began. Mr Arnold lay down there on his stomach across the coffin. An upper denture gleamed out in the clay beside him.

'I knew it,' said Miriam, later, 'I felt it in my bones when you two allowed him to walk alone to the graveside. Thank heaven *we* don't live here.' They were in the villa in conference. Mr Arnold had been taken to the county hospital with a fractured leg.

He stayed there two months. The first patient to be received out of a grave, he was the talk and pet of the hospital; as the night sister remarked: 'He must have been a devoted husband to throw himself into his wife's grave like that! I've never known a man grieve so much. How he calls out in the night for his Susan!'. . . . Cantankerous at first, he became astonishingly meek. The doctor allowed him a certain amount of whisky. The night sister, perhaps because she was shortly due for retirement, secretly allowed him a little more. She took quite a fancy to him, and some months later, thinking he had detected in her a flavour of Susan's character, Mr Arnold married her.

BOY WITH A TRUMPET

All he wanted was a bed, a shelf for his trumpet and permission to play it. He did not care how squalid the room, though he was so clean and shining himself; he could afford only the lowest rent. Not having any possessions except what he stood up in, the trumpet in an elegant case and a paper parcel of shirts and socks, landladies were suspicious of him. But he so gleamed with light young vigour, like a feather in the wind, that he kindled even in those wary hearts less harsh refusals.

Finally, on the outer rim of the West End, he found a bleak room for eight shillings a week in the house of a faded actress purply with drink and the dramas of a succession of lovers.

'I don't mind a trumpet,' she said, mollified by his air of a waif strayed out of a lonely vacancy. 'Are you in the orchestra, dear? No? You're not in a jazz band, are you? I can't have nightclub people in my house, coming in at all hours. No? . . . You look so young,' she said wonderingly. 'Well, there's no attendance, my charwoman is on war work; the bathroom is strictly engaged every morning from ten to half-past, and I do not allow tenants to receive visitors of the opposite sex in their rooms.' Behind the blowsiness were the remnants of one who had often played the role of a lady.

'I've just committed suicide,' he said naively. She saw then the bright but withdrawn fixity of his eyes, single-purposed.

'What!' she said, flurried in her kimono, and instinctively placed a stagey hand on her bosom.

'They got me back,' he said. 'I was sick. I didn't swallow enough of the stuff. Afterwards they sent me to a—well, a hospital. Then they discharged me. From the Army.'

'Oh dear!' she fussed. And, amply and yearning: 'Did your nerve go, then? . . . Haven't you any people?' There had been a suicide—a successful one—in her house before, and she had not been averse to the tragedy.

'I have God,' he said gravely. 'I was brought up in an orphanage. But I have an aunt in Chester. She and I do not love each other. I don't like violence. The telephone is ringing,' he said, with his alert but withdrawn awareness.

She scolded someone, at length and with high-toned emphasis, and returning muttering; she started to find him still under the huge frilled lampshade by the petunia divan. 'Rent is in advance,' she said mechanically. 'Number eight on the second floor.'

He went up the stairs. The webby carpet, worn by years of lodgers, smelt of old dust. A gush of water sounded above; a door slammed; a cat slept on a window-sill under sprays of dusty lacquered leaves. Later, as he was going out to the tea-shop, two young girls, silent and proud, sedately descended the stairs together in the dying sunshine. They, too, had that air of clear-cut absorption in themselves, unacknowledging the dangerous world. But they were together in that house of the unanchored.

And he was alone, not long back from the edge of the dead land, the intersecting country where the disconnected sit with their spectral smiles.

That evening, in the tiny room, he played his trumpet. His lips, as the bandmaster of his regiment had told him, were not suitable for a trumpet; they had not the necessary full, fleshy contours, and also there were interstices in his front teeth; his face became horribly contorted in his effort to blast 'Cherry Ripe' out of the silver instrument. Nevertheless, when the benevolent spinster in the cathedral town where he had been stationed and sung Elizabethan madrigals asked what she could buy him after he had left the asylum, he said: 'A trumpet.' And, alone, he had come to the great city with his neurosis and a gleaming second-hand trumpet costing sixteen guineas. On arrival he spent half his money on four expensive poplin shirts and in the evening went to a lecture on world reform; the night he had spent in Regent's Park, his trumpet case and parcel on his lap.

The landlady rapped and came in. Violet circles were painted round her eyes and her hair was greenish. Within a wrap large, loose breasts swam untrammelled as dolphins. She looked at him with a speculative doubt.

'It's very noisy. Are you practising? There are neighbours.'

'You said I could play my trumpet,' he pointed out gravely.

She said: 'I am artistic myself, and I have had actors, writers, and musicians in my house. But there's a limit. You must have a certain hour for practice. But not in the evenings; the mornings are more suitable for a trumpet.'

'I cannot get up in the mornings,' he said. The trim, fixed decision of the young soldier stiffened his voice. 'I need a great deal of sleep.'

'Are you still ill?' She stepped forward, her ringed hands outstretched. He sat on the bed's edge in his clean new shirt, the trumpet across his knees. From him came a desolate waif need. But his round, fresh-air face had a blank imperviousness, and down his indrawn small eyes flickered a secret repudiation. 'Are you lonely?' she went on. 'I play the piano.'

'I don't like trembling young girls,' he said. But as if to himself: 'They make me unhappy. I usually burst into crying when I'm with them. But I like babies; I want to be a father. I used to go into the married quarters in barracks and look after the babies. . . . Sometimes,' he said, with his grave simplicity, 'I used to wash their napkins.'

In her slovenly fashion she was arrantly good-natured and friendly. 'Did you have a bad time in the orphanage, dear?'

'No, not *bad*. But I cannot stand the smell of carbolic soap now; it makes me want to vomit. . . . I would like,' he added, 'to have known my mother. Or my father.'

'Hasn't anyone ever cared for you?' she asked, heaving.

'Yes. Both girls and men. But only for short periods.' Detached, he spoke as if he would never question the reason for this. The antiseptic austerity of his early years enclosed him like a cell of white marble; later there had been the forced, too early physical maturity of the Army, which the orphanage governor had induced him to join as a bandboy, just before the war. He had no instinctive love to give out in return for attempts of affection: it had never been born in him. 'People get tired of me,' he added, quite acceptingly.

After that, in her erratic fashion, he obsessed her. She occasionally fed him; in his room she put cushions and a large

134

oleograph of Dante and Beatrice on a Florence bridge; she even allowed him to play the trumpet when he liked, despite complaints from the other lodgers. She badgered her lover of the moment, an irate designer of textiles, to find him a job in the studio of the huge West End store. But the boy categorically refused all jobs that required him before noon. His head like an apple on the pillow, he lay in bed all the morning sunk in profound slumber.

In the afternoons he would sit at his window drinking her tea or earnestly reading a modern treatise on religious problems. He insisted to her that a fresh upsurge of religious awareness was about to arrive in the world. He had already passed through the hands of a hearty, up-to-date Christian group, and he corresponded regularly with a canon whose sole panacea, however, was an exhortation to pray.

'But I can't pray,' he grieved to her. There was a deadlock of all his faculties.

Only when playing his trumpet he seemed a little released. Harshly and without melodic calm, he blew it over a world in chaos. For all the contortions of his round face he bloomed into a kind of satisfaction as he created a hideous pattern of noise. Cast out of the Army as totally unfit for service, it was only in these blasts of noise that he really enjoyed his liberty—the first that had ever come to him.

'Your rent is a fortnight overdue,' she reminded him, with prudent urgency. 'You really must find work, dear. Think of your future; now is your opportunity, with so many jobs about.'

'What future?' he asked curiously. 'Why do you believe so confidently in the future?'

He could always deflate her with this grave flatness. But her habit of working up emotional scenes was not easily balked. She would call him into her sitting room and, stroking his hand, among the billowy cushions, heave and throb about the rudeness of her lover, who was younger than herself. 'We are two waifs,' she said, while the telephone concealed under the crinoline of a doll rang yet again.

But he did not want the sultry maternalness of this faded, artificial woman; unerringly he sensed the shallow, predatory egotism of her need. Yet neither did he want to know the two beautiful and serious girls, flaxen-haired and virginal, who lived on the same floor; he always ducked his head away from them. He wanted to pick up a prostitute and spend a furtive quarter of an hour with her in the black-out. But he could not afford this. He was destitute now.

'You are horrible,' she exclaimed angrily when, in a long talk, he told her of this. 'You, a boy of nineteen, wanting to go with prostitutes!'

'You see,' he insisted, 'I would feel myself master with them, and I can hate them too. But with nice, proud girls I cannot stop myself breaking down, and then I want to rush away and throw myself under a Tube train. . . . And that's bad for me,' he added, with that earnest naiveté of his.

'But *is* it bad for you to break down?' she asked with some energy.

'Yes; I can't stand it.' Beyond the fixed calm of his small crystal eyes something flickered. 'When I was discharged from the Army the MO advised me to attend a clinic. I've been to one. It made me feel worse. I don't want to feel I'm a case.'

'The clinic,' she said sagely, 'couldn't be expected to provide you with a mother. You've got nineteen years of starvation to forget.'

She had got into the habit of giving him a glass of milk and rum at nights. Nevertheless, she had her real angers with him, for she was of tempestuous disposition. She knew that he would not—it did not occur to her that he could not—unfold to her other than in these talks. He did not weep on her waiting bosom; he did not like his bright glossy hair to be stroked. And sometimes when he played the trumpet in his room she was roused to a transport of queer, intent fury and she would prowl about the staircase in helpless rage.

He had been in the house a month when one afternoon, after he had been playing for an hour, she walked into his room. Her green hair was frizzed out, the heavily painted eyes sidled angrily, the violet lips twisted like a cord. There was something both pathetic and ridiculous in the frenzy of this worn and used woman gallantly trying to keep up an air of bygone theatrical grandeur and, indeed, of ladylike breeding. But she was so brittle. Carefully looking at her, he laid the trumpet on his knees.

'Why must you *keep on!*' she fumed. 'That everlasting tune, it's maddening. The neighbours will ring up the police and I shall have them calling. You are not in a slum.'

'You said I could play my trumpet.'

And still there was about him that curious and impervious tranquillity, not to be disturbed, and, to her, relentless. It drove her to a vindictive outburst, her gaze fixed in hatred on the trumpet.

'Why don't you go out and look for *work*? Your rent—you are taking advantage of my kindness; you are lazy and without principle. Aren't you ashamed to sit there doing nothing but blowing noises on that damned thing?' She heaved over him in the narrow room, a dramatic Maenad gone to copious seed and smelling of bath salts.

He got up from the bed's edge, carefully disconnected the trumpet's pieces and put them in the elegant case and his shirts and socks into a brown paper carrier. She watched him, spell-bound; his crisp, deliberate decision was curbing. At the door he raised his hat politely. All recognition of her was abolished from the small, unswerving eyes.

'Good afternoon,' he said in a precise way. 'I will send you the rent when I earn some money. I am sure to find a position suited to me before long.'

He stored the trumpet in a railway station. On no account would he pawn it, though there was only a shilling or two left of the pound the canon had last sent him, together with a copy of *St Augustine's Confessions*. He knew it was useless to look for a job even as second trumpet in the cabarets; not even his fresh, shiny, boy appearance, that would look well in a Palm Beach jacket, could help him.

That night he hung about the dark, chattering Circus, not unhappy, feeling vaguely liberated among this anonymous crowd milling about in an atmosphere of drink, flesh, and boredom. He listened carefully to the soldiers' smudged catcalls, the female retaliations, the whispers, the ironical endearments, the dismissals. But as the night wore on and the crowd thinned, his senses became sharpened, alert, and at the same time desperate. Like a young hungry wolf sniffing the edge of the dark, he howled desolately inside himself. In the black-out the perfumed women, dots of fire between their fingertips, passed and repassed, as if weaving a dance figure in some hieratic ceremony; his mind became aware of a pattern, a design, a theme in which a restated lewd note grew ever more and more dominant. He wanted to play his trumpet. Startle the night with a barbaric blast.

He began to accost the women. He had heard that some would give shelter to the temporarily destitute, exercising a legendary comradeship of the streets. But none had use for him. After a brief assessment of his conversation they passed on rapidly. Only one was disposed to chatter. She told him he could find a job, if his discharge papers were in order, as a stagehand in a certain theatre; she gave him a name to ask for.

'Nothing doing, darling,' she replied promptly to his subsequent suggestion. 'No fresh pineapple for me tonight.'

Waiting for morning, he sat on a bench in the ghostly Square garden and returned to an earlier meditation on the nature of God. In this mental fantasy he continually saw the embryo of a tadpole which split into two entities. The force that divided the embryo was God, a tremendous deciding power that lay beyond biology. It was eternal and creative, yet could one pray to it, worship it? Would it be conscious of a worshipping acknowledgement, and, if so, could it reward with peace, harmony, and contentment? He ached to submerge himself in belief and to enter into a mystic identification with a creative force; he wanted to cast himself at the knees of a gigantic parent of the universe. But on every side were frustrations, and the chaotic world, armed for destruction, was closing in on him triumphantly. Yet he knew it was that creative force that had driven him to attempt suicide as a solution and a release; he had believed that the power within him would not die but return to the central force and be discharged again. But he shivered at the memory of the hours before that act of suicide, those furtive, secret hours that had ruptured his mind. Outside himself he had never been able to kill even a spider.

'You must think of your future!' he suddenly whinnied aloud, causing a bemused sailor on an adjacent bench to lift his round cap off his face. He tried to envisage a concrete picture of that future, but saw only a ravaged place of waste with a few tufts of blackened vegetation against a burnt-out sky.

He began working among acres of painted canvases depicting idealised scenes in a world devoted to song, hilarity, and dance. Rainbow processions of girls passed in and out, pearly smiles stitched into glossy faces, the accurate legs swinging like multi-coloured sausages. Watching these friezes in tranced gravity, he sometimes missed a cue, rousing the stage manager to threats of instant dismissal, despite the labour shortage. The hard-working young girl dancers, lustrously trim and absorbed in professional perfection, took no notice of the new stagehand fascinated in attempts to adapt their integrated patterns to his consciousness. But though hypnotized by this new revelation of idealized flesh and movements, he still could not identify himself with them. He was still cut off, he had not yet come through to acceptance that the world breathed, and that these pink and silver girls actually could be touched.

He started and listened carefully when a distinguished young man, a hero of the sky, sent a message backstage that he 'would like to collaborate' with a certain starry beauty of the chorus. 'She'll collaborate all right,' remarked another of the girls in the wings; 'I never heard it called that before.' That night he went home straight from the theatre and filled the house with the blasts of his trumpet.

He had rented a small partitioned space in the basement, its window overlooking the back garden. It contained a camp-bed and one or two bugs which he accepted as outcomes of the God-force. The street was not of good repute, but it was beyond the West End, and an amount of lace-curtained and fumed-oak respectability was maintained.

'You can blow your trumpet as much as you like,' Irish Lil said. 'Blow it in the middle of the night if you like—it might drive some of the bastards out. Can you lend me five bob till tomorrow morning?'

There had been a quarrel among the five prostitutes up-stairs: four accused the fifth of bringing in clients during the daytime—they declared the house would get a bad name. They were entirely daughters of the night; in daylight there was a moon glisten on their waxen faces, their hair looked unreal, and their voices were huskily fretful. They called him the Boy with a Trumpet, and he was already something of a pet among them. He shared the roomy basement with four refugees off the

139

Continent who came and went on obscure errands and everlastingly cooked cabbage soup.

Irish Lil was the disgrace of the house. Though she always
had real flowers stuck in the two milk bottles on her sideboard,
she was a slut. Her slovenly make-up, her regular OMS lover
in the Guards who got roaring drunk, and her inability to dis-
criminate and to insist on pre-payment angered the four
younger women. Blonde Joyce carried on a year-old vendetta
with her. Over a stolen egg. Irish Lil was creeping downstairs
one evening with the egg, which she had taken from Joyce's
room, when a bomb fell in the Avenue. Kathleen rushed out
of her room with a Free French client and found Lil struck
daft on the stairs with the crushed egg dribbling through her
fingers.

'Don't trust your trumpet to her,' Joyce said. 'She'll pawn
it.' For, as his room had no lock, he asked where in the house
he could hide his trumpet while he was at the theatre.

'She weeps,' he said gravely. 'I've heard her weeping.'

'If,' Joyce said, hard, 'she was on fire, I wouldn't pee on her
to put her out.'

But they all, in their idle afternoons, liked him about their
rooms. He fetched them newspapers and cigarettes; he was a
nice boy and, yawning in their dressing-gowns and irremediably
nocturnal, they discarded their professionalism with him. Their
calm acceptance of the world as a disintegration eased him;
his instinct had been right in seeking a brothel to live in.

Yet he saw the house, for all its matter-of-fact squalor, as
existing in a world still spectral to him. Still he lived behind
thick glass, unreleased and peering out in dumb waiting. Only
his old Army nightmare was gone—the recurrent dream in
which he lay sealed tight into a leaden pipe under a pavement
where he could hear, ever passing and returning, the heeltaps
of compassionate but unreachable women. But the tank-like
underwater quiet of the observation ward in the asylum was
still with him, always. And he could not break through,
smash the glass. Not yet.

It was Kathleen who took quite a fancy to him. They had
disconnected conversations in her room; she accepted him
amicably as a virginal presence that did not want to touch her.
She was plump as a rose, and a sprinkle of natural colour was

still strewn over her, the youngest girl in the house. She promised to try to find him a job as trumpeter in one of the clubs; he could earn a pound a night at this if he became proficient.

'But I don't want to earn a lot of money,' he said earnestly. 'It's time we learned how to do without money. We must learn to live and create like God.'

'I've met all types of men,' she said vaguely, tucking her weary legs under her on the bed. 'And I hate them all. I tell you I've got to have six double gins before I can bring one home. That costs them a quid or two extra; I make the sods spend.'

He said dreamily: 'When I took poison I felt I was making a creative act, if it was only that I was going out to search.' He could still rest in the shade of that release; the mysteriousness of that blue underworld fume was still there, giving him a promise of fulfilment. 'I saw huge shapes . . . they were like huge flowers, dark and heavy blood-coloured flowers. They looked at me, they moved, they listened, their roots began to twine into me, I could feel them in my bowels. . . . But I couldn't rise, I was lying in the mud. I couldn't breathe in the new way. I tried to struggle up . . . through. But I fell back, and everything disappeared—'

'Don't you go trying to commit suicide in this house,' she said. 'Mrs Walton would never forgive you. That Irish tyke's doing enough to advertise us already. . . . You're not queer, are you?' she asked, desultory. 'I like queer men, they don't turn me sick. . . . Always at one,' she ruminated of the others.

She attracted him more than the other four, but, to content his instinct completely, he wished her more sordid, lewd, and foul-tongued, more disintegrated. The ghostly lineaments of a trembling young girl remained in her. They conversed to each other across a distance. But she was the only one of the women who still appeared to observe things beyond this private world of the brothel. He sometimes tried to talk to her about God.

The taxicabs began to purr up to the front door any time after midnight. Sometimes he got out of his bed in the basement, mounted the staircase in trousers and socks, and stood poised in the dark as if waiting for a shattering revelation from behind the closed doors. There was the useless bomber pilot who broke down and shouted weepingly to Joyce that his nerve was gone—'Well,' Joyce had said in her ruthless way, 'you can stay if you like, but I'm keeping my present all the same, mind!' That pleased him, as he carefully listened; it belonged to the chaos, the burnt-out world reduced to charcoal. He laughed softly to himself. What if he blew his trumpet on this phantasmagoric staircase? Blew it over the fallen night, waken these dead, surprise them with a new anarchial fanfare?

One week when the elder tree and the peonies were in blossom in the once-cultivated back garden, Irish Lil declared the had a birthday. She opened her room on the Monday night--always an off night—to whoever wished to come in. Ranks of beer flagons stood on the sideboard, and Harry, her Guards sergeant regular, roared and strutted before them in his battle-dress like David before the Ark. Three refugees from the basement ventured in; Joyce forgot her vendetta, but refused to dress or make up; Pamela sat repairing a stocking. When he arrived from the theatre the beer was freely flowing. Irish Lil, in a magenta sateen gown, was wearing long, ornate earrings in a vain attempt to look seductive. Kathleen, on this off-night occasion, gazed at him with a kind of sisterly pensiveness.

'Heard that one about Turnham Green—?' bawled Harry, and took off his khaki blouse before telling it, owing to the heat.

He was a great tree of flesh. His roots were tenacious in the earth. The juice in his full lips was the blood of a king bull; the seeds of war flourished in the field of his muscular belly. For him a battle was a dinner, a bomb a dog bark, a bayonet a cat-scratch, and in the palm of his great blue paw statesmen curled secure. He was the salt of the earth. The limericks flying off his lips became more obscene.

But they fell flat. The prostitutes were bored with obscenity, the refugees did not understand English humour. Joyce yawned markedly.

'Hell, what's this?' Harry panted a bit—'The funeral of the duchess? . . . Reminds me. Heard that one about Her Grace and the fishmonger?'

'Fetch your trumpet, will you?' asked Irish Lil, feeling a little music was necessary.

'What!' shouted Harry, delighted. 'He's got a trumpet? I

been in the band in my time. A kick or two from a trumpet's jest what's needed.'

He snatched the beautifully shining instrument and set it to his great curled lips. The bull neck swelled, the huge face glowed red. And without mistake, unfalteringly, from harmonious lungs, he played the 'Londonderry Air'. A man blowing a trumpet successfully is a rousing spectacle. The blast is an announcement of the lifted sun. Harry stood on a mountain peak, monarch of all he surveyed.

Kathleen came in, hesitating, and sat beside him on the camppbed. 'What's the matter?' she asked. He had flung away with the trumpet as soon as Harry had laid it down. He sat concentratedly polishing it with a bit of chiffon scarf she had once given him, especially the mouthpiece. 'Has he spoilt it, then?' she murmured.

He did not answer. But his fingers were trembling. She said wearily: 'He's started reciting "Eskimo Nell" now.'

'I wish I could play like him,' he whispered.

'You do make an awful noise,' she said in a compassionate way. 'You haven't got the knack yet, with all your practising . . . I wonder,' she brooded after a while, 'if it's worth going down West. But they're so choosy on a Monday night.'

'Don't go.' He laid down the trumpet as if abandoning it for ever. 'Don't go.'

She seemed not to be listening, her preoccupied eyes gazing out of the window. The oblong of garden was filled with the smoky red after-fume of sunset. Their low voices drifted into silences. Two pigeons gurgled in the elder tree; a cat rubbed against the window-pane and became intent on the pigeons. Kathleen's mouth was pursed up thoughtfully. He was conscious of the secret carnation glow of her thighs. Her thick hair smelled of obliterating night.

'I won't ever play my trumpet.' His voice stumbled. 'I have no faith, no belief, and I can't accept the world . . . I can't *feel* it.'

'Christ, there's enough to feel,' she protested. 'This bloody war, and the bombs—'

'In the Army they taught us to get used to the smell of blood. It smells of hate. . . . And to turn the bayonet deep in the guts.

. . . There were nice chaps in our battalion who had letters and parcels from home . . . from loving mothers and girls . . . and they didn't mind the blood and the bayonets; they had had their fill of love and faith, I suppose. But I was hungry all the time, I wanted to be fed, and I wanted to create, and I wanted children. . . . I am incomplete,' he whispered—'I didn't have the right to kill.'

'But you tried to kill yourself,' she pointed out, though vaguely, as if her attention was elsewhere.

'My body,' he said—'that *they* owned.'

'Well, what can you *do*?' she asked, after another silence. 'You ought to take up some study, a boy with your brains. . . . It's a shame,' she cried, with a sudden burst of the scandalized shrillness of her kind: 'the Army takes 'em, breaks 'em, and chucks 'em out when they've got no further use for 'em. . . . What *can* you do?'

'There's crime,' he said.

'It don't pay,' she said at once.

'I believe,' he said, 'there'll be big waves of crime after the war. You can't have so much killing, so much teaching to destroy, and then stop it suddenly. . . . The old kinds of crime, and new crimes against the holiness in the heart. There'll be fear, and shame, and guilt, guilt. People will be mad. There's no such thing as victory in war. There's only misery, chaos and suffering for everybody, and then the payment. . . . There's only one victory—over the evil in the heart. And that's a rare miracle.'

His voice faltered in defeat. 'I've been trying to make the attempt. But the air I breathe is full of poison.'

She let him talk, pretending to listen. Clients sometimes talked to her oddly and, if there was time, it was professional tact to allow them their airings.

'Harry, up there,' he went on dejectedly, 'carries the world on his shoulders. But he'll rob his mother and starve his wife and pick his neighbour's pocket.' He took up the trumpet off the bed, turned it over regretfully, and let it drop back. 'I can't even play my trumpet like him,' he reiterated obsessively. 'Would I make a better criminal?'

'Now, look here,' she said, her attention arrested, 'don't you go starting down *that* street! Boys like you alone in London can

144

soon go to the bad. I've seen some of it. It won't pay, I'm telling you.'

'But crime as a protest,' he said earnestly. 'As a relief. And don't you see there's nothing but crime now, at the heart of things?'

Professionally comforting, she laid her hand on his, which began to tremble again. Yet his small crystal eyes remained impervious, with their single-purposed rigidity. She stroked his hand. 'Don't tremble, don't tremble. . . . Do you ever cry?' she asked, gazing into his face in the last light.

He shook his head. 'I can't.' But something was flickering into his eyes. He had leaned towards her slowly.

'If you could,' she said, but still with a half-vague inattentiveness—'I'm sure you ought to break down. You're too shut in on yourself.'

He breathed her odour of flesh. It seemed to him like the scent of milky flowers, living and benign, scattered in a pure air. As if it would escape him, he began to breathe it hungrily. His hands had stopped trembling. But the rigid calm of his appearance, had she noticed it in the dusky light, was more disquieting.

'There!' she said, still a little crouched away from him; 'you see, a little personal talk is good for you. You're too lonely, that's what it is.'

'Will you let me—'

'What?' she asked, more alert. The light was finishing; her face was dim.

'Put my mouth to your breast?'

'No,' she said at once. She shook her head. 'It wouldn't be any use, anyhow.'

But, now that the words were out, he fell on her in anguish. 'Stay with me! Don't go away. Sleep with me tonight.' He pressed his face into her, shuddering, and weeping at last. 'Stay!'

She heaved herself free, jumping off the bed with a squirm, like anger. 'Didn't I tell you that I hated men!' She raised her voice, very offended. 'I could spit on them all—and you, too, now.' She opened the door. 'But I will say this'—her voice relented a degree—'I wouldn't sleep with you if you offered me ten pounds! I know what I am, and I don't want any of your fancy stuff.' She flounced out with scandalized decision.

He rolled over and over on the bed. Shuddering, he pressed his face into the pillow. When the paroxysm had passed he half rose and sat looking out of the window. In his movement the trumpet crashed to the floor, but he did not pick it up. He sat gazing out into the still world as if he would never penetrate it again. He saw grey dead light falling over smashed cities, over broken precipices and jagged torn chasms of the world. Acrid smoke from abandoned ruins mingled with the smell of blood. He saw himself the inhabitant of a wilderness where withered hands could lift in guidance no more. There were no more voices and all the paps of earth were dry.

ALL THROUGH THE NIGHT

On this particular icy Wednesday in early January, Mrs Bessie Evans' routine followed its normal course for a drinking evening. Rhiannon, the afternoon help from the village, safely gone, the sitting room fire compactly built up, curtains closed against the bluely frozen night—all was set for three hours of slow pleasure. The isolation of the cottage among the cold-stiffened pines, even the ordinary fact that it was situated in a secret fold among the interior hills of Wales, seemed to give an additional relish to the coming session.

Bessie liked a hard winter: no vulgarly beaming sun nagging at one to go out and get healthy; no reproachful flowers to water in the damned garden; no malign wasps or mosquitoes; no birds yelling their little heads off at the crack of dawn. Also, a bitter frost, such as bruised the air this evening, raised (she was sure of it) a more fiery tang in her favourite beverage. She had arrived at the connoisseur's stage in such matters.

At seven o'clock, dressed in black satin, she ate boiled top-round beef with appreciation, neglecting none of the subsidiary dishes that Rhiannon—an excellent cook, ignorant village woman though she was—had prepared; there were preserved pears, a fat junket, local farm cheese and butter, home-baked bread and, finally, a slice of chocolate cake. She ate not so much out of greed as out of a realization, based on experience, that a solid foundation of food helped to generate from whisky the special rich, luxuriant glow she desired. She would go up to bed feeling a wonderful lack of contumaciousness towards the world.

At half-past seven, her bosom preceding her in royal solidity, she moved from the kitchen to the sitting-room, unlocked the old press of carved black oak, and drew out a glass and two bottles; one bottle was a third full, the other unopened. Her bosom, which was that of a handsomely endowed woman of forty, gave its usual preparatory heave; it suggested both a greeting and an admonishment.

Almost invariably she subjected herself to a strict practice of drinking exactly two-thirds of a bottle on alternate evenings of the week only, retiring to bed immediately after the sitting-room clock struck ten. It was a discipline from which she drew self-esteem and the deduction that she was not really going bad. On the rare occasions when she yielded to temptation and stayed up until eleven finishing a whole bottle, drastic scolding and punishment—such as doing without a meal or furiously working on the neglected garden—were administered the next day. As for the whiskyless evenings, these, of course, were hard to endure; and when, still more rarely, she broke her rule completely and enjoyed two consecutive sessions of intoxication, the lapse acquired a wicked splendour that almost made her topple over into the decision to give up the tenancy of Old Well Cottage and return, contritely, to the place she had come from.

The fire burned with purplish energy. An oil lamp cast a clear glow from its pretty shade; under it, a deeply upholstered chair took Bessie's body with a companionable sigh from its springs. A lady of leisure, secure in her domain, she had no difficulty, at least on such nights as this, in enjoying vicarious ownership of the charming old cottage and its kindred furnishings. She had rented it, two years before, from a man known locally as Shadrach the Gas (he managed the gas-works in the market town), and, because of its isolation and the lack of electricity and other main services, the rent was most reasonable.

After a few preliminary sips—the whisky was never tainted with other liquids—she turned on the battery wireless. There was a programme of rollicking variety turns. She enjoyed a good dirty laugh, liked boisterous comedians with red-nosed anecdotes of undignified disasters. What she *couldn't* stand was those women who heaved their guts up in some God-awful wail about love gone wrong. One of these upset the programme tonight, and Bessie, pouring her fourth large measure by then, shouted at the wireless cabinet: 'You silly cabbage, serve you

148

right if he let you down! We got to *fight* the devils, my gal!'

At nine-fifteen, a lecturer followed the variety turns, and she jeered good-humouredly: 'Ancient Egyptians—they were all like us, you fathead. You can't change human nature.' She shut him off, lit the single cigarette she allowed herself on whisky nights, and, as usual, sat back pondering plans.

Always, after about half a bottle had been consumed, problems acquired a roseate tinge. They would be solved with delicious ease. There was always her sister Susan, in Australia— Susan and her husband's expanding grocery business in Sydney; Susan who wanted a colleague experienced in business from the home country to help; Susan who, though she could be mean as cat's meat, valued her; Susan . . . Her drooping eyelids suddenly opened; she sat bolt upright, her eyes sidling round the room. Had a piece of coal exploded in the grate? She bent down to the low table and poured the last measured allowance from the second bottle. It was a quarter to ten.

She began to giggle. At tea-time, Rhiannon had told her more about Elfed, the widowed farmer who had been asking questions in the village about the tenant of Old Well Cottage. Why didn't she come down to the chapel on Sundays? He had seen her many times in the returning market bus, a heavily laden basket on her knees, and her face (Rhiannon herself enjoyed the inquisitive farmer's compliment) 'bright as a bunch of snapdragons'. Rhiannon thought he would soon be offering to carry that heavy basket the quarter mile from the village bus stop to the cottage above the slope of pines.

Bessie, sipping her drink and purring beautifully inside now, let out a guffaw. Those bottles in the basket! After her two years of residence, the villagers, even Rhiannon, had not found out about the whisky in the capacious wicker basket which sat, displaying a crust of groceries and fruit, on her lap in the bus after the twice-weekly visit to the market town, six miles away. But Rhiannon, her only link with the village, often hinted to her that the lone Mrs Evans, although thought of respectfully as a dignified woman of means, still roused speculation. Why had she chosen to live among strangers in such a quiet district?

'Tell the ladies and gentlemen of Sychan,' the recluse had said, 'that I've had my day with the best man that ever lived,

149

and I've come here to remember it undisturbed by other things.'

When she had arrived, she had told Shadrach the Gas that her late husband, William Evans, a war casualty, used to motor her on week-ends through this wonderful countryside, and that they had decided to retire hereabouts in due course. Still dressed in black, even after all that time of widowhood, she gave out the flavour of a woman who would mourn her loss forever. Yet acceptance of her became solidified when the villagers began to refer to her as Mrs Evans Old Well, and now she could enter the bus without the babble of voices dropping. There was a very deep seventeenth-century well, still functioning, near the cottage porch. The legend was that a sinful wife, in far-off, stricter days, had been dropped down it, and her ghost was said still to haunt the garden. Shadrach the Gas pooh-poohed all that, yet after buying and furnishing the cottage he had not lived long there himself.

At five minutes to ten, she exclaimed, still giggling, 'Elfed wants to carry my basket, does he! Well, his chance *might* come—if his oats show a good profit some year!' The giggling came to an abrupt stop. Her glass was empty. She frowned.

The price of Scotch! Thirty-six shillings the bottle! Occasionally a sort of paralysis gripped her in the region of the solar plexus when she approached her bank in the market town. Otherwise, she treated her legacy of three thousand pounds—it had arrived, indeed, with a fairy-wand unexpectedness from a bachelor uncle struck down untimely and intestate—as something subject at any moment to an equally unexpected magic removal from the granite building where it lay in a deposit account yielding two and a half per cent interest. Although only a glance was required, she found it increasingly difficult to examine the state of her finances. Anyhow, she could always go back to work at the drapery. Or disappear—assuming she still had the fare—to Australia. Beautiful, beautiful Australia.

When the mantelpiece clock began striking its ten crisp pings, she sat up rigid again and, arms folded across her chest, stared thunderously at the second bottle, now a third empty. 'No, Bessie!' she cried out. 'No! You can't afford it. You've got to go to Australia. Lolling around here, you big good-for-nothing!' She thrust the cork in the bottle, gave it a bang with her fist, and heaved herself up.

Then came the satisfaction of locking up the bottles and glass in the press. Tomorrow morning, the first empty bottle would be dropped down the well. This method of disposal amused her; she liked to hear the faraway splash. Perhaps, when she was safe in Australia, Shadrach the Gas or another tenant might discover a deposit of four or five hundred bottles in that choked-up old well, which was supposed to be the residence of a ghost!

After the press key had been safely hidden from Rhiannon's prying, the usual buoyant feeling of achievement, propriety observed, and self-admiration rewarded her. Bed now! Sleep would come easily—deep, warm sleep in that lovely bed of good linen, fleecy blankets, and red eiderdown, the world obliterated. What more could a woman want? She began to sing.

She bolted the front and back doors, still humming *Ar Hyd y Nos*. Every downstairs window was already fastened. Not that she was a nervous woman. Besides, burglars never functioned in these tranquilly unimportant parts; neither were tramps ever seen. She took the small lamp standing on a table in the hall—a place so cold that, despite the interior whisky warmth, she shivered. As, vaguely unsteady, she mounted the crooked staircase of black oak, the lamp's flame danced within the glass funnel under the cretonne shade. On the bulgy, fortress-thick walls, shadows danced clownishly. Sleepy though she was, she still hummed the popular, dirge-like old melody.

When she opened the door of the front bedroom, her attention was caught at once by a shape in the bed. Yet she did not cry out, and the lamp did not drop from her hand. She only stared at the shape with the same thunderous intensity as that with which she had looked at the bottle downstairs when the hour struck.

The shape—clearly it was that of a man, with the head visible on the farther of the two pillows—had its back to her. The old-fashioned double bed stood against the wall, and its occupant had taken the inner position. No sound of breathing came. Bessie's eyes roved, with an effort, to garments dropped on a chair. A pair of shoes stood neatly together on a rug. Most conspicuous of all, a soft felt hat hung, rakish-looking, on the knob of one ebony bedpost.

These evidences of outrageous intrusion did not exert on her, a married woman, the effect they might have achieved with a spinster. Nevertheless, in the long moments of silence her face became drained of its opulent colour. A dim memory came to her of an old, now abandoned country custom—*caru yn y gweli*, it was called. A suitor climbed through a bedroom window—a ladder was usually left conveniently handy—and, if acceptable, was allowed to stay an hour or two, with marriage in view. It was just possible that in remote and unspoiled villages like Sychan the custom was still followed, if only in a jesting manner. Those earthy glances she got sometimes in the bus from men old enough to know better!

Fury rescued her. Her voice thick but bridling, she spoke. 'If you don't leave my house this instant,' she declared, 'I'll call the police.'

At once, she was aware of the fatuity of this—no telephone, and the nearest neighbour hopelessly beyond the range of the loudest scream.

Slowly, unalarmed, the man turned his head on the pillow. Bessie's free hand, opening and closing, clutched her satin dress. She still held the lamp; otherwise, she might have sunk to the floor. But her legs buckled somewhat. '*William*,' she stammered.

Her husband looked at her with assessing curiosity—a square-headed man with hard, unblinking eyes and a mouth that had become tightened as though from driving ruthless business transactions. 'What's that you said about the police?' he asked, still not budging from under the blankets.

'I'll—I'll call them,' she panted.

'Shouldn't think you'd want to do that.' He spoke with slow, exactitude, but mildly. 'There's only one in the village, I expect, and *he* wouldn't be used to a case like this—not in these nice, respectable parts.' His steady eyes, not moving from her, shone greenish in the lamplight. 'Sit down, Bessie,' he suggested. 'Unless you're coming into bed?'

He watched her turn and, with the slow, waddling movements of a person exercising will-power after the petrification of a shock, walk to the high chest of drawers and place the lamp on it. 'What did you think was in your bed?' he asked, entirely without amusement. 'A wolf?' And suddenly, rapidly, he flung back the bedclothes and leaped out—a short, solid-fleshed man of mature cast, with strong, thick arms. He filled, with comfortable tightness, the striped shirt he had left on. Bessie shrank back a step, clutching the bodice of her dress, her eyes bared. But he did not touch her. He only locked the door, drew out the key, and leaped back into bed, thrusting the key under the farther pillow.

'Brrh! It's warmer in here,' he said. 'A pity you haven't got a stove in the room.'

She had watched with the strained inertia of someone hopelessly lost in a no man's land of mist. Then, carefully lowering herself, she sat on a hard chair placed against the wall where the chest stood. A little heat, perhaps sufficient for a doll's house, came from the lamp. The room was very cold. The sitting room downstairs, the three hours of cosy drinking, already seemed remote. Something drastic had happened. Her mind kept on fumbling towards realization, but so far all she felt was that a great black cloud had suddenly clamped down on the pretty cottage. She no longer looked at the man in the bed. He was saying something about having come in by the back door after keeping watch on the house for hours . . . helping himself to bread and cheese in the kitchen . . . examining the layout of the house with a torch. She made an effort to clear a way through the muddle in her mind.

'How did you find where I was living?' she whispered at last. The ordinariness of the inquiry seemed to reassure her. His presence was perfectly acceptable and, somehow, logical. But still she did not look at him—only stared in turn at the wardrobe, at the dressing-table, and, finally, up at the gently burning little lamp, as though seeing them for the first time.

'Took me a long time to track down a pal of yours,' William replied. Perhaps because of his success in this, he even sounded affable. 'She's in furs now, Monica is—a wholesale house in Cardiff. I expect you know about that. Cost me a four-quid dinner in the Angel to make her slip the bit of information—pretending she wasn't slipping it, of course.' He eased himself up, and gave the pillow a pugilist's blow. 'You shouldn't have written her asking for that twenty quid you lent her, Bessie. You must have been drunk when you did it.'

She bridled a little. 'I don't get drunk.'

'No? Well, it was your tightness about money, then.' He chuckled, with a queer, throaty sound she had never heard from him before. He was not a man given to jokes.

'Wait till I get hold of Monica!' she said, her voice too shaky for vindictiveness.

'You won't,' William said.

She bent her head as though the strength of her neck had dwindled.

There was a long silence, and when, finally, she spoke, her sluggishness suggested a lack of interest in or focus on what she was asking: 'Have you still got the restaurant?'

'No. Sold it months ago. Been on the prowl since then.' He stretched, and snuggled down like any married man in bed at home. The heaving eiderdown shone luxuriously warm. 'Got a fair price for the premises from a big firm of caterers. They said the goodwill of the business wasn't worth much—your fault, Bessie.' She said nothing, and he, calm in his deductions, although his tone seemed to imply long and bitter reveries, presently went on: 'If you'd put the money you had from your Uncle Charles—and I bet he's boiling in hell at the thought *you* got it—if you'd put it into the restaurant, we'd soon have been well off, Bess. That scheme they had to build a factory estate outside Dinas has got going—the Government is encouraging it. Dinas town is going to be a big noise in a couple of years or so.'

She drew her feet, which were getting cold, under her skirt. 'Why didn't you hold on to the premises, then?'

There was a long pause before he replied. 'I lost interest in the business. I got sour, Bessie, see? When I'd go down in the morning to let Sally and Mrs Bevan in, and notice them looking at me sideways, wondering about my state of temper— well, I got to hate myself, too. After you did a bunk from me, I took to staying at home all on my own . . . night after night.' In his voice was all the bleak solitude of the home over the restaurant, all the deserted silence of the small-town street after the shops closed.

'You used to go to meet the Chamber of Commerce men in

154

The White Hart often enough, leaving *me* at home,' she reminded him.

'You drove me out, with your moods. You could have kept me at your side, loving as a silly spaniel.' Still, he sounded only mildly concerned about all that now. 'After you bunked off, leaving that note of three lines on the mantelpiece, I couldn't get myself to go to The White Hart any more, knowing how all the boys would push drinks on me and slap me on the back, cheerful as a lot of undertakers. . . . But the money, Bessie, the money! If you had run off *before* you got the solicitor's letter about your uncle's money, it wouldn't have been quite so bad. The thought of the money stuck in my gullet. We could have used that money well, and in ten years you'd have had your jewellery and sables and ride about fat as a duchess. But, no! You wanted the legacy all to yourself. Yourself, yourself!'

She didn't like his further chuckle. Although stupor still held her body inert, her mind formulated a clear little patch of opinion. Sounding detached from any wish to give offence, she began: 'I hated Dinas, and you could not have made the restaurant into anything. You're a fighter, I dare say, but you just can't think *big*. You're not the master type, William; you haven't got the employer's temperament. Those two waitresses used to laugh at you. After being in a large drapery business for fifteen years, I know what's what in business—' She stopped, dimly aware of incautiousness.

'A good woman ought to try to make a man feel larger, not smaller,' he replied to this, only a shade censorious. 'You're a mean and selfish woman, Bessie. One of the kind that only wants a man to keep her in comfort and expects it as her right— amen and no two opinions about it.'

They were approaching the old trouble, the ancient warfare, the eternal trap. For some reason, she remembered hearing, in a Welsh wireless talk on bygone courting customs, how a couple would be sewn inside a sack together by the girl's parents and left all night as a test of mutual suitability. 'I'm as God made me,' she found herself mumbling.

For the first time, his voice betrayed a dark, glowering anger. 'I wonder what we have schools and upbringing for! Did God set out purposely to make you a humbug, a liar, a greedy hypocrite, and a thief? Do you think I didn't know how

155

you used to help yourself to money in the restaurant till and spend it in Cardiff on flighty clothes that you said you got at wholesale prices? Ha! Always wanting to play the lady in Dinas, you shifty bitch!'

She did not deal with this. It seemed unimportant and normal beside the fact of his presence and the key under the pillow—unimportant, even, in comparison with the fact of her defunct feet and the moribund apathy of faculties elsewhere in her body. The room was getting colder. Or had something else—shock and fear—reduced her stamina? Whisky was fraudulent; there might be something in the belief that ale gave one more lasting warmth and energy. For a moment, she contemplated placing the lamp at her feet. But she lacked the initiative for the act; a rigid unwillingness to budge from the chair against the wall governed her. If she made a movement, would he spring? She sat with her arms folded across her chest, as if to retain the last warmth there, and still she did not look directly at him, though her eyes sidled now and again in the direction of the bed.

This silence was even longer than the others. She broke it. Again in that reminding but not conciliatory way, she said: 'I didn't run off with another man. It's what they usually get cross about.'

He replied in the reflective manner of a man who has dwelt with long deliberation on a problem or scheme but will not reveal his final decision until the time is ripe. 'It would have been better if you had run off with another chap. It was just plain, cold, murdering selfishness.'

She preferred the abusive anger. 'I can't think why you were so fond of me,' she said. 'I didn't run after *you*. I never thought you much of a catch. You got me when I had a nasty row over pay with the firm I worked for in Cardiff—the tykes. You're no handsome oil painting, William—' Again she stopped, vaguely astonished at herself. Did she *want* him to spring?

That peculiar chuckle! He had developed into a different person, calculating, uncharacteristically voluble, chuckling to himself. Had he gone off his head? Why hadn't he called at the front door, in the normal way? The strange calculation of his trick struck her forcibly now. He had gone mad! She moved uncomfortably, and the chair creaked.

156

'Getting cold out there? Warm enough in here!'

'I'm all right,' she mumbled.

'That's the worst of getting yourself an outlandish cottage for a bolt hole—no heating in the bedroom when a thing like this happens. Never mind; it won't be a chill or influenza you'll be catching.'

As though rejecting what she heard, she stared more fixedly at the wall. A fancy preoccupied her that the veins of her feet had stiffened into sprays of icicles and it was impossible to walk. But her mind kept on making efforts to grapple with subjects suitable and, indeed, necessary for discussion. Anything to break those prolonged silences that were laden with something undeclared. After a while, she resumed: 'You doted on me too much, William. Your doting got on my nerves. I don't think I like men. I ought to have married a retired old man who just wanted not to die alone.' A further fancy came to her that, but for the stupefying cruelty of the cold, it would be pleasant and fruitful to sit talking like this all through the night. Matters could be wound up, a personal bankruptcy declared void; pacified contestants might even make amicable farewells.

But William ignored her last observations. He asked: 'What do you do with yourself all day in this place?'

'Nothing.' She answered as if glad of his apparently sociable inquiry. 'At first, I thought I'd stay only a few months. I wanted to think. All my life I promised myself a time to myself, with no nagging employer—or anyone else, for that matter— to answer to. I kept on trying to make up my mind to go to Susan in Australia. But somehow I couldn't make the move—'

'Ah!' he said, and chuckled.

'I eat well, and take a little whisky some evenings. I keep an afternoon maid. I listen to good-class concerts and lectures on the wireless. The weeks go by . . .' The sloth of the slow, eventless days lay in her trailing-away voice.

'You mean you came here to guzzle. Australia, my Aunt Fanny! True, you've got a lot of the gypsy in you. I'm not saying that's a nasty thing; it can make a woman shine out and set a man ticking faster than usual. I bet when you'd finished guzzling your way through that legacy you'd have set about hooking some well-off fellow in these parts. You know all right there's some chaps that *like* being hooked and done down.'

'I intend going back to the drapery in Cardiff when the money is gone,' she said meekly.

'Isn't there some old buffer running after you here? I see you've got a lot of your looks left.'

At this, she turned her head and gazed at him. His eyes were fixed on her as if they had never moved away. He had placed the vacant pillow on top of his own, so that his head was propped up; he looked comfortable and warm but relentlessly wideawake, the greenish glint of his eyes clear and hard. She said: 'If you've come here thinking of a divorce, William, there isn't anyone to name. But I won't give you any trouble. I deserted you.' A glimmer of eagerness had struggled into her face.

'I don't want a divorce. No need for all that fuss and expense. Not now.'

Her mouth opened to ask the obvious question—'Why not now?'—but she only looked at him glassily. She could hardly discern his head. Was the cold disabling her sight? Why was he there? It no longer seemed shocking that he had arrived, with such dramatic calculation, in her bed (but why, why?); she accepted the actual fact of his presence now—even, she fumblingly thought, almost welcomed it. The two dormant past years were smashed, and the thing that had fugitively haunted her had taken on, at last, concrete stature and power. She looked towards the bed as a homeless wanderer might look through a window into a firelit room.

'Come in,' he said, as if aware of her thoughts.

She did not reply but, draggingly, shook her head before turning it, with an automaton's movement, away from the hazed bed. A few moments later, the lamp began to fade. 'If you give me the key,' she said, quivering out of her passivity, 'I'll fetch oil from the can in the kitchen.'

'No, Bessie.'

Her remaining vestiges of warmth and strength seemed to ebb with the sinking light. She couldn't even bring herself to get up and fetch coats and other garments from the wardrobe to wrap herself in. Neither could her mind dwell on the refusal of the key. Almost there was a sense of release, an elusive, lapping seduction, in her resolution not to move from the chair.

I'll be found frozen to death in the morning, she thought. In the flickering light, the furniture began to look insubstantial, withdrawing its familiar identity; the dressing-table mirror became lifeless—an oval for ghosts to look in.

The last edge of blue on the lampwick vanished. She was surprised to find herself, suddenly conversational, saying: 'I often sit downstairs in the dark when the lamp goes out and I can't be bothered to fill it. I sit thinking. Living alone here has cured me of fright. It isn't as if you're a stranger.'

William said nothing. He was not a stranger? All people were strangers in the dark.

At the window, where the curtains were only half drawn, an anonymous night greyness seeped in, but it did not reach any object in the room. The last links with fact and reality were broken. There was not the faintest sound from the frozen world outside. All natural things were cast into the abeyance of this deepest and darkest hour. Was it midnight? What did it matter? Time mattered no more. The only thing existing—and it still remained a mystery—was the unseen element of judgement in the room; she recognized it fully now and waited for it to declare itself. It belonged to the dark.

She found herself saying, as if testing this judgement: 'You were silly to feel disgrace when I left you. A woman that runs off like that is a good riddance. Your friends at The White Hart would realize that, I expect.'

He said nothing. Had he fallen asleep? Buried his ears under the bedclothes? She could hear no breathing. Oh, if only he would hurl a heap more of abuse! Even the daft chuckle would be better than this silence. Now and again, her knees gave little convulsive jerks, as if making protest on their own account. The savage cold left her no dominion at all over her body now. Yet her mind, detached from her body, seemed to become clear of its confusion. She heard her own hesitating voice from a distance. 'William . . . If you've come wondering if I'll go back with you . . . it will need some talking . . . thinking about.' In her chest, a dead sort of pain followed the hard breathing necessary to get the words out.

Still there was no reply. Her head swerved from the direction of the hidden bed to the greyness at the window space. She thought of the bereft foothills and, beyond, the heights of the

Brecknock Beacons impregnable with marble snow. All the world was pinioned in stony silence. If only she could hear the soft thud of a pine cone falling into the withered ferns of the garden! Loneliness, oblivion and freezing death were all about her. Hours must pass before a small, dim glimmer would crack the night.

When her mouth opened again, it felt grotesquely not her own. 'William . . .' Her lower jaw seemed to lock. She sat pondering.

Blue, blue . . . Why did she think of a blue, sun-curled sea with foam swirling on a picnic beach? Tenby! The day trip she took to Tenby last summer . . . She saw a florist's shop filled with riotous blooms of July—roses, sweet peas, zinnias, carnations. In a café, a sundae heaped with nuts and marshmallow cream was placed before her. A man with a sports-club crest on his blue blazer lowered a newspaper and eyed her from a face as brown as a football. She wore a red dress and a hat she had just bought. Tenby was a good-class town. Not like rough, coal-mining Dinas, where a lady couldn't really be a lady . . . Her cheeks began twitching. Tenby vanished. Even the grey window space had gone. Her body gave a long, dislocated jerk; she was aware of it from afar.

Why was she on her feet? She did not remember getting up. Had he spoken? There was no sense of sound about her, and her eyeballs gained nothing from the dark. But she knew now where she must go. Carefully, laboriously, her feet moved. She trudged without a bending of her knees. Her body moved as towards a command, blindly without error. Her knee pressed against the bed.

'Come in,' he chuckled.

She heard the poplin swish of the thrown-back eiderdown. A faint eddy of warmth touched her face briefly. She fell into the opened bed, in all her clothes. The bedclothes closed round her. But she did not feel the warmth; the blankets seemed only to hold her immobile. When he turned and pressed the pillow over her face, she quivered only once. The long, silent apathy of the two past years contracted into a massive strength of obliteration, and, acquiescent, she sank under it.

Light, a pure morning light, was seeping into her eyes. But she could not see it clearly. A pillow was on her face. Pulling it away—why was it there?—she sat up in astonishment. A shaft of sunlight came from the space between the curtains. For long moments, her mouth open like a startled child's, she remained looking down at the man beside her in the warm bed. He lay fast asleep, mouth open, too, a patina of sweat on his short, thickly rooted nose. For the first time, she recognized the nose as a pugnacious one. The wart on his chin somehow made him seem less sternly menacing.

Stealthily, keeping concentrated watch on his face, she slid a flat hand under his pillow and found the key. Then, with long pauses, she eased herself out of the bed. Her body, already wonderfully thawed, felt abounding as she stood safely on the woollen rug. She shook herself down like a dusty fowl; the black satin dress was badly creased. Her eyes did not move from William's face as she backed to the door. She unlocked and opened the door without noise, gave William a last look, and crept out.

When she returned, she carried a tray that held a teapot, two cups and a plate of biscuits. The night's residue of sloth was off her powdered face; her hair was tidied. She placed the tray on the bedside table; and stood looking at William's far-gone face again before crossing to the window. Brass rings clanged briskly as she flung back the curtains as far as they would go, releasing into the room the full, crisp morning. It was still very cold, and the light, spinning back from the dazzling frost in the garden, had the fiery bounce of diamonds. Night's claustrophobic assembly of threats had slunk away and the morning rang alive with victory.

'*William!*' At once, she reduced the hectoring shout. 'William!' There was something abridged, if not obsequious, in her gait and manner as she went to the tray and poured the tea. 'Another cold morning, William!' She did not look at him now. But she fetched a purple silk wrap from the wardrobe and, as Clytemnestra flung the net over the warrior returned from Troy, wrapped it round his shoulders. William, still a bit manacled in his heavy sleep, struggled up in the bed. Bessie found a pink woollen cardigan for herself.

As he took the cup of tea from her hand, he glanced at her

from under swollen lids. He was always a thick sleeper. She shook out that other pillow, gave it a pronounced scrutiny, and placed it behind his shoulders. Bemused, he looked into the cup. 'There's nothing in it except tea,' she assured him. 'I've got no use for rat poison. When I want to get rid of you, I'll shoot you like a dog.'

She tittered as she crossed with her own cup to the chair on which such hours of agony had been endured the night before. William tasted the tea. Bessie swallowed two good mouthfuls herself, and after a silence, which seemed neutral, she asked: 'How much did you get for the restaurant from those caterers?'

'Five thousand pounds for the lease of the premises, seven hundred for the contents.' They were his first words. Had he returned to his old surly meagreness of speech?

'Why, William, that's not at all bad! Judging by the way you talked last night, anyone would think you had a grudge. You must have fought them like a man.'

He glanced at her. Something lurked in his face; it did not suggest anything to do with smiling. 'What time is it?' he asked abruptly, and looked at the soft felt hat still hanging on the ebony bedpost.

'About half-past eight. Plenty of time yet. You'll have to go by two. A woman from the village comes then. I'm supposed to be a widow.'

'I'm not going,' he said slowly.

She did not deal with this. 'I took a day trip to Tenby last summer,' she began, 'and I thought to myself, if William had adventure in him, this is a nice place to open a restaurant in. I like seaside places. . . . What's the matter with you?' she suddenly challenged across the room. 'Can't you look me straight in the eye?'

He looked her straight in the eye. His thick, hard neck and square head lunged out from the purple wrap, and he growled: 'You can count yourself lucky you're sitting there drinking tea in comfort, like a bloody hypocrite sozzling after a funeral.'

'Now, William!' Bessie reproved, not without admiration dipping in her voice. 'Language!'

They drank their tea. Presently, ruminative, he said: 'The thought crossed my mind to do you in.'

'Well, you tried to, William.' She swallowed the last drop of tea. 'I could have you up for attempted murder, William.'

He looked with curiosity into the sharp blaze of light at the window. 'Something suddenly broke inside me,' he said. 'I went to sleep.'

'In your way,' Bessie said, putting her empty cup on the floor, 'you're a good man, William. I intend coming back to you.'

'Do I want you?' Curiosity still mused in his voice.

'Yes, William. Otherwise you wouldn't have gone to such trouble to nose me out here. I like a man to show spirit.' Her hand gave a large gesture, but the characteristic heave of her bosom was a curtailed one. 'It was romantic, William—you breaking in here, just for me! It's like Romeo and Juliet! Last night, when I came in that door with the lamp and found it was you in the bed, I felt myself going double my size. . . . Though I did go weak in the knees, too,' she said in afterthought. 'I never believed you had it in you, William.'

'*Now*,' he said, staring into his empty cup as though it might reveal the future, 'you know what I've got in me.'

'Yes, William,' she replied soberly, 'I do.'

CANUTE

As the great Saturday drew nearer most men asked each other: 'Going up for the International?' You had the impression that the place would be denuded of its entire male population, as in some archaic tribal war. Of course a few women too intended taking advantage, for other purposes, of the cheap excursion trains, though these hardy souls were not treated seriously, but rather as intruders in an entirely masculine rite. It was to be the eternal England versus Wales battle, the object now under dispute being a stitched leather egg containing an air-inflated bladder.

The special trains began to leave round about Friday midnight, and thereafter, all through the night until Saturday noon, these quaking, immensely long vehicles feverishly rushed back and forth between Wales and London. In black mining valleys, on rustic heights, in market towns and calm villages myriads of house doors opened during the course of the night and a man issued from an oblong of yellow light, a railway ticket replacing the old spear.

The contingent from Pleasant Row, a respectable road of houses leading up to a three-shafted coal-mine, came out from their dwellings into the gas-lit winter midnight more or less simultaneously. Wives stood in worried farewells in the doorways. Their men were setting out in the dead of night to an alien land, far away from this safe valley where little Twlldu nestled about its colliery and usually minded its own business.

'Now be careful you don't lose your head, Rowland!' fretted his wife on their doorstep. 'You take things quiet and behave yourself. Remember your trouble.' The 'trouble' was a hernia, the result of Rowland rescuing his neighbour, Dicky Corner House, from a fall of roof in the pit.

Rowland, grunting a repudiation of this anxiety, scuttled after a group of men in caps. 'Jawl,' shouted one, 'is that the whistle of the 'scursion train? Come on!' Out of the corner house ran Dicky, tying a white muffler round his neck. Weighted though they all were with bottles for the long journey, they shot forward dramatically, though the train was still well up the long valley.

The night was clear and crisp. Thousands of stars briskly gazed down, sleepless as the excited eyes of the excursion hordes thronging all the valley's little stations. Stopping every few minutes, the train slid past mines deserted by their workers and rows of houses where, mostly, only women and children remained. It was already full when it stopped at Twlldu, and, before it left the smallest men were lying in the luggage-racks and sitting the floor, placing their bottles safe. Some notorious passengers, clubbing together, had brought crates of flagons.

Dicky Corner House, who was squat and sturdy, kept close to Rowland, offering him cigarettes, or a swig out of his bottle and a beef sandwich. Ever since Rowland had rescued him he had felt bound to him in some way, especially as Rowland, who was not a hefty chap, had that hernia as a result. But Rowland felt no particular interest in Dicky; he had only done his duty by him in the pit. 'Got my own bottle and sandwiches,' he grunted. And: 'No, I am not feeling a draught.' The train rocked and groaned through the historic night. Some parts of it howled with song; in other parts bets were laid, cards played, and tales told of former Internationals.

Somewhere, perhaps guarded by armed warriors, the sacred egg lay waiting for the morrow. In its worship these myriads had left home and loved ones to brave the dangers of a foreign city. Situated in a grimy parish of that city, and going by the name of Paddington, the railway terminus began to receive the first drafts at about 4 am. Their arrival was welcomed by their own shouts, whistles and cries. From one compartment next to the Pleasant Row contingent a man had to be dragged out with his legs trailing limply behind him.

'Darro,' Rowland mumbled with some severity, 'he's started early. Disgrace! 'Gives the 'scursionists a bad name.'

'Hi!' Dicky Corner House tried to hail a vanishing porter, 'where's the nearest public-house in London?'

165

'Pubs in London opened already, then?' asked Shoni Matt in wonder and respect, gazing at 4.30 on the station clock.

'Don't be daft, man,' Ivor snarled, surly from lack of sleep. 'We got about seven hours to wait on our behinds.'

A pitchy black shrouded the great station. Many braved the strange dark and wandered out into it. But in warily peering groups. A watery dawn found their numbers increased in the main thoroughfares; early workers saw them reconnoitering like invaders sniffing out a strange land.

'Well, well,' said Rowland at ten o'clock, following his nose up the length of Nelson's column, 'how did they get that man up there? And what for?'

'A fancy kind of chimney-stack it is,' Dicky declared. 'A big bakehouse is under us.' He asked yet another policeman—the fourth—what time the public-houses opened, but the answer was the same.

'Now, Dicky,' said Rowland, in a severe canting voice like a preacher, 'you go on behaving like that and very sorry I'll be that I rescued you that time . . . . We have come here,' he added austerely, 'to see the International, not to drink. Plenty of beer in Wales.'

'I'm cold,' bleated Shoni Matt; 'I'm hungry; I'm sleepy.'

'Let's go in there!' said Gwyn Short Leg, and they all entered the National Gallery, seeing that Admission was Free.

It was the Velasquez 'Venus' that arrested their full attention. 'The artist,' observed Emlyn Chrysanthemums—he was called that because he was a prize-grower of them in a home-made glasshouse—'was clever to make her turn her back on us. A bloke that knew what was tidy.'

'Still,' said Rowland, 'he ought to have thrown a towel or something across her, just by here—'

'Looking so alive it is,' Ivor breathed in admiration, 'you could smack it, just there—'

An attendant said: 'Do not touch the paintings.'

'What's the time?' Dicky Corner House asked the attendant. 'Are the pubs open yet?'

'A disgrace he is,' said Rowland sharply as the contingent went out. 'He ought to have stayed home.'

By then the streets were still more crowded with gazing strangers. Scotland had sent tam-o'-shantered men, the North

166

and Midlands their crowds of tall and short men in caps, bowlers, with umbrellas and striped scarves, concertinas and whistles. There were ghostly-looking men who looked as if they had just risen from hospital beds; others were unshaven and still bore the aspect of running late for the train. Many women accompanied the English contingents, for the Englishman never escapes this. By noon the invaders seemed to have taken possession of the metropolis and, scenting their powerful majority, they became noisy and obstreperous, unlike the first furtive groups which had arrived before dawn. And for a short while a million beer-taps flowed ceaselessly. But few of the visitors loitered to drink overmuch before the match. The evening was to come, when one could sit back released from the tremendous event.

At two-thirty, into a grey misty field surrounded by huge walls of buzzing insects stickily massed together, fifteen red beetles and fifteen white beetles ambled forward on springy legs. To a great cry the sacred egg appeared. A whistle blew. The beetles wove a sharp pattern of movement, pursuing the egg with swift bounds and trim dance evolutions. Sometimes they became knotted over it as though in prayer. They worshipped the egg and yet they did not want it: as if it contained the secret of happiness, they pursued it, got it, and then threw it away. The sticky imprisoning walls heaved and roared; myriads of pin-point faces passed through agonies of horror and ecstasies of bliss. And from a great quantity of these faces came frenzied cries and urgings in a strange primitive language that no doubt gave added strength to the fifteen beetles who understood that language. It was not only the thirty below the walls who fought the battle.

The big clock's pallid face, which said it was a quarter to midnight, stared over the station like an amazed moon. Directly under it was a group of women who had arranged to meet their men there for the journey back. They looked worried and frightened.

And well they might. For surely they were standing in a gigantic hospital-base adjacent to a bloody battlefield where a crushing defeat had been sustained. On the platforms casualties lay groaning or silently dazed; benches were packed with

167

huddled men, limbs twitching, heads laid on neighbours' shoulders or clasped in hands between knees. Trolleys were heaped with what looked like the dead. Now and again an ambulance train crawled out packed to the doors. But still more men kept staggering into the station from the maw of an underground cavern and from the black foggy streets. Most of them looked exhausted, if not positively wounded, as from tremendous strife.

But not all of them. Despite groans of the incapacitated, grunting heaves of the sick, long solemn stares of the bemsued helplessly waiting for some ministering angel to conduct them to a train, there was a singing. Valiant groups of men put their heads doggedly together and burst into heroic song. They belonged to a race that, whatever the cause, never ceases to sing, and those competent to judge declare this singing something to be greatly admired. Tonight, in this melancholy place at the low hour of midnight, these melodious cries made the spirit of man seem undefeated. Stricken figures on floors, benches and trolleys stirred a little, and far-gone faces flickered into momentary awareness. Others who still retained their faculties sufficiently to recognize home acquaintances shouted, embraced, hit each other, made excited turkey-cock enquiries as to the activities of the evening.

A youngish woman with parcels picked a zigzag way to under the clock and greeted another there. 'Seen my Glynne, have you?' she asked anxiously; 'I've been out to Cricklewood to visit my auntie. . . . Who won the match?' she asked, glancing about her in fear.

'You can tell by the state of them, can't you!' frowned the other.

Another woman, with a heave of hostility, said: 'Though even if Wales had lost they'd drink just the same, to drown the disappointment, the old beasts. . . . Look out!' The women scattered hastily from a figure who became detached from a knot of swaying men, made a blind plunge in their direction, and was sick.

'Where's the porters?' wailed one woman. 'There's no porters to be seen anywhere; they've all run home. . . . Serve us right, we shouldn't have come with the men's 'scursion. . . . I'm feeling ill, nowhere to sit, only men everywhere.'

168

Cap pushed back from his blue-marked miner's face, Matt Griffiths of Gelli bellowed a way up No 1 platform. He was gallantly pulling a trolley heaped with bodies like immense dead cods. 'Where's the backwards 'scursion train for Gelli?' he shouted. 'Out of the way there! We got to go on the night-shift tomorrow.'

'The wonder is,' said a woman, fretful, 'that they can find their way to the station at all. But there, they're like dogs pointing their snouts towards home.'

Two theological students, solemn-clothed as crows, passed under the clock. They were in fierce converse and gesticulated dangerously with their flappy umbrellas. Yet they seemed oblivious of the carnal scenes around them; no doubt they were occupied with some knotty biblical matter. The huddled women looked at them with relief; here was safety. 'We'd better get in the same compartment as them,' one of them said to her friend; 'come on, Gwen, let's follow them. I expect they've been up for a conference or an exam.' Soon the two young preachers-to-be were being followed by quite a band of women though they remained unconscious of this flattering retinue.

'That reverse pass of Williams!' one of the students suddenly burst out, unable to contain himself, and prancing forward in intoxicated delight. 'All the matches I've been to I've never seen anything like it! Makes you want to grab someone and dance ring-a-ring-o'roses.'

Elsewhere, an entwined group of young men sang *Mochyn Du* with an orderly sweetness in striking contrast to their mien; a flavour of pure green hills and neat little farmhouses was in their song about a black pig. On adjacent platforms other groups in that victorious concourse sang *Sospan Fach* and even a hymn. As someone said, if you shut your eyes you could fancy yourself in an eisteddfod.

But in the Gentlemen's Convenience under No 1 platform no one would have fancied this. There an unusual thing had occurred—the drains had clogged. Men kept on descending the flight of steps only to find a sheet of water flooding the floor to a depth of several inches. They had to make-do with standing on the bottom steps, behind them an impatient block of others dangerously swaying.

169

And this was not all. Far within the deserted convenience one man was marooned over that sheet of water. He sat on the shoeshine throne which, resting on its dais, was raised safely—up to the present—above the water. With head lolling on his shoulder he sat fast asleep, at peace, comfortable in the full-sized armchair. Astonished remarks from the steps failed to reach him.

'Darro me,' exclaimed one man with a stare of respect across the waters, 'how did he get there? No sign of a boat.'

'Hoy,' another bawled over, 'what train you want to catch? You can't stay there all night.'

'Who does he think he is,' someone else exclaimed in an English voice—'King Canute?'

The figure did not hear, though the head dreamily lolled forward an inch. Impatient men waiting on the crowded steps bawled to those in front to hurry up and make room. Soon the rumour that King Canute was sitting below passed among a lot of people on No 1 platform. It was not long before someone—Sam Recitations it was, the Smoking Concert Elocutionist—arrived at the bottom step and recognized that the figure enthroned above the water was not King Canute at all.

'I'm hanged if it isn't Rowland from Pleasant Row!' he blew in astonishment. 'That's where he's got! . . . Rowland,' his chest rose as in a recitation, 'wake up, man, wake up! Train is due out in ten minutes. Number 2 platform. . . .'

Rowland did not hear even this well-known Twlldu voice. Sam, himself not in full possession of his faculties, gazed stupidly at the sheet of water. It looked deep; up to your calves. A chap would have soaking wet socks and shoes all the way back to Wales. And he was appearing at a club concert on Tuesday, reciting four ballads; couldn't afford to catch a cold. Suddenly he pushed his way through the exclaiming mob behind him, hastened recklessly through the platform mobs, reached No 2 platform and began searching for the Pleasant Row contingent.

They were sitting against a kiosk plunged in torpid thought. Sam had to shake two or three of them. 'I've seen him!' he rolled. 'Your Rowland! He isn't lost—he's down in the men's place under Number 1, and can't budge him. People calling him King Canute—'

They had lost him round about nine o'clock in crowded Trafalgar Square. There the visiting mob had got so obstreperous that, as someone related later at a club in Twlldu, four roaring lions had been let loose and stood lashing their tails in fury against these invaders whose nation had won the match; an someone else said that for the first time in his life he had seen a policeman who wore spectacles. While singing was going on, and two or three cases of assault brewing, Rowland had vanished. From time to time the others had missed him, and Dicky Corner House asked many policemen if they had seen Rowland of Twlldu.

Sam Recitations kept on urging them now. 'King Canute?' repeated Shoni Matt in a stupor. 'You shut up, Sam,' he added crossly; 'no time for recitations now.'

'He's down in the Gents under Number 1,' Sam howled despairingly. 'English strangers poking fun at him and water rising up! He'll be drowned same as when the Cambrian pit was flooded!' He beat his chest as if he was giving a ballad in a concert. 'Ten minutes and the train will be in! And poor Rowland sitting helpless and the water rising round him like on the sands of Dee!'

Far off a whistle blew. Someone hear-by was singing *Cwm Rhondda* in a bass that must have won medals in its time. They shook themselves up from the platform, staring penetratingly at Sam, who was repeating information with wild emphasis. Six of them, all from Pleasant Row. Awareness seemed to flood them simultaneously, for suddenly they all surged away.

By dint of pushing and threatening cries they got down all together to the lower steps of the Convenience. Rowland had not moved in the shoe-shine throne. Still his head lolled in slumber as if he was sitting cosy by his fireside at home after a heavy shift in the pit, while the waters lapped the dais and a yellow light beat down on the isolated figure indifferent to its danger. They stared fearfully at the sheet of water.

'Shocking it is,' said Gwyn Short Leg, scandalized. 'All the Railway Company gone home, have they, and left the place like this?'

'In London too!' criticized Ivor, gazing below him in owlish distaste.

Then in one accord they bellowed: 'Hoy, Rowland, hoy!'

He did not stir. Not an eyelid. It was then that Shoni Matt turned to Dicky Corner House and just looked at him, like a judge. His gaze asked—'Whose life had been saved by Rowland when that bit of roof had fallen in the pit?' Dicky, though he shivered, understood the long solemn look. 'Time to pay back now, Dicky,' the look added soberly.

Whimpering, Dicky tried to reach his shoe-laces, on the crowded steps. But the others urged excitedly: 'No time to take your shoes off. Hark, the train's coming in! Go on, boy. No swimming to do.'

Dicky, with a sudden dramatic cry, leapt into the water, foolishly splashing it up all round his legs. A pit-butty needed to be rescued! And with oblivious steps, encouraged by the applause of the others, he plunged across to the throne. He stepped on the dais and, being hefty, lifted Rowland across his shoulders without much bother. He staggered a bit as he stepped off the dais into the cruelly wet water.

'Careful now,' shouted Emlyn Chrysanthemums; 'don't drop him into the champagne.'

It was an heroic act that afterwards, in the club evenings, took precedence over tales of far more difficult rescues in the pits. Dicky reached the willing arms of the others without mishap. They took Rowland and bore him by his four limbs up the steps, down the platform and up the other, just as the incoming train was coming to a frightened standstill. After a battle they got into a compartment. Dicky took off his shoes, hung up his socks over the edge of the rack and wiped his feet and calves in the white muffler that had crossed his throat.

'Wet feet bad for the chest,' he said fussily.

All the returning trains reached the arms of Wales safely, and she folded the passengers into her fragrant breast with a pleased sigh of 'Well done, my sons'. The victory over her ancient enemy—it was six points to four—was a matter of great Sunday celebration when the men's clubs opened in the evening, these having a seven-day licence, whereas the ordinary public-houses, owing to the need to appease old dim gods, were not allowed to open on Sundays.

The members of the Pleasant Row contingent, like most others, stayed in bed all the morning. When they got up they related to their wives and children many of the sights and marvels of London. But some weeks had passed before Rowland's wife, a tidy woman who starched her aprons and was a great chapel-goer, said to him in perplexity: 'Why is it people are calling you Rowland Canute now?'

Only that evening, Gwyn Short Leg, stumping to the door on his way to the club, had bawled innocently into the passage: 'Coming down, Rowland Canute?' Up to lately Rowland had been one of those who, because he seemed to have no peculiarity, had never earned a nickname.

'Oh,' Rowland told his wife, vaguely offhand, 'some fancy name or other it is they've begun calling me.'

'But a reason there must be for it,' she said inquisitively. 'Canute! Wasn't that some old king who sat on his throne beside the sea and dared the tide to come over him? A funny name to call you.'

'What you got in the oven for my supper?' he asked, scowling at the news in the evening paper.

She knew better than to proceed with the matter just then. But of course she did not let it rest. It was the wife of Emlyn Chrysanthemums, living three doors up, who, in the deprecating way of women versus the ways of men, told her the reason. There are nicknames which are earned respectably and naturally, and indeed such nicknames are essential to identify persons in a land where there are only twenty or so proper baptized names for everybody. But, on hearing how Rowland earned Canute, his wife pursed in her lips like a pale tulip, opening them hours later to shout as Rowland tramped in from the pit:

'Ah, *Canute* is it! . . . Sitting there in that London place,' she screamed, 'and all those men—' She whipped about like a hailstorm. 'You think I'm going to stay in Twlldu to be called Mrs Rowland Canute, do you? We'll have to move from here— you begin looking for work in one of the other valleys at once.'

And such a dance she led him that in a couple of months they had left Pleasant Row. Rowland got taken on at the Powell pit in the Cwm Mardy valley, several stout mountains lying between that and Twlldu.

Yet give a dog a bad name, says the proverb, and it will stick. Who would have thought that Sam Recitations, growing

173

in fame, would visit a club in far-away Cwm Mardy to give selections from his repertoire at a Smoking Concert? And almost the first man he saw when he entered the bar-room was Rowland. 'Why now,' his voice rolled in delight, 'if it isn't Rowland Canute! Ha, ha—' And not noticing Rowland's dropped jaw of dismay, he turned and told all the clustering men what had happened under Paddington platform that time after the famous International—just as the history of the rescue had been told in all the clubs in the valley away over the mountains.

THE DILEMMA OF
CATHERINE FUCHSIAS

Puffed up by his success as a ship-chandler in the port forty miles away, where he had gone from the village of Banog when the new town was rising to its heyday as the commercial capital of Wales, Lewis had retired to the old place heavy with gold and fat. With him was the bitter English wife he had married for her money, and he built the pink-washed villa overlooking Banog's pretty trout stream. And later he had set up a secret association with an unmarried woman of forty who was usually called Catherine Fuchsias, this affair—she receiving him most Sunday evenings after chapel in her outlying cottage—eluding public notice for two years. Until on one of those evenings, Lewis, who for some weeks had been complaining of a 'feeling of fullness', expired in her arms on the bed.

In every village there is a Jezebel or the makings of one, though sometimes these descend virtuous to their graves because of lack of opportunity or courage, fear of gossip or ostracism. Lewis the Chandler was Catherine Fuchsias' first real lover, so that for her to lose him like that not only dreadfully shocked her but, it will be agreed, placed her in a serious dilemma. She was not a born bad lot and, as a girl, she had been left in the lurch by a sweetheart who had gone prospecting to Australia and never fulfilled his promise to call her there. Thereafter she had kept house for her father, a farm worker, until he had followed her mother into the burial-ground surrounding Horeb chapel, which she cleaned for five shillings a week; in addition she had a job three days a week in the little wool factory a mile beyond Banog. It was in Horeb chapel during service that Lewis first studied her and admired her egg-brown face, thick haunches and air of abundant health. Her cottage stood concealed on a bushy slope outside the village, and she had a great liking for

175

fuchsias, which grew wonderfully in the rich lap of the cottage.

When her paramour died on her bed she at first refused to believe it, so pertinacious and active was he and so unlike her idea of a man of sixty-four. Nevertheless, she ran howling downstairs. There she madly poked the fire, flung the night cloth over the canary's cage, ran into the kitchen and swilled a plate or two in a bowl, straightened a mat, and tidied her hair. In the mirror *there* was her face, Miss Catherine Bowen's face, looking no different, a solid unharmed fact with its brown speckles. The autumn dusk beginning to arrive at the window was quiet and natural as the chirp of the bird winging past the pane. For a moment she listened to the grandfather clock ticking away the silence. Then, with a bustling haste, she filled the kettle, lit the oil cooker, took an apple tart out of a zinc safe, looked at it, and put it back. She stood still again. And groaned.

She crept half-way up the stairs and called: 'Mr Lewis . . . Mr Lewis, here I am! Just put the kettle on. Time's going, boy. Come down straight away . . . Mr Lewis!' She raised her voice. 'Lewis, stir yourself, boy. Come on now!' Only the clock replied. She sat on the stairs and groaned. 'Lewis,' she whimpered, 'there's a trick you are playing on me! Don't you come here again, I am offended . . . Yes, offended I am. I'll go for a walk, that's what I'll do. And don't you be here when I'm back.'

She tramped noisily down the stairs, unlocked the front door, and slammed it behind her.

Bats were flying round the cottage. The sunflowers were hanging their half-asleep heads, and the old deep well among the luxuriant chrysanthemum bushes at the bottom of the garden, on which her eye rested for a dazed but speculative minute, stood in secret blue shadow. But she hurried out of the garden by the side gate where a path led into a coppice of dwarf trees and bushes. 'I'll go and pick mushrooms in Banner's fields, that's what I'll do,' she assured herself. 'Gone he'll be by the time I'm back.' But she did not descend the slope to the farm's fields. She scrambled into a ring of bushes and hid herself there on a patch of damp grass. One eye remained open in palpitating awareness, the other was half closed, as if she was in profound thought.

A bad shock can work wonders with a person's sensibility.

176

Buried talents can be whisked up into activity, a primitive cunning reign again in its shady empire of old instincts. Or such a shock can create—women especially being given to escape into this—a fantasy of bellicose truth, a performance of the imagination that has nothing to do with hypocrisy but is the terrified soul backing away from reality. Catherine sprang up and hurried back to her whitewashed cottage. Already in the long dusky vale and the distant village a few lights shone out. She shot into the cottage and ran upstairs.

'Well, Mr Lewis,' she exclaimed loudly, 'better you are after your rest?' She went close to the bed and peered down at the stout dusky figure lying on the patchwork quilt. 'Well now, I am not liking the look of you at all,' she addressed it, half scoldingly. 'What have you taken your jacket off for? Hot you were? Dear me, quite bad you look. Best for me to fetch your wife and the doctor. But you mustn't lie there with your coat off or a cold you will catch.' Volubly tut-tutting, she lit a candle and set about the task. Already, in the hour that had escaped, he had begun to stiffen somewhat. She perspired and groaned, alternately blenching and going red. He was heavily cumbersome as a big sack of turnips: she was obliged to prop up his back with a small chair wedged against the bedstead. Luckily he had removed only his jacket, but (since of late he had got stouter) this, which was of chapel-black vicuna, fitted tight as the skin of a bladder of lard. Downstairs, the grandfather clock ticked loud and hurried.

Finally, buttoned up complete, he rested tidy, and she staggered back sweating. To lay out her father she had got the assistance of the blacksmith's wife.

For a minute she stood in contemplation of her work, then ran downstairs to fetch up his hat, umbrella, and hymn-book. She dropped the umbrella beside the bed, placed the hat on the bed-side table, and laid the hymn-book on the quilt as though it had fallen from his hand. And all the time she uttered clamorous remarks of distress at his condition—'Oh, Mr Lewis, you didn't ought to have taken a walk, unwell like you are. Climbing! Lucky I saw you leaning over my gate. Dropped dead in the road you might have, and stayed there all night and got bitten by the stoats! You rest quiet now, and I won't be long.' At another thought she placed a glass of water by the bedside. Then, giving her own person a quick look-over, she put on a raincoat and a flowered hat, blew out the candle, and hastened from the cottage. It was past nine o'clock and quite dark, and she never rode her bicycle in the dark.

Half an hour later she banged at the costly oaken door of the pink villa, calling excitedly: 'Mrs Lewis, Mrs Lewis, come to your husband!' Milly Jones, the servant, opened the door, and Catherine violently pushed her inside. 'Where's Mrs Lewis? Let me see her quick.' But Mrs Lewis was already standing, stiff as a poker, in the hall.

'Catherine Fuchsias it is!' exclaimed Milly Jones, who was a native of Banog. 'Why, what's the matter with you?'

Catherine seemed to totter. 'Come to your husband, Mrs Lewis, crying out for you he is! Oh dear,' she groaned, 'run all the way I have, fast as a hare.' She gulped, sat on a chair, and panted: 'Put your hat on quick, Mrs Lewis, and tell Milly Jones to go to Dr Watkins.'

Mrs Lewis, who had the English reserve, never attended chapel, and also unlikably minded her own business, stared hard. 'My husband has met with an accident?' she asked, precise and cold.

'Wandering outside my gate I found him just now!' cried Catherine. 'Fetching water from my well I was, and saw him swaying about and staring at me white as cheese. "Oh, Mr Lewis," I said, "what is the matter with you, ill are you? Not your way home from chapel is this!" . . . "Let me rest in your cottage for a minute," he said to me, "and give me a glass of water, my heart is jumping like a toad." . . . So I helped him in and he began to grunt awful, and I said: "Best to go and lie down on my poor father's bed, Mr Lewis, and I will run at once and tell Mrs Lewis to fetch Dr Watkins." . . . Bring the doctor to him quick, Mrs Lewis! Frightened me he has and no one to leave with him, me watering my chrysanthemums and just going to lock up for the night and seeing a man hanging sick over my gate—' She panted and dabbed her face.

Milly Jones was already holding a coat for her mistress, who frowned impatiently as Catherine went on babbling of the fright she had sustained. Never a talkative person, the English-woman only said, abrupt: 'Take me to your house . . . Milly, go for the doctor and tell him what you've just heard.' And she did not say very much as she stalked along beside Catherine, who still poured out a repeating wealth of words.

Arrived at the dark cottage, Catherine bawled comfortingly on the stairs: 'Come now, Mr Lewis, here we are. Not long I've been, have I?'

'You ought to have left a light for him,' remarked Mrs Lewis on the landing.

'What if he had tumbled and set the bed on fire!' said Catherine indignantly. In the heavily silent room she struck a match and lit the candle. 'Oh!' she shrieked.

Mrs Lewis stood staring through her glasses. And then, in a strangely fallen voice, said: 'John!...John!' Catherine covered her face with her hands, crying in dramatic woe. 'Hush, *woman* . . . hush,' said Mrs Lewis sternly.

Catherine moved her hands from her face and glared. *Woman*, indeed! In her own house! When she had been so kind! But all she said was: 'Well, Mrs Lewis, enough it is to upset anyone with a soft heart when a stranger dies in her house. . . . *Why*,' she began insidiously, 'was he wandering in the lanes all by himself in his bad state? Poor man, why is it he didn't go home after chapel? Wandering lost outside my gate like a lonely orphan child!'

Mrs Lewis, as though she were examining someone applying for a place in her villa kitchen, gave her a long, glimmering look. 'Here is the doctor,' she said.

'Yes indeed,' Catherine exclaimed, 'and I am hoping he can take Mr Lewis away with him in his motor.' The glance she directed at the corpse was now charged with hostility. 'He is a visitor that has taken advantage of my poor little cottage.' And was there a hint of malice in her manner as she swung her hips past Mrs Lewis, went to the landing, and called down the stairs: 'Come up, Dr Watkins. But behind time you are.'

Having verified the death and listened to Catherine's profuse particulars of how she had found him at the gate and strained herself helping him up the stairs, Dr Watkins, who was of local birth and a cheerful man, said: 'Well, well, only this evening it was I saw him singing full strength in chapel, his chest out like a robin's. Pity he never would be a patient of mine. "You mind that heart of yours, John Lewis," I told him

once, free of charge, "and don't you smoke, drink, or sing."
Angina he had, sure as a tree got knots.'

'He liked to sing at the top of his voice,' agreed Mrs Lewis.
She took up the hymn-book from the quilt, turned quickly to
Catherine, and demanded: 'Did he take this with him to the
bed, ill as he was?'

'No!' Catherine's voice rang. With Dr Watkins present, the
familiar local boy, she looked even more powerful. 'After I had
helped him there and he laid a minute and went a better colour, I said: "Now, Mr Lewis, you read a hymn or two while I
run off; strength they will give you." '

'But you put the candle out!' pounced Mrs Lewis. 'It must
have been getting quite dark by then.'

'There,' Catherine pointed a dramatic finger, 'is the box of
matches, with the glass of water I gave him.' She stood aggressive, while Dr Watkins' ears moved. 'Candles can be lit.'

'This,' proceeded Mrs Lewis, her eyes gazing around and
resting in turn on a petticoat hanging on a peg and the women's
articles on the dressing table, '*this* was your father's room?'

'Yes,' Catherine said, defiant; 'where he died and laid till
they took him to Horeb. But when the warm weather comes, in
here I move from the back; cooler it is and the view in summer
same as on the postcards that the visitors buy, except for the
old Trout Bridge. . . . What are you so inquisitive about?' She
began to bridle. 'Tidy it is here, and no dust. You would like
to look under the bed? In the chest?'

Mrs Lewis, cold of face, turned to the doctor. 'Could you
say how long my husband has been dead?'

He made show of moving the corpse's eyelids, pinching a
cheek, swinging an arm. 'A good two hours or more,' he sad
with downright assurance.

'Then,' said Mrs Lewis, 'he must have been dead when he
walked up those stairs! It takes only half an hour to reach my
house from here.' She turned stern to Catherine: 'You said you
came running to me as soon as you helped him up here to your
father's room.'

'A law of the land there is!' Catherine's voice rang. 'Slander
and malice is this, and jealous spite!' She took on renewed
power and, like an actress towering and swelling into rage,
looked twice her size. 'See,' she cried to Dr Watkins, 'how it is

180

that kind acts are rewarded, and nipped by a serpent is the hand of charity stretched out to lay the dying stranger on a bed! Better if I had let him fall dead outside my gate like a workhouse tramp and turned my back on him to water my Michaelmas daisies. Forty years I have lived in Banog, girl and woman, and not a stain small as a farthing on my character.' With her two hands she pushed up her inflated breasts as though they hurt her. 'Take out of my house,' she sang in crescendo, 'my poor dead visitor that can't rise up and tell the holy truth for me. No husband, father, or brother have I to fight for my name. Take him!'

'Not possible tonight,' said Dr Watkins, bewildered but appreciative of Catherine's tirade. 'Late and a Sunday it is, and the undertaker many miles away.'

'The lady by there,' said Catherine, pointing a quivering finger, 'can hire the farm cart of Peter the Watercress, if he can't go in your motor.'

'I,' said Mrs Lewis, 'have no intention of allowing my husband to remain in this house tonight.' The tone in which she pronounced 'this house' demolished the abode to an evil shambles.

'Oh, oh,' wailed Catherine, beginning again, and moving to the bedside. 'John Lewis!' she called to the corpse, 'John Lewis, rise up and tell the truth! Swim back across Jordan for a short minute and make dumb the bitter tongue that you married! Miss Catherine Bowen, that took you innocent into her little clean cottage, is calling to you, and—'

Dr Watkins, who had twice taken up his bag and laid it down again, interfered decisively at last, for he had been called out by Milly Jones just as he was sitting down to some slices of cold duck. 'Hush now,' he said to both women, a man and stern, 'hush now. Show respect for the passed away. . . . A cart and horse you would like hired?' he asked Mrs Lewis. 'I will drive you to Llewellyn's farm and ask them to oblige you.'

'And oblige me too!' Catherine had the last word, swinging her hips out of the room.

The corpse, though not much liked owing to its bragging when alive, was of local origin, and Llewellyn the Farmer agreed readily enough to disturb his stallion, light candles in the cart lanterns, and collect two village men to help carry the

181

heavy man down Catherine Fuchsias' stairs. Already the village itself had been willingly disturbed out of its Sabbath night quiet, for Milly Jones, after calling at the doctor's, was not going to deprive her own people of the high news that rich Mr Lewis had mysteriously been taken ill in Catherine's cottage. So when the farm cart stopped to collect the two men, news of the death was half expected. Everybody was left agog and expectant of the new week being a full one. What had Mr Lewis been doing wandering round Catherine's cottage up there after chapel? Strange it was. Married men didn't go for walks and airings after chapel.

On Monday morning, before the dew was off her flowers, Catherine's acquaintance, Mrs Morgans, who lived next door to the Post Office, bustled into the cottage. 'Catherine, dear,' she exclaimed, peering at her hard. 'What is this, a man dying on your bed!'

'My father's bed,' corrected Catherine. And at once her body began to swell. 'Oh, Jinny Morgans, my place in Heaven I have earned. I have strained myself,' she moaned, placing her hands round her lower middle, 'helping him up my stairs after I found him whining like an old dog outside my gate. A crick I have got in my side too. So stout he was, and crying to lay down on a bed. I thought he had eaten a toadstool for a mushroom in the dark.'

'What was he doing, walking about up here whatever?' Mrs Morgans breathed.

'Once before I saw him going by when I was in my garden. He stopped to make compliments about my fuchsias—Oh,' she groaned, clasping her stomach, 'the strain is cutting me shocking.'

'Your fuchsias—' egged on Mrs Morgans.

'Very big they hung this year. And he said to me, "When I was a boy I used to come round here to look for tadpoles in the ponds." Ah!' she groaned again.

'Tadpoles.' Mrs Morgans nodded, still staring fixed and full on her friend, and sitting tense with every pore open. As is well known, women hearken to words but rely more on the secret information obtained by the sense that has no language.

Catherine, recognizing that an ambassador had arrived, made a sudden dive into the middle of the matter, her hands

182

flying away from her stomach and waving threatening. And again she went twice her size and beat her breast. 'That jealous Mrs Lewis,' she shouted, 'came here and went smelling round the room nasty as a cat. This and that she hinted, with Dr Watkins there for witness! A law of slander there is,' she shot a baleful glance at her visitor, 'and let one more word be said against my character and I will go off straight to Vaughan Solicitor and get a letter of warning sent.'

'Ha!' said Mrs Morgans, suddenly relaxing her great intentness. 'Ha!' Her tone, like her nod, was obscure of meaning, and on the whole she seemed to be reserving judgement.

Indeed, what real proof was there of unhealthy proceedings having been transacted in Catherine's cottage? Mrs Morgans went back to the village with her report and that day everybody sat on it in cautious meditation. In Catherine's advantage was the general dislike of proud Mrs Lewis, but, on the other hand, a Jezebel, for the common good and the protection of men, must not be allowed to flourish unpunished. All day in the Post Office, in the Glyndwr Arms that evening, and in every cottage and farmhouse, the matter was observed from several loquacious angles.

On Wednesday afternoon Mr Maldwyn Davies, BA, the minister of Horeb, climbed to the cottage, and was received by his member and chapel cleaner with a vigorous flurry of welcome. Needlessly dusting a chair, scurrying for a cushion, shouting to the canary, that at the minister's entrance began to chirp and swing his perch madly, to be quiet, Catherine fussily settled him before running to put the kettle on. In the kitchen she remembered her condition and returned slow and clasping herself. 'Ah,' she moaned, 'my pain has come back! Suffering chronic I've been, off and on, since Sunday night. So heavy was poor Mr Lewis to take up my stairs. But what was I to be doing with a member of Horeb whining outside my gate for a bed? Shut my door on him as if he was a scamp or a member of the Church of England?'

'Strange,' said Mr Davies, his concertina neck, that could give forth such sweet music in the pulpit, closing down into his collar, 'strange that he climbed up here so far, feeling unwell.' He stared at the canary as if the bird held the explanation.

'Delirious and lighted up he was!' she cried. 'And no wonder.

Did he want to go to his cold home after the sermon and singing in chapel? No! Two times and more I have seen him wandering round here looking full up with thoughts. One time he
stopped at my gate and had praises for my dahlias, for I was
watering them. "Oh, Mr Lewis," I said to him, "what are you
doing walking up here?" and he said, "I am thinking over the
grand sermon Mr Davies gave us just now, and I would climb
big mountains if mountains there were!" Angry with myself I
am now that I didn't ask him in for a cup of tea, so lonely he
was looking. "Miss Bowen," he said to me, "when I was a boy
I used to come rabbiting up here."'

'Your dahlias,' remarked Mr Davies, still meditatively
gazing at the canary, 'are prize ones, and the rabbits a pest.'

'Oh,' groaned Catherine, placing her hands round her lower
middle, 'grumbling I am not, but there's a payment I am
having for my kindness last Sunday! . . . Hush,' she bawled
threateningly to the canary, 'hush, or no more seed today.'

Mr Davies, oddly, seemed unable to say much. Perhaps he,
too, was trying to sniff the truth out of the air. But he looked
serious. The reputation of two of his flock was in jeopardy, two
who had been nourished by his sermons, and it was unfortunate
that one of them lay beyond examination.

'Your kettle is boiling over,' he reminded her, since in her
exalted state she seemed unable to hear such things.

She darted with a shriek into the kitchen, and when she
came back with a loaded tray, which she had no difficulty in
carrying, she asked: 'When are you burying him?'

'Thursday, two o'clock. It is a public funeral. . . . You will
go to it?' he asked delicately.

This time she replied, sharp and rebuking: 'What, indeed,
me? Me that's got to stay at home because of my strain and can
only eat custards? Flat on my back in bed I ought to be this
minute. . . . Besides,' she said, beginning to bridle again, 'Mrs
Lewis, the *lady*, is a nasty!' She paused to take a long breath
and to hand him a buttered muffin.

'Her people are not our people,' he conceded, and pursed
his lips.

Fluffing herself up important, and not eating anything herself, Catherine declared: 'Soon as I am well I am off to
Vaughan Solicitor to have advice.' Black passion began to

scald her voice; she pointed a trembling finger ceilingwards. 'Up there she stood in the room of my respected father, with Dr Watkins for witness, and her own poor husband not gone cold and his eyes on us shiny as buttons, and her spiteful tongue made remarks. Hints and sarcastic! Nearly dropped dead I did myself. . . . The hand stretched out in charity was bitten by a viper!' She began to swell still more. 'Forty years I have lived in Banog, clean as a whistle, and left an orphan to do battle alone. Swear I would before the King of England and all the judges of the world that Mr John Lewis was unwell when he went on the bed up there! Swear I would that my inside was strained by his weight. A heathen gypsy would have taken him into her caravan! Comfort I gave him in his last hour. The glass of water by the bed, and a stitch in my side racing to fetch his wife, that came here stringy and black-natured as a bunch of dry old seaweed and made evil remarks for thanks. . . . Oh!' she clasped her breasts as if they would explode, 'if justice there is, all the true tongues of Banog must rise against her and drive the bad-speaking stranger away from us over the old bridge. Our honest village is to be made nasty as a sty, is it? No!'

Not for nothing had she sat all these years in close attention to Mr Davies' famous sermons, which drew persons from remote farms even in winter. And, as she rocked on her thick haunches and her voice passed from the throbbing of harps to the roll of drums, Mr Davies sat at last in admiration, the rare admiration that one artist gives to another. She spoke with such passion that, when she stopped, her below-the-waist pains came back and, rubbing her hands on the affected parts, she moaned in anguish, rolling up her big moist eyes.

'There now,' he said, a compassionate and relenting note in his voice, 'there now, take comfort.' And as he pronounced: 'There must be no scandal in Banog!' she knew her battle was won.

'Put your hands by here,' she cried, 'and you will feel the aches and cricks jumping from my strain.'

But Mr Davies, a fastidious look hesitating for a moment across his face, accepted her word. He took a slice of apple tart and ate it, nodding in meditation. A woman fighting to preserve the virtue of what, it is said, is the most priceless

185

treasure of her sex is a woman to be admired and respected. Especially if she is a Banog one. And it was natural that he was unwilling to accept that two of his members could have forgotten themselves so scandalously. Nevertheless, as Catherine coiled herself down from her exalted though aching state and at last sipped a little strong tea, he coughed and remarked: 'It is said that nearly every Sunday night for two years or more Mr Lewis never arrived home from chapel till ten o'clock, and no trace is there of his occupation in these hours. "A walk," he used to tell in his home, "a Sunday-night walk I take to think over the sermon." That is what the servant Milly Jones has told in Banog, and also that in strong doubt was Mrs Lewis concerning those walks in winter and summer.'

'Then a policeman she ought to have set spying behind him,' said Catherine, blowing on a fresh cup of tea with wonderful assurance. 'Oh, a shame it is that the dead man can't rise up and speak. Oh, wicked it is that a dead man not buried yet is turned into a goat.' Calm now, and the more impressive for it, she added: 'Proofs they must bring out, strict proofs. Let Milly Jones go babbling more, and *two* letters from Vaughan Solicitor I will have sent.'

'Come now,' said Mr Davies hastily, 'come now, the name of Banog must not be bandied about outside and talked of in the market. Come now, the matter must be put away. Wind blows and wind goes.' He rose, gave a kind nod to the canary, and left her.

He would speak the decisive word to silence offensive tongues. But, as a protest, she still stayed retreated in the cottage; serve them right in the village that she withheld herself from the inquisitive eyes down there. On Friday morning the milkman told her that Mr Lewis had had a tidy-sized funeral the previous day. She was relieved to hear he was safely in the earth, which was the home of forgetfulness and which, in due course, turned even the most disagreeable things sweet. After the milkman had gone she mixed herself a cake of festival richness, and so victorious did she feel that she decided to put an end to her haughty exile on Sunday evening and go to chapel as usual; dropping yet another egg in the bowl, she saw herself arriving at the last minute and marching to her pew in the front with head held high in rescued virtue.

On Saturday morning the postman, arriving late at her out-of-the-way cottage, threw a letter inside her door. A quarter of an hour later, agitated of face, she flew from the cottage on her bicycle. The village saw her speeding through without a look from her bent-over head. She shot past the Post Office, Horeb chapel, the inn, the row of cottages where the nobodies lived, past the house of Wmffre, the triple-crowned bard whose lays of local lore deserved to be better known, past the houses of Mr Davies, BA, and Mrs Williams Flannel, who had spoken on the radio about flannel-weaving, past the cottage of Evans the Harpist and Chicago Jenkins, who had been in jail in that place, and, ringing her bell furious, spun in greased haste over the cross-roads where, in easier times, they hanged men for sheep stealing. She got out on to the main road without molestation.

'Judging,' remarked Mrs Harpist Evans in the Post Office, 'by the way her legs were going on that bike the strain in her inside has repaired quite well.'

It was nine miles to the market town where Vaughan the solicitor had his office, which on Saturday closed at midday. She stamped up the stairs, burst into an outer room, and demanded of a frightened youth that Mr Vaughan attend to her at once. So distraught was she that the youth skedaddled behind a partition of frosted glass, came back, and took her into the privacy where Mr Vaughan, who was thin as a wasp and had a black hat on his head, hissed: 'What are you wanting? Closing time it is.' Catherine, heaving and choking, threw down the letter on his desk and, after looking at it, he said, flat: 'Well, you can't have it yet. Not till after probate. You go back home and sit quiet for a few weeks.' Accustomed to the hysteria of legatees, and indeed of non-legatees, he turned his back on her and put a bunch of keys in his pocket.

She panted and perspired. And, pushing down her breasts, she drew out her voice, such as it was—'Oh, Mr Vaughan,' she whimpered, 'it is not the money I want. Come I have to ask you to let this little business be shut up close as a grave.' A poor misused woman in mortal distress, she wiped sweat and tears off her healthy country-red cheeks.

'What are you meaning?' He whisked about impatient, for at twelve-five, in the bar-parlour of the Blue Boar, he always

187

met the manager of the bank for conference over people's private business.

She hung her head ashamed-looking as she moaned: 'A little favourite of Mr Lewis I was, me always giving him flowers and vegetables and what-not free of charge. But bad tongues there are in Banog, and they will move quick if news of this money will go about.'

'Well,' he said, flat again, 'too late you are. There is Mrs Lewis herself knowing about your legacy since Thursday evening and—'

Catherine burst out: 'But *she* will keep quiet for sure! She won't be wanting it talked that her husband went and left me three hundred pounds, no indeed! For I can say things that poor Mr Lewis told me, such a nasty she was! It is of Horeb chapel I am worrying—for you not to tell Mr Davies our minister or anyone else that I have been left this money.' She peeped up at him humble.

'Well,' he said, even flatter than before and, as was only proper, not sympathetic, 'too late you are again. Same time that I wrote to you I sent a letter to Mr Davies that the chapel is left money for a new organ and Miss Catherine Bowen the cleaner left a legacy too: the letter is with him this morning. In the codicil dealing with you, Mr Lewis said it was a legacy because your cleaning wage was so small and you a good worker.'

The excuse would have served nice but for that unlucky death on her bed. She groaned aloud. And as she collapsed on the solicitor's hard chair she cried out in anguish, entreating aid of him in this disaster. Pay him well she would if he preserved her good name, pounds and pounds.

'A miracle,' he said, 'I cannot perform.'

Truth, when it is important, is not mocked for long, even in a solicitor's office. The legatee went down the stairs with the gait of one whipped sore. She cycled back to her cottage as though using only one leg, and, to avoid the village, she took a circuitous way, pushing the cycle up stony paths. At the cottage, after sitting in a trance for a while, she walked whimpering to the well among the chrysanthemums, removed the cover, and sat on the edge in further trance. An hour passed, for her thoughts hung like lead. She went into the dark night of the

188

soul. But she couldn't bring herself to urge her body into the round black hole which pierced the earth so deep.

Then, on the horizon of the dark night, shone a ray of bright light. For the first time since the postman's arrival the solid untrimmed fact struck her that three hundred poounds of good money was hers. She could go to Aberystwyth and set up in partnership with her friend Sally Thomas who, already working there as a cook, wanted to start lodgings for the college students. The legacy, surprising because Mr Lewis had always been prudent of pocket—and she had approved of this respect for cash, believing, with him, that the best things in life are Free—the legacy would take her into a new life. She rose from the well. And in the cottage, shaking herself finally out of her black dream, she decided that Mr Lewis had left her the money as a smack to his wife the nasty one.

No one came to see her. She did not go to chapel on the Sunday. Three days later she received a letter from Mr Davies, BA, inviting her to call at his house. She knew what it meant. The minister had sat with his deacons in special conclave on her matter, and he was going to tell her that she was to be cast out from membership of Horeb. She wrote declining the invitation and said she was soon to leave Banog to live at the seaside in quiet; she wrote to Sally Thomas at the same time. But she had to go down to the Post Office for stamps.

She entered the shop with, at first, the mien of an heiress. Two women members of Horeb were inside, and Lizzie Post-mistress was slicing bacon. Catherine stood waiting at the Post Office counter in the corner. No one greeted her or took notice, but one of the customers slipped out and in a few minutes returned with three more women. All of them turned their backs on Catherine. They talked brisk and loud, while Catherine waited drawn up. Lizzie Postmistress sang: 'Fancy Lewis the Chandler leaving money for a new organ for Horeb!'

'The deacons,' declared the wife of Peter the Watercress, 'ought to say "No" to it.'

'Yes, indeed,' nodded the cobbler's wife; 'every time it is played members will be reminded.'

'Well,' said single Jane the Dressmaker, who had a tape-measure round her ncek, 'not the fault of the organ will that be.'

189

They clustered before the bacon-cutting postmistress. On a tin of biscuits, listening complacent, sat a cat. The postmistress stopped slicing, waved her long knife, and cried: 'Never would I use such an organ—no, not even with gloves on; and *I* for one won't like singing hymns to it.'

'A full members' meeting about *all* the business there ought to be! Deacons are men. Men go walking to look at dahlias and fuchsias—'

'And,' dared the cobbler's wife, 'drop dead at sight of a prize dahlia.'

Catherine rapped on the counter and shouted: 'Stamps!'

The postmistress craned her head over the others and exclaimed: 'Why now, there's Catherine Fuchsias! . . . Your inside is better from the strain?' she enquired. The others turned and stared in unison.

'Stamps!' said Catherine, who under the united scrutiny suddenly took on a meek demeanour.

'Where for?' asked the postmistress, coming over to the Post Office corner, and snatching up the two letters Catherine had laid on the counter. 'Ho, one to Mr Davies, BA, and one to Aberystwyth!'

'I am going to live in Aberystwyth,' said Catherine grandly.

'Retiring you are on your means?' asked Jane the Dressmaker.

'Plenty of college professors and well-offs in Aberystwyth!' commented Peter's wife.

'Well,' frowned the postmistress, as if in doubt about her right to sell stamps to such a person, 'I don't know indeed. . . . What you wasting a stamp on this one for,' she rapped out, 'with Mr Davies living just up the road? Too much money you've got?'

'Ten shillings,' complained unmarried Jane the Dressmaker, 'I get for making up a dress, working honest on it for three days or more. Never will *I* retire to Aberystwyth and sit on the front winking at the sea.'

'What you going there so quick for?' asked the cobbler's wife, her eyes travelling sharp from Catherine's face to below and resting there suspicious.

'Two stamps.' The postmistress flung them down grudgingly at last, and took up Catherine's coin as if she was picking up a

190

rotten mouse by the tail. 'Wishing I am you'd buy your stamps somewhere else.'

Catherine, after licking and sticking them, seemed to regain strength as she walked to the door, remarking haughtily: 'There's wicked jealousy when a person is left money! Jealous you are not in my shoes, now *and* before.'

But, rightly, the postmistress had the last word: 'A cousin I have in Aberystwyth. Wife of a busy minister that is knowing everybody there. A letter *I* must write to Aberystwyth too.'